CAPITOL CRIMES

2021 ANTHOLOGY

CEMETERY PLOTS

OF NORTHERN CALIFORNIA

ISBN: 978-1-7369391-2-3

Cemetery Plots of Northern California is an anthology of fiction. While some
locations desribed are real places and, on occasion, historical figures may be
referenced, the stories told and the characters who populate them are the
product of the authors' imaginations.

Cover design and formatting by Karen Phillips, PhillipsCovers.com

Published by Capitol Crimes, the Sacramento, California Chapter
of Sisters in Crime
CapitolCrimes.org

Dedicated to Sonja Hazzard-Webster (1971-2020)
who had the best laugh in the world.
Wherever you are now, I know you can see this.
I hope it gives you as much joy as you gave all of us, and
it makes you proud.

—*Penny Manson, Capitol Crimes President*

Contents

Foreword

Catriona McPherson

When the Capitol Crimes anthology committee asked if I would write this foreword, my reply was: "Would I read fifteen stories and call it working? Why, yes, I believe I might." If I could have worked out how to spell "Aauurrrnchh!" in time, I would have said that, too. (It's the sound of an arm being bitten off. I'm still not sure I've cracked it.) Boy, was I ever right to grab this gig with both hands.

It's not just the quality of the writing; the range of these fifteen stories is astonishing, too. As soon as I had read them, I started daydreaming about a sequel—*Crème de la Crematorium*—because I was in no way done with where my siblings' imaginations had led them. That's for another day, though. For now, let me say that *Cemetery Plots* is a box of delights.

Meet the 12-stepper sheriff of a town haunted by a prohibitionist benefactor in "Intemperance"; a ruthless Christmas tree farmer in the twisty "Not the Killing Kind"; a cop whose traumatic past has left her with one last puzzle to solve in "Over Me"; a determined young lady with an excellent reason to stop at the cemetery en route to the airport in "The One"; a seasoned reporter far too jaded to fall for a Halloween hustle in "A Teeny Weeny Drop"; and a drug dealer with elder-care problems in "The Plot Thickens."

Come and roll sushi for the annual bazaar of a Buddhist church in "Cranes in the Cemetery"; try the chili at the hill-billy BBQ in "The Secret of Thompson's Hill"; hop a 1940s freight train in "Hot Box"; stroll through Colma with a plucky mortician's daughter in "Nameless"; and take a drive through the state's drought-ravaged interior in "One Tossed Match."

Eavesdrop on the deliciously entertaining bickering of two old gal pals as they mourn a third in "Murder in the Days of COVID-19"; play gooseberry at the romantic picnic from hell in "Strange Place for a Date"; listen to the strains of blues guitar among the headstones in "The 27 Club"; and ponder the unique problem facing the Yolo County officials in "Unknown Male and Parts of Two Others."

And there's more! The chapter has partnered with 916 Ink, a Sacramento charity empowering children and youth through creative writing, and a wonderful story by one of the 916 Ink students is included here. Hugo de León's "Dreamscape" is part biblio-mystery, part action adventure and all wrapped up in a tender tale of grief and friendship. Watch out, world—Hugo de León is coming!

It's no surprise that "Dreamscape" emerged from 916 Ink, nor that Capitol Crimes has produced such a cornucopia of terrific short fiction. You see, besides our founding mission of working for gender equity, our organization is passionately dedicated to the kind of all-around writing excellence show-cased here. These are just two of the reasons I am as proud to be a Sisters in Crime lifetime member as I am to be introduc-ing *Cemetery Plots*.

The volume is bittersweet for the Capitol Crimes chap-ter, however. It is dedicated to our late president and long-time sister, Sonja Hazzard-Webster, who died suddenly and much too soon, leaving a painful hole in our little community where her steady hand and inventive fun streak used to be. Sonja, we love you and miss you and offer this anthology to your memory.

Murder in the Days of COVID-19

Virginia Kidd

F at rays of sunlight reached between the tall pines and cedars that shade East Lawn Memorial Cemetery, highlighting rows of worn gravestones sunk in the dark green grass and staunch upright headstones fighting decades of erosion. The August morning was quiet; even traffic on nearby Folsom Boulevard faded into background white noise. Facing COVID-19 restrictions, few mourners gathered at East Lawn, but intermittent neighborhood walkers exercised along the roads that curved through the parklike setting, some with dogs clearly relishing their outdoor adventure.

Pearl and Arlene stood together reading a new black granite headstone: Rosalie Murnan, 1957—2020. Pearl's voice came out as a hoarse growl through the black cloth mask covering her nose and mouth. "She shouldn't have gone this young."

"No, no, she shouldn't have," Arlene agreed. "Just at the beginning of retirement. Finally time for adventures." She leaned forward to place a bouquet of pink roses beside the headstone, stopping with a grimace and a hand to her back. With a sigh she let the flowers drop in a random array and slowly pulled herself upright. "Face it, Pearl, COVID is deadly for people our age. That's just the way it is."

"Horse hockey!" Having driven Arlene from her 1930s Curtis Park home, Pearl had already had time to express her view on this once. "Wearing masks is just the way it is. Staying home for months watching *Diagnosis Murder* reruns and squinting at people on Zoom is just the way it is. Rosalie is gone because Gordon killed her. That's just the way it was for her."

"Oh, don't start again, Pearl." Arlene lifted her face into a soft breeze that carried the scent of floral wreaths nearby. She adjusted her lilac mask that was just the color of her linen blouse. She had found the mask at (of all places!) Emigh Hardware. "The world is in a pandemic. People our age die."

Pearl snorted. "I am quite aware that COVID discriminates against the elderly, or what snarky young broadcasters with the life experience of a gnat call 'the elderly,' but we protect against it. Gordon won't wear a mask. He flaunts his disdain of medical advice. From the beginning, he wouldn't shelter at home. He was Mr. Cool taking Rosalie out to fancy places to rub elbows with COVID."

"She went with him, Pearl. He didn't drag her."

"We don't know how he made her go. He exposed her to COVID. Think about it. Flying to Hilton Head—*why*? In a plane all the way across the U.S. Drinking margaritas in a hotel bar. You saw that selfie, didn't you? Breathing air indoors when an ocean was just blocks away—*why*? He killed her as surely as if he put arsenic in her afternoon tea. Or nicotine in her cocktail."

"Nicotine in her cocktail? Re-reading Agatha, are we?"

Pearl grinned. *"Murder in Three Acts."*

"Right. Well, whatever Gordon did, he exposed himself to COVID too, and he's still doing it. Karma doesn't need your help, so don't say anything to him when he gets here."

"Wonder where he is. I expected him to be standing around holding court. Maskless. Generating business for the funeral industry."

Arlene took Pearl's stout arm and pulled her away from Rosalie's gravesite. "Let's walk around a while. It's so peaceful here. A retreat right in the middle of town for people seeking 'surcease of sorrow,' as Poe put it. It's restful and calming and lovely, too. This view could be a painting."

"Yeah, I can just see it hung in a mortician's reception room."

The two women walked along the edge of the street in the shade of overhanging trees. "I never thought I'd miss funerals," Arlene remarked. "The Zoom ceremony for Rosalie was moving with all the photographs of her as a child and then in her nurse's uniform, but I miss being together with people who share the same loss I do."

"I guess that's what today is in some mini-way. A day for Rosalie's mourners to come to the grave at somewhat the same time."

Their path curved into the sun, turning Arlene's white hair into a shining halo and Pearl's black jacket into an oven. She began struggling with her sleeves. Arlene tugged the jacket off, exposing a faded gray T-shirt proclaiming NEVERTHELESS SHE PERSISTED, and they crossed to a shaded, cooler area beside a single mausoleum. Pearl read the inscription. It was for Tom LaBrie, who had hosted movies on Sacramento TV for fourteen years and owned the big LaBrie's Waterbed Warehouse when such beds were the peak of fashion.

Pearl said, "Remember his TV show, *Night Comfort Theater*?"

"Remember waterbeds?"

"Definitely. I had one in the fourplex, remember?"

"Oh, Pearl, that's when we first met. You needed help filling your bed when you and Cedric moved in! The beginning of our adult lives. We were so young."

"Didn't know it, though. I felt so mature. Married and in our own apartment."

"It was a charmed unit. Rosalie and Gordon upstairs on the left, Ted and I on the right. You and Cedric downstairs and—who was in the fourth unit? That young guy going to McGeorge Law School who always sat up till the early hours studying?"

A deep voice behind them answered. "That would be Grant Ruiz, I believe."

Pearl responded first. "Grant! How good to see you." She resisted her impulse to hug him, instead joining in an elbow-touching threesome. "You haven't changed much," she said, thinking that he was still a handsome man, not tall, just Arlene's height and as thin as she, with a full head of hair gone gray, not white. He wore a dark suit and tie and a disposable mask.

Arlene said, "We were going back in time."

"It's been a long while," he agreed.

"Yes. Couples socialized together back then. At least we did. I sort of remember you were closer to Rosalie and Gordon—" She stopped at the smack from Pearl on her back. "It's a sad occasion that's brought us back together."

"Yes. Especially here." He gestured toward the area beside them.

Arlene looked toward a section of East Lawn marked by small graves. "Oh," she said, and fell silent.

"Little ones who lived a day, a month," Grant said. "With Rosalie on my mind, it brings back her miscarriage."

"She wanted kids so much," Pearl said.

"Gordon didn't." Grant's voice had a sharp edge. He pointed over toward Rosalie's grave. "Is that Rosalie's sister over there?"

They turned to watch a dark-haired, maskless woman maneuver her way in high heels across the grass to Rosalie's gravesite. She was followed by a stout, ruddy-faced man in slacks and a sports coat.

"Lillian, is it?" Pearl asked. "Lanell?"

"Lillianne," Arlene said.

"Think their parents wanted to name their girls Rose and Lily and wimped out?"

Lillianne's navy heels matched the A-line skirt and tailored jacket that set off her soft ivory blouse—"Bound to be silk," Pearl muttered to Arlene—and double string of white beads—"Bound to be pearls," Arlene replied, adding, "real ones, from Tahiti, not Penney's."

"Six feet of space," Pearl said as they walked back, "between us and them, between them and Rosalie."

"Don't joke. That's her sister."

As they neared the couple, Lillianne raised a wrist to glance at a gold watch, then spoke over her shoulder to the man behind her. Her voice was lowered but still audible to the trio. "We can't stay long, Doug. If we want that property, we need to get there early." She raised her voice to speak as the group neared. "Oh, you're here for Rosalie, aren't you?"

"Yes," Arlene answered for them.

"Is Gordon here yet? We stopped by the house earlier and he said he was coming right over."

Pearl answered. "We haven't seen him."

"I guess it's a ritual to come to a grave to say goodbye," Lillianne said, "although I thought the service on Zoom was quite adequate. We don't have time for this."

"We'll miss Rosalie," Arlene said. "We knew her for forty years."

"You're even wearing masks," Lillianne noticed. "How nice. Rosalie argued with Gordon about that, but he wouldn't give in. And he didn't let her wear one either." She shot a quick glance at the grave.

Pearl said, "Gordon prevented a lot of things, didn't he?"

"What do you mean?"

"The advanced nursing degree she wanted to get, for one."

"Oh, there was no reason for that. Gordon made enough money for both of them. I wish he'd show up. We have to go soon. We've been here for ages, haven't we, Doug?"

The man beside her said, "We came in on the wrong side. Then Lilli wandered off somewhere and got lost."

"Cemeteries take up so much good city land," Lillianne said.

Grant requested, "Could I talk to you for a minute?" and stepped toward the duo.

Lillianne said to Pearl and Arlene, "It's so considerate of you two to show up here. You've done such a good job being friends to her. You've done all the right things." She turned to her husband and Grant, and the trio drew away.

"Spit on a gut, Arlene," Pearl hissed under her breath as they started walking. "How did Rosalie stand her?"

"A tad condescending, you think?" Arlene snickered.

"Come on. I left my jacket over where we were."

"Why did you smack me on the back when I mentioned Grant being closer to Rosalie and Gordon than to us back in the fourplex?"

"Oh, Arlene! Seriously?"

"What?"

"Are you telling me you don't remember the rumors about Rosalie and Grant?"

Arlene frowned. "I don't remember any rumors. What were they? Surely not romantic. Rosalie was at least ten years older. Grant was still in law school."

Pearl heaved a theatrical sigh. "Sometimes I wonder how we've kept our friendship all these years. Pay attention now. Ten years difference in age doesn't mean dog spit when lust is involved. Especially to people in their twenties and thirties."

"You really think they had an affair? She was married."

"To Gordon. Stodgy, in-it-for-himself Gordon. And there was Grant. Charming, naïve, available. Think about it, Arlene. We haven't seen Grant for what—thirty years? We all moved on, exchanged a few Christmas cards, then he faded away. And suddenly here he is. After all this time. Doesn't that say 'affair' to you?"

"No. It says 'courtesy' to me. And drop the subject, I see him coming back."

"Okay, but quick—why did he bring up the miscarriage?"

"Oh, I don't—you aren't saying—oh, Pearl!"

They had reached Tom LaBrie's memorial. "I'll get your jacket." Arlene stepped toward the other side of the mausoleum.

Pearl said, "Do you think Gordon is avoiding Lillianne and Doug? He'll probably show up here as soon as they leave and moan about them not staying."

Arlene's voice came in a thin whisper. "I don't think Gordon will do that." She staggered toward Pearl, squeezing her eyes closed.

Pearl grabbed her. "What's wrong? What happened? Sit down, Arlene! Come on, sit down. Here, just sit on the grass. Put your head down if you're feeling faint."

She stepped over to where Arlene had been. Gordon's body lay sprawled across the grass. A dark line trailed down from his mouth, and dried white liquid coated his lips. His eyes stared upward toward the hot blue sky. She didn't need a closer look to know he saw nothing. Beside him lay a stain-less-steel travel cup labeled HILTON HEAD.

Looking back, she saw Grant catch a glimpse of the action and start running. He reached them, breathing heavily. "It's Gordon." Pearl pointed.

"Heart attack?"

Before she could answer, Grant had his phone out and was clicking 9-1-1.

Arlene murmured. "I don't think that's heart attack. Look at his face, his mouth. It looks like he vomited."

The first police officer arrived in five minutes that felt like at least fifty. He told them to "go wait over there with the others." *Over there* was a vague destination under a Chinese Pistache tree where Doug and Lillianne already stood.

As they neared it, Grant said, "Sometimes spouses die at the shock of losing their mate."

"Fat chance of that in this case," Doug said. "Rosalie was a total drag on Gordon. He already has tickets for a cruise when those finally start up again. She didn't want to go. Afraid. Not that he was any better when it came to work. I'm sorry I ever started in business with him. Was a great relief to dissolve it."

"Now's not the time, Doug," his wife said.

Pearl and Arlene settled to the side on the grass. In a low voice Pearl said to Arlene, "Are you okay?"

Arlene nodded. "It was such a shock."

"Yeah. You don't expect—oh. I was going to say you don't expect to find dead people in the cemetery. Never mind."

They waited, listening to a slight rustle of leaves, an occasional bark from an excited dog, and soon the sounds of emergency assistance rolling in. An ambulance, a fire engine, and several police cars pulled up. The morning grew hotter despite little playful breezes sending them fragrant aromas off and on. Pearl watched Grant become their link to the official action going on. "Why is Grant suddenly our spokesperson?" she asked Arlene. "Because he's male, because he's wearing a suit, because he's a lawyer?"

"Because he wants to be," Arlene answered.

"Frankly, it's okay with me to be left out. From the beginning this has been a totally miserable morning. Totally. When we can leave here, let's treat ourselves to a luxurious lunch at Biba's and try to forget about all this for a while. Have wine, some special ravioli, then a luscious dessert radiating calories, the whole works."

"Biba's is closed because of the pandemic."

"Crap. Well, Tower Café then?"

"Closed."

"Celestine's?"

"Open for take-out in the evening four days a week, and this isn't one of the days."

"Have I mentioned how irritated COVID-19 makes me?"

"Only every time we've talked since the stay-at-home order March nineteenth."

Lillianne approached them. "We have a problem. As tragic as Gordon's death is, we're due in San Francisco this afternoon for several days of actual in-person meetings. And—"

"And who's going to clean out Gordon's refrigerator and lock up the house?" Pearl finished Lillianne's thought. "We'd be glad to." She saw Arlene's eyes widen.

"Just the immediate things, you know," Lillianne said. She offered a weak smile and started threading her fingers through her pearls. "We just called Gordon's sister. She'll fly out and deal with the funeral home. It seems cold to just go on with our business, but we've been planning for months, and, well . . . what can we do?"

Grant brought the official news when they were allowed to leave. "They're guessing it was some kind of drug overdose. These are EMTs, not the coroner, but they're experienced."

In the car, Pearl pulled off her mask and turned the air-conditioner on full blast. She handed Arlene the key Lillianne had given her.

"And why are we volunteering to close up Gordon's place, may I ask?" Arlene folded her mask and slipped it into her pocket.

"To look around. Why not? Something's really weird, Arlene. Why didn't Gordon come straight to Rosalie's gravesite this morning? So far as I know, only three people here knew him: Lillianne, Doug, and Grant. I don't know how one of them could have slipped something in his travel cup, but we know two of them went by his house this morning. And Grant—well, now that it matters, why *did* he appear out of the past this morning? Maybe at the house we'll find signs of some connection, some link. Don't worry. We'll get a scrumptious lunch first. Taco Bell or McDonald's?"

Rosalie and Gordon's house assaulted them with the mingled odors of dirty socks, spoiled food and fetid water in a long-abandoned vase of rotting flowers. All of the interior lights burned, and Me TV blasted out the latest episode of *Gunsmoke*. Gordon's clothes lay strewn about the house. Dirty plates, glasses, cups, aluminum food trays, and Styrofoam containers rested on the week's issues of *The Sacramento Bee* and unopened junk mail. In the kitchen, a pungent aroma reminiscent of barbecue sauce and mustard was traced to the garbage bin marked RECYCLE.

The pain of loss hit them only when in a back room they came to Rosalie's desk with its rosewood pen, stained-glass lamp, box of creamy stationery, and silver vase with a now-dead single rose. Pearl caught Arlene brushing away tears, and she could feel herself clenching her teeth the way her dentist had specifically warned her against. "Look," she said, pointing a stubby finger at a scrap of paper stuck under the vase. "Grant's address."

In the kitchen Arlene found a container of Clorox wipes and cleaned the end of the dining table while Pearl poured the reeking contents of the vase down the drain. Taking clean plates from the cabinet, they settled down with two Chicken Quesadilla Combos and large Cokes.

Pearl surveyed the cluttered table to her left. Lifting Sunday's comics from beside her, she uncovered an engraved silver flask lying on a greeting card. She tilted the flask to read its message: *To Gordon from Rosalie. For all you've done.* She opened the flask, smelled, then shrugged as she closed it. "Alcohol. At least half empty. It's got jam on it. Toast and Irish coffee for breakfast, you think?" She set it down and picked up the card.

"Don't read that, Pearl!" Arlene gasped. "You shouldn't read other people's mail."

"Oh, excuse me, Jane Austen! One, the card is to Gordon and he's dead, so he won't mind. Two, it's from Rosalie and she's dead and won't mind. Three—" She stopped. "I can't think of a three. How about 'I want to see what it says.' I'll read it aloud, so you're guilty too. 'Gordon, if you are reading this, then I am gone and you found the flask in your desk. Right now I feel dreadful and I'm going to the clinic."

"Oh, poor Rosalie."

"'I had the flask engraved for our anniversary. I have filled it just for you. Keep it while you can, remembering me. Happy anniversary, Rosalie.' That's it."

"It feels so tragic. 'Dear Gordon,' and as he's reading it, he knows she's gone."

"It doesn't say 'Dear.' And there's no 'with all my love' or 'be at peace, my darling.'"

"Maybe she was just too weak to write endearments to console him."

"Oh, belching bears, Arlene! She's got COVID and it's his fault. He dragged her out into the infectious COVID world. Why would she still love him or want to console him?"

"Well, if she didn't love him, why would she leave him a gift? And even fill it with...what? Scotch? Bourbon? Kahlua? Or...or..."

"Brandy with a touch of Raid?"

Silence settled over the table. After a minute, Pearl asked, "How long does poison take to work?"

"I guess it depends on the poison."

They each glanced at the flask, then concentrated attentively on lunch.

Finishing up, Pearl said, "Let's gather up the mess, water the plants, lock everything up, and get out of here. If Gordon's death is natural, that's that. If it isn't natural, police will search the house and they'll check the flask and see what's in it."

"Or Doug and Lillianne will wash it out and donate it to Goodwill before police get here."

Pearl leaned back in her chair with the last of her Coke. "I feel like one of those mothers whose son is running from the law and comes home. Does she hide him or turn him in?"

"We don't know there's poison in the flask. We don't even know Gordon was poisoned."

"No, but we know we have to either give the flask to police or risk letting it disappear. If you knew he was poisoned and knew the flask from Rosalie had poison in it, what would you do?"

Arlene frowned. "Where would Rosalie get poison?"

"You're avoiding the question. But, just speculating, she had been a nurse. She could have access to chemicals we don't know. The wrong mix of prescription drugs can kill. Remember all the warnings you told me you got when you first hurt your back and were taking several drugs?"

Arlene gathered up her food wrappings. "Let's get to work."

Closing up the house went quickly: all throw-away items gathered in a big garbage bag, dishwasher loaded and started, electrical appliances unplugged, plants watered, windows closed and locked, air-conditioner set at a temperature environmentalists would applaud. They ignored Gordon's dirty clothes and personal items and had just mutually chosen not to make the bed when the doorbell rang.

Arlene opened the door to Grant. He no longer wore a jacket or tie and showed signs of the hot day outside. Arlene led him to the table while Pearl found a bottle of cold water in the refrigerator. Grant dropped into a dining chair and laid an open envelope on the table, then tore off his mask and took a long swallow of the water. Pearl stepped over to the temperature gauge to abandon her environmental impulse in favor of a cooler room.

"Thanks. I needed that." Grant set his plastic bottle down. "I'm glad you're still here. I heard Lillianne ask you two to come over. I tried to talk to her at the cemetery—I mean, she's Rosalie's sister—but she was too focused on whatever's coming up in San Francisco. Then I thought of you two. You were both longtime friends of Rosalie." He glanced up to take in their nods. "The thing is, I got this letter Rosalie wrote just before she died." He indicated the envelope. "Letters plural, I guess I should say. There's another letter underneath."

He paused, noted Pearl's hand reaching for the envelope, then stopping. "Go ahead. That's why I brought it. Read it aloud. I'd like your advice on what to do."

Pearl removed and unfolded the letter. "Dear Grant," she read, then glanced at Arlene.

"What's the matter?" Grant asked.

"Nothing. Just—a contrast. 'Dear Grant, I have tested positive for COVID-19. Maybe I'll sail through with just a terrible flu. If so, PLEASE SHRED—' It's in all caps and underlined. 'PLEASE SHRED the enclosed letter without opening it and meet me for a glass of wine.'"

"It would have been so nice to visit with her again." Grant's voice was wistful.

"'If I don't make it, would you keep an eye on Gordon.' On Gordon?" Pearl said. "Why? Too weird. 'If he remains alive, shred the enclosed letter. But if he is murdered, and someone is charged with his death, open it.' Why would she say this?"

"Keep reading," Grant said.

"'I know this sounds melodramatic, and I don't have strength to explain. If no one is charged, just keep the letter in a safe place for a while and finally shred it.' Now everything's in caps again. 'IF SOMEONE IS ARRESTED OPEN THE ENCLOSED LETTER. USE YOUR JUDGMENT.' Then a new paragraph. 'I can't thank you enough, Grant. I turn to you at this terrible time out of an abiding trust. Thank you so, so much. With love, Rosalie.'" Pearl dropped the letter on the table and leaned back. "What are you going to do?"

"Right now, wait for the official judgment on Gordon's cause of death. It really blew me away when they said it looked like drugs."

"What do you think the cause is?"

"That. An overdose of drugs. I never thought he was an addict, so legal ones. A mix-up of medicine, maybe."

"Because you think he's been sick or because Rosalie was a nurse?"

He looked at them, then shook his head. "You both know her better than I do these days. What do you think?"

Pearl handed Grant the flask and card. "We found these here."

Grant read the card. "'Keep it while you can.' What does that mean?"

Arlene said, "For all we know Gordon had something wrong with him."

"I keep telling myself that surely he died naturally," Grant agreed. "I started to just shred all this, but—"

"Do you know what's in the second letter?" Arlene pointed to the unopened envelope.

"No. I'm doing what she asked about not opening it. You agree with that?"

"Yes. She knew who to trust."

"Still, as an attorney, I don't want to do anything illegal."

"Yes, I can see that. And what's in the letter could be misleading."

"Or it could be helpful. We can't forget she was ill and could be—"

"Oh, give me a bubbling break!" Pearl grabbed the sealed letter and ripped it open. "Okay, listen. Here's Rosalie. 'I write this so no one will be falsely accused of killing my husband. I left him a flask of his favorite Scotch and Valium. By the time you read this, I will be gone myself, so I have no need to tell you why.'"

"I can't—I can't believe it," Grant said. "Rosalie! Rosalie deliberately . . ."

"Even though she writes this," Arlene said, "maybe that didn't kill him."

Pearl folded her arms and sat taking in Grant's response. "You know what? This letter is two things."

"What do you mean?"

"It's a confession, of course." She watched Grant, turned her eyes to Arlene, then back to Grant. "And, also, it's a get-out-of-jail-free card for anyone who knew about it. Such a person could kill Gordon then hand over Rosalie's letter." She flung it back on the table.

"Why?" Grant's face tightened; his jaws clenched. "Why would this nameless person do that?"

Pearl shrugged. "I have no idea."

"And how?" asked Arlene.

"Bringing Gordon a loaded latte?"

Grant's face had turned red and the veins on his neck stood out as he said, "I presume you mean me, and I can assure you I did not do that!"

"Come on, Pearl," Arlene said. "Rosalie confessed."

"To doing something that may have failed. I'm just pointing it out."

"Well, you're wrong," Grant said.

They sat in silence listening to the hum of the air-conditioner, the shifting of bodies when any of them moved, the discordance of a leaf blower outside the house.

Finally, Arlene said, "Rosalie trusted him, Pearl."

"Yes," Grant said, "and I came to consult you two. I'll leave it to you. What do you want to do?"

Arlene said, "I don't know. Pearl?"

Pearl leaned forward. "Well, if it comes to a vote, I'll tell you who I'll vote for. Arlene's candidate for murderer: Karma. In my opinion Gordon contributed to Rosalie's death. Maybe she caused his or maybe not. Either way, Karma has put a check mark in the balance column.

"So here's my suggestion. Grant, you keep the letter Rosalie asked you to keep. The flask is part of our cleaning up and goes in that big plastic bag over there, and that goes out in the bin."

"And then what?" Arlene asked.

"And then," Pearl answered in her strongest voice, "we three abandon this foul abode, unearth at least one watering hole still open somewhere in Sacramento County where we can get glasses of chilled champagne, and we go there, even if we have to take our crystal flutes outside and sit six feet apart in the heat. And we drink a long, cold toast to our dear Rosalie.

"Frankly, I think Gordon died naturally, but I kind of hope he didn't. I mean, really, it's not every day a husband is killed by his dead wife."

Unknown Male and Parts of Two Others

Chris Dreith

July 1, 1934

"Most guys don't have three left arms," Arnie Ramos said, leaning against my porch railing, laughing and slapping his knee. The kid thought he was funny, but I figured it was just the gin.

"He doesn't have three left arms," Doc Thatcher said to his young helper. The doc never had much of a sense of humor. Whenever he came to talk on my porch, he stood erect and stiff, but at no time refused a glass of my homemade hooch.

"So how many bodies do you think we have here, Doc?" Sheriff Langley got to the point.

"At least three!" Arnie was still snickering. At seventeen, he was smart enough to appreciate a paying job, even if it meant pulling corpses out of the river, but the kid had no respect for the dead.

I watched Liam McDowell's back muscles tighten. The big Irishman's brawn came from years of cutting granite by hand for our county cemetery's headstones. He had what it took to be an artist but no sense of humor either. Not since his wife died a few months ago. Liam did not usually spend time on my raised porch overlooking the Sacramento River, but this was important, and I needed him here. He had stood with his back to me since Louisa handed him gin and offered him one of my precious cigars. He took the glass in that big bear-paw hand of his, refused the smoke and turned to gaze across the river at the booming city of Sacramento. The motor from the barge dredging the river made a low vibrating growl. It reminded me of McDowell, big, slow, powerful.

Doc Thatcher shook his head, took a sip and said, "Some of the parts we just fished out of the river today look like a couple arms, yes, two left ones." His stern glance at Arnie shut the kid up for a while. "There are more parts, but not as easily identified. Might be human but could be pig or a big fish even. I figure they've been underwater for at least a month. Probably ripped from their bodies by the dredger." He nodded toward the river. We all looked in that direction, half expecting to see more body parts pop up out of the water. "I wouldn't be surprised that all those old pilings from the M Street Bridge were like an underwater net, seizing everything that got caught in the current from upriver. And now that the old bridge is being torn down to build the new Tower Bridge, we might find all sorts of things floating to the surface."

He took another sip. "The body that came up yesterday was mostly intact. Except for his roughed-up face. He looked like he was in the water for only about a week. I'll know more when I have time to do an autopsy."

"The best dressed body I ever pulled outa the river. Dressed to the nines," chirped the kid. "He's wearing a yella vest the doc says is real silk! I could sure use a vest like that one, Judge." Arnie looked at me, thick eyebrows raised above a mud-smudged face.

I chewed on my cigar, moving it from one side of my mouth to the other. I wanted to give the kid the impression that I would consider it, but Doc spoke up first, losing his patience. "You can't have the man's clothes. I already told you that."

"There's only one little hole in it, and the guy ain't gonna need it anymore anyway." Arnie slumped against the railing.

"A hole? Like from a gunshot?" Langley asked, always the copper.

"Can't tell for sure yet."

"It looked like a star or an X," said the kid. "I think I can stitch it up just fine."

Liam choked on his gin, growled a bit to clear his throat. I thought for a moment he was going to say something, but he just slowly turned to stare at Arnie. The kid got the point this time, slurped his gin and looked innocently at the river.

"Any identifying marks on the body?" The sheriff.

The doc shook his head again. "None that I could find after a quick look last night. I was about to start a thorough study this morning but rushed right back over here to Broderick when we got the call that more body parts were dredged up. I figure we might as well stick around until the *Natomas* is done dredging, in case more float up," Doc Thatcher continued. "No use heading the twenty-six miles back to Woodland if we just need to turn around to pick up additional bodies. Or their parts."

The sheriff nodded. "Ain't had any missing person reports for a long time." He hesitated. "I'll check down at the gambling barges at the dock. Drifters come and go so often it's hard to tell if any of them are missing. Poor slobs. Nobody to miss them, I guess."

I glanced past McDowell at the Yolo County coroner's panel truck parked on the dirt road in front of my house. A few people walked back up the slope from the public dock, glancing at the truck. I wondered if the stench of the waterlogged body parts was causing the attention.

"So, Judge…" I knew the sheriff was going to bring up Yolo County business. I was the local justice of the peace. This was my territory. I ruled the west side of the river, but he liked to remind me that he was responsible for the whole county and was much more fiscally duty-bound than I was. "How much are we going to have to pay to bury all of this mess? The Woodland Cemetery only has a few plots left in Potter's Field after we used up several from the big barge fire two years ago."

McDowell carefully put his glass on the top rail and turned toward me. "I only got one slab. If you want more, I have to drive all the way to the quarry up at Auburn." His Irish Rs and Ls rolled around in his throat as he spoke.

Langley smiled. "We all know that this side of the river has always been Sacramento County's dumping ground. Those bodies are probably from them. Let's just row these parts back across the river tonight and drop them over the side. Save Yolo County residents a bundle!" Sometimes the sheriff's professional qualities slipped a bit and allowed his animosity toward the more affluent county to show.

"Uoo-ee! I'm with you, Sheriff!" Arnie slapped his knee again.

I rolled my cigar around to the other side of my mouth once more. Louisa always said that was my "tell." She might have been right, so I had practiced in front of the mirror, rolling my cigar, looking judicial, considering all angles before reaching a brilliant resolution. Sometimes the cigar trick worked, and I wouldn't have to make a decision right away. I was hoping it would work today. Why did all these body parts have to show up on my side of the river?

"Only got one slab," McDowell said again.

"It would be a bit obvious if these body parts magically appeared on the east side of the river." Doc Thatcher spoke slowly and clearly, as if he were talking to a group of school children. "The *Natomas* crew all live in Sacramento, and I'm pretty sure the word is already out that they found more body parts again today."

"Doesn't mean that the bodies didn't come from their side," the sheriff argued, but he knew he had lost that battle.

We all looked up at the sudden silence. The *Natomas* was closing down for the day. More people were climbing up to the road. They probably figured the show was over, and no more bodies were to be seen.

"Hey, Irish! Ain't that your pretty daughter down there?" Arnie leaned over the railing. McDowell flinched and glared at the kid. "I heard she was sellin' smoked salmon down at the dock. I could sure use some of that kind of smoked salmon." He smacked his lips. The kid was an idiot. McDowell was slowly reaching for his neck when Doc Thatcher rushed over, grabbed Arnie's shirt and pulled him away.

"Time to go, kid. Thanks for the gin, Judge. I'll let you know what I find out as soon as I can." Doc pulled Arnie down the stairs and shoved him into the truck.

Louisa came through the screen door with a package wrapped in the *Independent Leader* newspaper. "Siobhan is such a lovely girl, Liam," she said as she handed McDowell the bundle. I was sure it was filled with her special biscuits, and I hoped she hadn't given them all away. "You should be so proud of her, helping out since dear Clodagh died. I've heard that her smoked salmon is the best around."

McDowell bowed slightly to my wife, turned to me. "If you want more headstones, I'll have to drive up to Auburn. Only got one slab," he reminded me yet again. I wondered if he thought I had already forgotten how many slabs he had. "Ma'am." He nodded to Louisa and stomped down the stairs.

Louisa picked up the glasses left on the porch railings, stood in front of the sheriff until he drained his and handed it over to her. She gave me a frown and walked back into the house. The screen door slammed behind her. The party was over, and I hadn't had to decide on how the county would pay for a grave and headstone, or for that matter, how many we needed.

The sheriff and I both moved to the edge of the porch and watched McDowell walk down the road to meet his sixteen-year-old daughter. She handed him the empty box that had SMOKED LOCAL SALMON painted on the side and skipped beside him, dust from the road dancing around her bare legs.

"One thing the kid got right," said the sheriff. "That Siobhan McDowell has sure turned out to be a pretty one."

She turned slightly, tilting her head, and looked over her shoulder directly at me. Her dazzling smile was seductive. I had to fight the wildest notion to jump off the porch and run after her. When she laughed, shook her blonde hair out of her face, took her father's arm and walked away, I realized that I could finally breathe again, but my hands had a death grip on the railing.

The sheriff coughed and muttered, "See you later, Judge." He hurried down the steps and headed in the opposite direction. The back of his neck was bright red. Seemed the girl's smile had affected him the same way.

I propped my elbows on the top rail and leaned further forward to watch the blue of her dress catch the light of the lowering sun until she disappeared behind the tall Valley Oak trees that lined the levee. I allowed myself to fantasize that smile was for me and me alone, until Louisa appeared at my side. I never knew how she managed to catch me like that. I knew that she couldn't really know what I was thinking, but I managed to look guilty each and every time anyway.

"You going to be ready for the Independence Day rally, Judge?" she asked, accompanied by one of her sugary sweet smiles. Maybe she really could read my mind. That thought made me focus on something else.

"What's to get ready? Governor Merriam will be set up with the Cal Band from Berkeley on the two barges at the public dock. He'll have all his newspaper hacks with him and try to run the whole show. No room for me." Louisa rolled her eyes. She knew that I would force my way to the podium whether I was invited or not. This was my home base. Not the Governor's. "And I won't be surprised if that greaseball, Sinclair, will try to steal some thunder."

"I heard he's got quite a contingency coming to support his EPIC plan," Louisa said quietly. I knew she said it just to get me riled, but I jumped in anyway.

"How the hell does he think his plan to 'End Poverty In California,'" I said this with the most sarcasm I could muster, "is going to float in *my* county?" I pounded the railing to make sure Louisa heard the point. She ignored me. "That commie socialist thinks *my* Yolo County farmers are going to simply give up their land to this genius' government so he can run farms to feed the poor? Hell, no!" I gave the rail one more slap. That one really stung, but I acted like it didn't.

Louisa turned toward the house. "Well, don't stay out too late, dear. The skeeters are coming out, and they will eat you up." Was that a smile on her face?

I sat back down on my rocker and poured another shot of gin from my thermos, thinking I might be able to use some of that argument for the rally. Then I swatted a mosquito on my neck.

***

July 4, 1934

Independence Day had threatened to be the hottest that I could remember, but it didn't stop the festivities. The Cal Band pounded out a military march from two barges on my side of the river, while the California Ramblers blasted swing music from the deck of the *Delta King* on the Sacramento side. Governor Merriam was balancing in a rowboat, throwing candy to the kids along both the shores, while his flunkies tried to keep the boat from tipping over. His opponent, the commie Sinclair, was hollering from a canoe how he will take over farms and factories for the good of all. His women followers, dressed in white lace and surrounding him in their own canoes, were singing hymns and cheering every word he cried.

Louisa's church ladies had decorated half of the I-Street Bridge, the north boundary of the festival. The abundance of red, white and blue bunting and streamers of flowers covered the railroad bridge, but only to its center. The county line ran down the middle of the river. No use giving those Sacramento ladies credit, Louisa told me, when all the work was done by the West side women.

I felt pretty proud of my speech. I'd been able to rush to the podium before anyone else to get the first word in about the new Tower Bridge. The roar of cheers led me to believe that my ability to stretch the truth a bit convinced the crowd that the original design of this impressive vertical-lift bridge had been mine and the new jobs that would be coming soon were because of me. But I was generous enough to point out Alfred Eichler in the crowd as the bridge's architect when I saw him scowling at me. What could he do? People rushed up to him to shake his hand and pat him on the back.

I had then graciously introduced Governor Merriam, glazing over the fact that he hadn't actually won a gubernatorial election yet, since he was placed in the office after the death of Governor Rolph only a few weeks earlier. But I had told the audience, "He will win this one!" The crowd went wild. I knew Merriam would owe me a couple favors because of my fantastic presentation. The state might even spring for the price of a couple more plots in the Woodland Cemetery for the body parts we hauled out of the river. Louisa's church ladies would think of me as a highly moral leader, honoring the souls of the dead that progress forgot. I would be a hero of the women of Broderick, Bryte and Clarksburg. It felt good.

It was a beautiful sight from my perch at the top of the levee as I munched on a pig-in-a-blanket from the Odd Fellows booth. Sheriff Langley joined me with an ice cream cone melting down his arm.

"I still can't believe we were able to get some firecrackers for tonight." He beamed. "My deputies have been collecting coins for a whole year to pay for this. They are so excited. We're going to be able to show those losers from the Sacramento Sheriff's Department a thing or two!" The sheriff started licking the melting ice cream off his arm, which would have turned my stomach if I hadn't been in such a good mood.

Doc Thatcher ambled up the levee road with a bag of popcorn. He carefully ate one kernel at a time. I was about to ask how long it would take to finish when a small tornado of a woman in a flowered housedress dashed past us.

"Uh oh," said the doc, as we watched Arnie's mother run straight as an arrow toward her son, who had his back to her while talking to a couple of the gambling-barge women at the edge of the river.

"Arnold Randall Ramos!" she shouted, fists on her hips. Arnie spun around, grabbing the lapels of his dirty brown jacket, and pulled them across his chest, but he wasn't fast enough to hide the vibrant yellow silk vest he was wearing underneath. We couldn't hear what was being said, but we could see the color drain from his face. He dropped his head and walked up the hill, his mother herding him home.

"I'll get that damn vest to you tomorrow, Doc," she said through gritted teeth as she passed.

"Thank you, Mrs. Ramos," the doc said quietly. The three of us knew better than to laugh out loud if Helen Ramos could hear us. A moment passed.

"So, Sheriff," Doc Thatcher said, "any info about our dead fellow?"

"No name yet." The sheriff was still licking the ice cream off his arm. "A couple women from the gambling-barges said they might have seen some joe with nice clothes a few weeks ago, but nothing definite."

"We got to do something with him and the parts, Judge." Thatcher turned to me. "It's getting really bad in my office. It costs so much for refrigeration. The county supervisors are in an uproar."

I nodded and moved my cigar to the other side of my mouth.

A loud bang came from the river's edge, followed by laughter.

"Those idiots!" The sheriff dropped his cone in the dirt. "They're going to accidentally shoot off those fireworks too early! That, or they'll shoot off a finger!"

He rushed down the hill toward his men at the river's edge, where they were preparing tonight's fireworks extravaganza. Thatcher looked after him and said, "Well, if someone is going to shoot off a finger, I should probably be there. I don't want another body part landing in the river that I would have to identify."

I was shoving the rest of the pig-in-a-blanket in my mouth past my cigar when I heard a soft, whispery voice.

"Hello, Judge Marino." Siobhan McDowell was standing next to me, holding her empty salmon box. Her Irish lilt and her flimsy blue dress enticed me.

I choked on the pig, pulled a handkerchief out of my back pocket, and was able to spit out the wiener while maintaining my cigar and professional demeanor.

"Why, hello there, dear," I managed to say as I dropped the chewed hot dog out of my handkerchief onto the ground behind me. "Are you enjoying the festivities?"

"It's been a wonderful day." She flashed that killer smile. "I've sold out of everything that I brought, so I'm going back home to get more fish."

"Lovely." That was all I could think to say.

She turned slowly toward the levee road and said over her shoulder, "I might need a little help carrying all the fish back."

Did I hear that right? Maybe this was one of my fantasies. I quickly looked for Louisa and spotted her at the Church Bake Sale booth, frantically selling cookies and pies. The gambling-barge ladies had a Kisses for $1 booth right next to my wife's. That was incentive enough to keep her busy, I figured. She'd hate to raise less money than those gambling hussies, so I turned to offer Siobhan my masculine help. She was already gone.

I tried to catch up, but all I caught were glimpses of that blue dress as she walked through the trees. A couple times she would turn back to me and smile. I think I heard a little laugh as she moved nearer to the small house under the I Street Bridge she shared with her father.

I was breathing heavily but didn't know if it was the exertion or the guilt creeping into my chest. An invisible cord seemed to pull me toward her.

As I came past tall tule plants on the water's edge, their long green stalks waving in the breeze, I found her. She had removed her shoes and stood on a small dock that protruded into the river. I wondered what else besides her shoes was she planning to remove? That thought stopped me. My heart was beating faster than the Cal Band's military march, but I couldn't move forward. My shoes were sinking in the heavy mud at the river's edge.

I moaned as I watched Siobhan kneel on the dock and run her hands gently along the surface of the water. Large salmon emerged from the depth, nibbling at her fingers. She looked at me and beamed. It was like she was sharing a secret while I stood there, stuck and entranced.

She reached into a small bucket on the dock and scattered some grain onto the water. More and more fish appeared, jumping, splashing, fighting for food, climbing over the top of each other like a mass of slimy snakes.

Siobhan stood up, grinning at the frenzy of fish, and lifted a long wooden shaft that had been lying alongside her on the dock. Running both hands up and down the shaft, she held my attention. I started to get dizzy.

Then I noticed the shiny end of the shaft. Its metal cover caught the sunshine and points of light sparkled across her face and down the front of her dress. She ran a delicate finger along the sharp edges of the crossed metal ridges. Blood coated her finger. She put it in her mouth and stared at me.

I couldn't move. My shoes sunk deeper in the mud.

Keeping her eyes locked on mine, Siobhan lifted the staff high and slammed it into the water. When she raised it above her head, a large salmon had been skewered, flopping, gasping for breath. Water and blood poured onto her upturned face. She opened her mouth and laughed and danced like she was playing in a gentle spring shower.

She brought the fish to the dock, stepped on it with her bare toes, and pulled the shaft out. The fish was almost dead when she stabbed into the water for the next victim. Soon she had a pile of fish with glistening X-shaped holes in their sides.

I started gasping for breath like the dying fish on the dock, but before I could release myself from the sucking mud, a strong hand clamped down on my shoulder and pulled me backward toward solid ground. My muddy feet felt as heavy as the granite headstone Liam McDowell held under his other arm.

He loomed over me blocking the view of his killer daughter. His bare arms looked like the solid granite he worked with. Sweat rolled down his face and darkened the slab of rock he held. His eyes were pleading and frightened. I could still hear splashing behind him.

"I will be taking my daughter away," he said quietly.

I nodded.

"Where will you go?" Laughter and fish bodies slapped on the dock.

"We still have kin in Ireland. Portmagee. We will be able to take care of her," he said. His eyes seemed to plead with me to let him take her, to not hold her responsible for the deaths of …how many men? "I will work with my brothers at the quarry there." He nodded.

I nodded.

He bent slowly and placed the heavy stone at my feet. Like an offering, I thought.

"We will leave tonight," Liam said.

I nodded again and chomped on my wilting cigar.

Quietly he turned around and held his hand out to his daughter. She dropped the shaft and walked toward him. Gently he put his arm around her and pulled her away. She turned and smiled at me, raising a dainty, bloody hand.

I started to wave back but clamped my shaking hand over my mouth instead to stifle the scream that wanted to come.

Siobhan and Liam disappeared through the thicket of oaks and tule.

I heard a pop of firecrackers downstream and thought the sheriff might not have anything left to show off by the time the sun sets. I took out my cigar and tried to get control of my breathing. The end of my stogie had been bitten off. I spit out the tobacco leaves and looked down at the stone at my feet.

Liam's only slab. Already engraved. In his precise way, he had taken care of my dilemma. We would have only one grave for all those lost souls, after all.

His last headstone for the Woodland Cemetery read:

Unknown Male and Parts of Two Others
July 1, 1934

Strange Place for a Date

Jenny Carless

Mary winced at the strength of Ed's grip as he wrapped a weather-worn hand firmly around the neck of the wine bottle. He held the bottle against his chest and stabbed firmly with the corkscrew, forcing its sharp end into the soft cork. Nerves in overdrive, Mary's mind shot in a dark direction: She didn't want to think of the bottle as her own neck, or the cork as her chest, but once she'd let the images seep into her mind, heck if she could erase them.

Sweat trickled and itched every which-way across her skin, and the red and green plaid wool blanket she sat on wasn't helping. Thank goodness it wasn't August; at least in late September, the oven that was the Central Valley dialed it down to a bearable temperature by late afternoon.

A flurry of honking drew Mary to squint at the searing sky. A small team of ducks, in perfect V formation, headed in for a landing in the slough far down the sloping hill upon which she and Ed sat. Enveloped in the shade of an ancient valley oak, she exhaled with the ducks' descent, trying to relax into the moment while still debating with herself at this late stage whether this date was a good idea.

Mary loved that Sacramento sat on the Pacific Flyway and thought briefly that if the conversation stalled, at least they could watch the birds. But then she remembered how chatty Ed had been when they met on the plane last week. Lack of conversation wasn't going to be a problem.

With a start, she pulled herself back to the present. Ed had said something and was waiting for a response.

"Sorry, I…"

"You're not paying attention." A tinge of annoyance colored his voice. He towered over her, kneeling while he handed her a glass of the wine he'd finally opened. He made a point of looking her in the eye when they clinked glasses.

Mary's eyes followed his muscular hands up to a beige dress shirt, sleeves rolled partway up in military-like folds. Crisp and clean jeans, too. Salt and pepper hair framed a face with deeply etched lines—less like wrinkles and more like crevices worn over time into ancient rock. He'd probably had them his entire life.

Mary leaned back, shifting her weight onto her right hand, the one farthest from him. In fact, she *was* paying close attention, attuned to his every move. For example, he still had a tight grip on the neck of the wine bottle.

"Just enjoying the view. I love that there's so much bird life around Sacramento." She indicated the slough with a nod of her head. She smiled and hoped she wasn't going to have to appease this man's ego for the next two hours.

Ed redirected Mary's attention to his bounteous picnic and went on to describe, in encyclopedic detail, the origins of the various fruits and cheeses laid out before them. She already knew—and loved—the Point Reyes Original Blue and the Cowgirl Creamery Mt Tam, but Ed had also brought a goat cheese from a local farm she hadn't heard of.

"Nice of you to go to so much trouble." Her mouth salivated from the rich, creamy cheese she nibbled.

He rewarded her with a grin, almost self-deprecating, and thought maybe he'd realized that he'd just been kind of a jerk. She let out a breath again. She could do this. Dating was like getting back on a horse, right? No need to be so jumpy.

That made Mary think of her colleagues at work—mostly younger, less experienced but more arrogant men. For the past week, they'd been making jokes at her expense. Surprised that Ed had actually asked her out, taking bets about whether she'd make it through the afternoon without things going horribly wrong…that kind of thing.

Was it so hard to imagine a man asking her out? Slightly north of 40, she hardly had a foot in the grave. Trim and fit, she enjoyed soft, clear skin, and once a month she forked out for a top-notch hairdresser to make the most of her graying hair. Men could do a lot worse. The "ribbing" at the office felt more like bullying to her. She wanted to prove them wrong in the worst way.

She licked a salty drop of perspiration from her upper lip and tuned in again to Ed, who had switched from talking about the cheese and grapes to extolling the virtues of the wine—a Sonoma County sauvignon blanc he'd picked up from one of his favorite wineries, he said. He knew the winemaker, he said. He really could ramble on. But that suited her just fine. The less she had to talk, the less likely her nerves would betray her.

He put his glass down on the cheese board between them. "Why don't you take off your sweater and relax?" He reached toward her shoulder as if to start pulling it off.

Mary flinched and pulled one side of her cardigan across her stomach as she leaned away. The soft cotton felt comforting. "I'm fine, thanks." She glared until he dropped his arm and settled back down. Immediately, her cheeks flushed in embarrassment at her overreaction. She looked down and started pushing a juicy green grape around her glass plate. She had to pull herself together.

"Not too hot?"

"Nope." Yes, of course she was! But she wasn't about to take off the damn sweater.

Mary thought back to when Ed had helped her *on* with her sweater, just last week on the flight from Dallas, in the frigid airplane cabin. Then, he'd seemed helpful. Why did she interpret his move less generously now? Just those nerves, she supposed.

On the plane, he'd started chatting before they'd even pulled back from the gate. Then, too, he'd needed little prompting, and that was okay with Mary. She was more of an observer than a talker. You could learn more about a person by watching them than by talking to them, anyway—the kind of information they didn't necessarily want you to learn. For example, Ed used flattery to try to get what he wanted. He'd spread it on pretty thick, and he focused more on himself than on others. And what did she have to say of interest, anyway? She didn't want to talk about her past relationships. Or her job.

By the time they'd landed in Sacramento, Mary had learned a lot about subjects she'd never thought much about before, including pioneer cemeteries like this one. It seemed like a strange place for a date. Especially a first date. But from the minute she'd sat down next to Ed on that plane, she'd thought about her colleagues' endless teasing and had hoped that he would ask her out. Thankfully, he did—and she wasn't going to let a little thing like spending an afternoon among departed souls stop her from accepting.

Mary had nothing against cemeteries. Ed had asked her, when he texted her the address, if she was afraid of ghosts. To the contrary, she liked the idea of souls settling in together for the long haul. As long as you didn't get stuck next to someone who would talk your ear off. Like Ed. She sure wouldn't be able to take his nattering for eternity.

And this cemetery was very pretty. They sat on a rise, protected from the worst of the afternoon sun by the enormous spidery oak branches. A smell of dust and parched Central Valley earth filled the air. Several other oaks and a few small mausoleums broke up the repeating pattern below: row upon row of gravestones protruding from the unnaturally green grass. It was clearly a well-maintained cemetery because the grass would be dead otherwise at this time of year. But where were the gardeners?

Being at a cemetery *per se* didn't bother her. Being at an isolated one—light traffic on the drive here and no one else on the grounds—put her a little on edge. Was it part of a test of some sort to see how far Ed could push her, or simply to see how gullible or naïve she was? She'd enjoyed the hint of surprise on his face when she'd said yes. Yep, she could surprise people, too.

That made her think about her colleagues again. She really did want to show them and pull this off. The alternative wasn't worth thinking about.

When Mary focused back on Ed, he was wrapping up the story of how he'd first met the winemaker. She hoped there wouldn't be a test. He finally took a breath and, without asking, scooped up her still half-full glass. He turned toward the cooler, his back to her.

"Tell me about your dating history, Mary." The wet pop of the cork as he re-opened the bottle almost drowned out his quiet voice.

"I really don't want anymore, thanks."

"No more dating?" He laughed at his little joke.

"No more wine."

He was doing something else besides filling her glass, but Mary couldn't see around his back. Was he messing with her wine? *Stop letting your imagination run wild*, she scolded herself. If Ed had wanted to drug or poison her, he could just as easily have spiked the cheese beforehand. And it was too late, if that was the case, she thought, as she popped another cheese-laden cracker into her mouth.

"Sure, you want some more." He turned and handed her the glass.

The brimming glass glowed pale gold. Mary hesitated for a moment before accepting it. Definitely tempting. She was enjoying the zesty blend of citrus tones and had made a note of the name, to look it up at her local wine shop. And it felt criminal to waste a nice wine. She'd settle for sipping at it. Slowly.

"Not much to tell about my dating life, if I'm honest. Always busy, and online dating seems dangerous, you know? It's hard to meet people," she said. "So, when we found ourselves together on the plane, it felt...right."

"But how's that different than online dating? You don't know anything about me," Ed said, settling back down opposite her.

He obviously didn't realize how much he yacked.

"Well, I do think I'm a pretty good judge of character. And I feel like I got to know you on the plane," she said. "Anyway, I know how to take care of myself." Take that, Mr. 'I dare you to come to a cemetery.' It was good to remind herself that she *could* handle this. Nothing was going to get out of control or go horribly wrong, despite her colleagues' predictions. She hoped.

"So...a cemetery for a first date, huh? Definitely a first for me." She suspected that it wasn't for him. Men were such creatures of habit.

"They hold so many fascinating stories. I thought you'd enjoy learning about some of the people here. Some of them are my old friends."

Mary thought about that for a second but had no idea how to reply, so she changed the subject. "You mentioned the

Forty Niners—the old prospectors. I'm interested to see how some of those old grave markers have fared after all these years." In the cemetery below them, Mary tried to see if she could identify the oldest part with the Gold Rush graves. The southern section, with uneven rows and tilting headstones, looked most likely.

"I'll take you on a little tour. But first, drink up!"

He reached toward her, and Mary scrambled up and stepped back, spilling most of her wine on his wool blanket.

"Now look what you've done!" His booming voice bounced off the thick oak trunk. She took another step back, almost tripping on the edge of the blanket.

"Oh, gosh, sorry. Clumsy me." Actually, that's what happens when you overfill a glass, especially when someone said they didn't want any more, she wanted to say.

Using her sandal, she made an indent in the edge of the blanket to let the excess wine flow off onto the grass. Out of the corner of her eye, she gauged Ed's reaction, but after the initial outburst, he seemed to let it go.

"See, I told you I didn't need anything more to drink!" She smiled and attempted a laugh. "Sorry to waste that great wine, though."

They stood and faced each other. What remained of the picnic lay between them, a few soft mounds of melting cheese and the skeleton of a grape bunch.

Mary's legs appreciated the stretch, and she didn't miss the itchy wool. Out across the flat landscape in the distance, the sun had drifted lower. Closer to home, she had another look around the cemetery but still didn't see anyone else. But what had she expected—throngs of visitors?

"Let's go on that tour you mentioned," she said. The wooded part of the cemetery below them lay in deep shade already. She'd rather be out of there by dark. "How 'bout we tidy all this up afterward?"

"Sure you don't want to take off that sweater and relax a little?"

"Nope."

Despite her initial misgivings about Ed's choice of the cemetery, Mary looked forward to seeing the gravestones of some of the optimistic pioneers who had rushed into California's Gold Country in the late 1840s and the 1850s. She recognized the poignancy—and irony—of so many adventurers, most with their dreams unfulfilled, now lying buried in the very soil they'd hoped would be their salvation.

Mary pulled her cardigan across her again, settled her hands into the pockets and began to walk down the hill, hoping Ed would follow. Within a few steps, he caught up and overtook her. She followed him across uneven ground as he cut through designated sections rather than following the orderly paths.

Ed first stopped in front of a tall, thin headstone made of smooth granite that looked almost new. A few pebbles from the nearby path sat scattered across the base of the stone. He leaned down, plucked them and tossed them back onto the walkway.

Mary read everything out loud, including the dates and inscription. "Eleanor Baptiste. March 12, 1957—December 11, 2018. In God's Garden."

A gust of hot wind rattled the branches above them, sending some of the driest leaves swirling away into the air.

"Eleanor was a gardener."

Ed's voice made Mary jump.

"Her roses always won prizes at the county fair." He leaned down and ran his finger along the delicately engraved rose in the stone.

Mary opened her mouth, about to ask Ed to tell her how he knew Eleanor, but he had turned and walked away. Next, they passed through a freshly painted wrought-iron gate into a new section of the graveyard, where, after cutting across several rows, Ed stopped again.

Once more, Mary read the text aloud. "Jean Stafford. February 2, 1943—September 13, 2008. Toward the sun rising. Joshua 1:15."

She waited for a comment about Jean. Nothing. Ed simply stared at the gravestone, seemingly lost in thought, his head tilted slightly to one side.

Two rows over, the next headstone on Ed's tour—wide, with a slight curve across the top—sat on a small pedestal. The design included a pair of praying hands. Mary read out loud: "Genevieve Thomas. January 23, 1961—October 31, 2009. Generous heart, blessed spirit."

Ed snorted. "In the end, Gen really *wasn't* very generous."

"What?" What kind of a thing was that to say about the dead?

"She mostly thought about herself."

You're a fine one to talk, Mary thought.

Ed stood with his head down for several seconds before turning to her. "You're not like that, are you, Mary?" His tone leaned toward whiny.

"How did you know all these women?" Probably a wasted question, Mary figured. Would he even tell her the truth?

"I dated them." A hint of a smile slipped across his face, and he reached out to touch her shoulder. "Don't worry. It's purely coincidental that they died after we broke up."

"You're saying that these women all died *right after you dated them*?"

"Pretty soon after, yep."

Ed seemed to be having fun trying to scare Mary. Little did he know, she didn't scare easily.

"I'd much rather see the more historic part of the cemetery."

"Patience, Mary. I told you, this is a tour of special places. I wanted you to meet some of these women. My friends."

He used the past tense, but it seemed almost as if these women were still alive to Ed—the way he'd swept the pebbles from Eleanor's grave, had gently touched the others' headstones.

One mausoleum they passed had an oversize metal door. Ed grasped the handle and shook it, but it didn't budge.

"Imagine if you got locked inside something like that," he said. "The walls too thick for anyone to hear you cry for help."

Mary shuddered but reminded herself that he was just playing games. At least, she hoped he was.

They walked on, across a pea gravel path, the crunch of their footsteps disturbing a pair of sparrows. The next grave Ed stopped in front of brought Mary up short. Lying flat on the ground, more like a pillow, this one had an elaborate engraving along the left side featuring a cross, lilies, a prayer book and a rosary.

Mary Francis Harlow
March 22, 1978 — November 28, 2019
Beloved sister

Same first name as her own, Mary thought, *and not only born the same year, but the same month that she was. Mary Francis even had a sister. Ed couldn't know these things about Mary, could he?* For a moment, her mind darted to an image of her sister Clare having to select a headstone for her grave. She shook her head, chasing away the macabre thought.

"Tell me about her," Mary whispered as she kneeled down. She slipped her right hand out of her sweater pocket briefly to touch the cold, still-shiny marble.

"Ah, Mary Francis. A very interesting story, actually."

They stood on a slight incline—Mary on the lower side, dwarfed by Ed. He described how he'd met Mary Francis at a single's event and then went off on another long-winded story, which Mary eventually tuned out. She thought about Clare, whom she hadn't spoken to in months, and determined to call her soon. She looked around at the mausoleums and remembered Ed's veiled threat.

She let him go on for a while but began to feel frustrated with the game-playing. After all, he'd lured her here with interesting stories about the old miners, and she wanted to see that part of the cemetery.

"You're not going to show me the Gold Rush graves, are you?"

She hadn't hidden the sharpness to her voice, and Ed's reaction came swiftly. His large hand clamped around her right arm as it had done with the wine bottle just an hour earlier.

"Why are you so impatient? I have a plan!"

Mary turned away to hide the tears brimming in her eyes. She hadn't expected that outburst. Her arm hurt, but she tried not to show it. Instead, she concentrated on getting things back on track. She stepped back, forcing him to either hold on tighter or let her go. He released his grip.

"That's *enough*, really!" Mary's voice dissolved across the empty grounds.

This wasn't how she'd imagined things going when she'd been getting ready that afternoon. Her stomach did a little flip and her eyes shot back and forth, taking in the massive trees, the mausoleums. Where *were* the gardeners? And were there no graveside services this afternoon? Were they really alone?

Doubts and self-recriminations pulsed through her mind. Why had it been so important to her to prove to everyone at work that she could reel this man in?

"Now, are you ready to continue the tour?" Ed's voice was quiet—not much more than a whisper.

Of course, she wasn't. At this point, she wanted to put this man in his place and get out of there. Settle into a warm bath and nurse the bruise now blooming on her arm. But she'd come this far, and dammit, she was going to see it through.

"Sure," she managed.

A chill hung in the air as the sun slipped farther down and they headed deeper into the wooded area. Mary tripped on a root and stumbled forward. Ed caught her and pulled her close for just a moment—his firm hands locked onto her arms—before releasing her. She stepped away, fighting a growing dizziness. Maybe he *had* slipped something into her wine, or the food.

"You haven't asked me about *my* dating history." His eyes drilled into hers.

Sweat slipped down Mary's back, no longer due to the heat. She didn't want to ask. She just wanted to see another face, another living human there in the darkening grave-yard. She took a deep breath, trying to quash a rising wave of nausea.

Up the hill, something flashed among the detritus of their picnic. But it was just the last rays of sun hitting one of the tiffin boxes Ed had brought the food in. Were her chances for this to end well fading, too? She'd thought she was so clever, that she had everything under control. She'd been looking forward to gloating to her colleagues. But what had seemed brave and self-affirming now seemed stupid and reckless.

They had reached the most remote part of the ceme-tery, steeped in chilly shade. Mary's knees wobbled, and she leaned against a tall headstone for support. She rubbed her hand over the engraved letters to help her read them, but everything seemed blurry now, too.

"Shall I tell you about my time with Eleanor, Jean, Genevieve and Mary Francis?"

"Honestly, I think I've just had enough for one day," she said.

"This is the most interesting part."

"Really. Can we...can we just wrap this up now?"

"No need to shout." Ed smiled and turned slowly around, one arm out wide, indicating the whole cemetery. "I don't think there's anyone else to hear you, if that's what you're thinking."

That was, in fact, exactly what Mary was thinking. She followed his gaze. The sun had left their picnic spot at the top of the rise now. Long, twisted shadows from the oaks enveloped them both.

Ed moved in close to her, forcing her to step back. She bumped up against a thick trunk. A shiver spasmed through her, and she drew her sweater tighter around her body.

"I said, that's *enough*!"

"Cold? Good thing you kept that sweater on after all, I suppose," Ed said, grabbing her cardigan by its collar and sliding his thumb up to her throat. She squirmed and coughed, trying to release the pressure that threatened to cut off her breath.

Good thing I did, Mary thought. It wasn't big, the switchblade she'd been guarding in the sweater pocket, but it would slow him down at least.

With one hand, Ed forced her neck harder against the trunk. Her scalp scraped against the rough bark. His other hand pressed a sharp object to her cheek. Mary could just make out the curve and the forked end of a cheese knife below her eye. One solid push and it would put an even bigger dent in her already limited dating life.

She fumbled with the switchblade, trying not to alert Ed by moving her arm too much. Everything seemed fuzzy, whether from something he'd put in her wine or her fear, she wasn't sure. Maybe both.

"I told you I was very close to those women," he whispered, his face inches from hers, his breath sour from the wine. "Would it surprise you to know that I killed them all?" He pressed the knife harder. A warm trickle slid down Mary's cheek. "You didn't really think it was a coincidence that they all died after we dated, did you?"

Mary slid a couple of inches down the oak trunk, the rough bark scraping her back and shoulders. She had to hold on just a few minutes more. Finally, she managed to get the switchblade in the right position. At least, she hoped so. Ed's hand still up against her neck, she took as deep a breath as she could, eased her right hand out of the pocket, pressed the button on the knife's handle and plunged the blade into Ed's side. He screamed and stepped backward. She wrestled out of his loosened grasp and flung herself to one side, tumbling onto the grass.

Ed's hands held his bloody side, and he groaned. But he was still on his feet. He took a few uneven steps in her direction. She crab-walked backward.

From over her shoulder, heavy footsteps and loud voices pounded toward them. *About time*, she thought.

"You didn't really think I'd come here all on my own, did you?" she managed, finally allowing herself to collapse into the cool grass. But she made a mental note to have a word with her team about taking so long; she'd been signaling to them for at least the past ten minutes.

Ed protested and scuffled with the three policemen who'd been monitoring the date—the young men who'd been predicting her failure all week. When the click of the handcuffs told her it was over, Mary lifted herself onto her elbows to look at him. Their eyes met, and she pulled back her cardigan and turned to one side, revealing the recording device she'd been wearing. She couldn't resist one last smile. This one was genuine.

There would be time to explain everything to Ed during his interrogation. She looked forward to detailing how she'd set him up from the beginning, booking the seat next to his on the flight from Dallas. Mostly, she looked forward to being in the office tomorrow. Her colleagues would have to admit that she'd managed to get Ed to take her bait, that she'd pulled it off.

This 40-something still had it.

A Teeny Weeny Drop

Elaine Faber

It was late October, and the nation continued to mourn the September 11, 2001, New York World Trade Center attack, where nearly 3,000 innocent victims lost their lives. Newspapers were still filled with stories of human and canine heroes who continued to scour the rubble, hoping to retrieve any evidence of human remains…some small comfort to grieving families.

I work at the *Sacramento Daily Sun* newspaper where conversations around the water cooler continued to focus on the inexplicable tragedy and its aftermath. Who was behind the attack? Would the United States declare war on the perpetrators? If nothing else, the stories increased the number of newspaper sales.

One afternoon, my editor, Tom Googenfeld, stuck his head around the corner of the cubical I share with another reporter, Julie Trowbridge. "Clive, Julie? Reporters' meeting in the lunch room in ten minutes for a special announcement."

He had me at *lunch room*! With yet another gut-wrenching article on my desk about one of the 341 firemen lost in the Twin Towers, I was ready for anything to get away from the twenty-four-seven news cycle.

I joined Tom and the four other *Daily Sun* reporters in the crowded break room. I stood beside Julie, close enough to touch. Her sleeve brushing against my jacket made my heart beat a little faster. Unfortunately, she's blonde and beautiful and never gives me a second look, an old guy with gray hair and a paunch. She wasn't the only one. I haven't had a girl-friend since bell bottoms and 'big hair' were in fashion.

Julie held a notepad and a pen, eager to take notes and make a good impression. "What's up, boss? Is someone get-ting promoted?" Julie giggled nervously. She always was a suck-up. I expected the editor might announce more office cut-backs rather than a promotion. We all held our breath, anxious to hear what he had on his mind. Was someone about to get fired?

Tom gazed at the five of us. "Believe it or not, this month, on October 31, the moon will be full for the first time in twen-ty-seven years. It's a Halloween phenomenon that occurs only three or four times a century. To commemorate the occasion, I've decided to hype the event, and give the subscribers some-thing else to think about besides 9/11. I'm sending all of you out to find the most compelling Halloween stories you can. We'll print all five stories next week before Halloween and the public will score each story. Scores will be tallied and the win-ning reporter will get an all-expense-paid Lake Tahoe week-end for you and your plus-one. One of the voting subscribers' names will be drawn to win a similar weekend vacation."

A collective sigh of relief from the five of us almost whooshed from the room. It wasn't a promotion for anyone, but it wasn't cutbacks or layoffs either. Hadn't we heard enough bad news lately?

"There's more. You're each to pick a small town some-where within thirty miles of Sacramento. Go there and write about how the town celebrates Halloween. Is there a haunted house or a local ghost story? Maybe a special event or a parade? They can be humorous, spooky, poignant, or straight reporting. The newspaper will provide an expense account for food and lodging, so plan an overnight." He looked at his watch. "Your stories are due this Friday by five o'clock. We'll start printing them in the Monday edition with the last one Friday. Votes will be tallied and the winner announced on Saturday, the day before Halloween."

Julie and I walked back to our desks together. "Where are you going, Julie?"

"I think Placerville. A lot of miners lived there during the gold rush. There must be some good ghost stories there. You?"

I nodded. "I think I'll head up to that little town near Jackson, Mokelumne Hill? I hear they have a haunted hotel and a boot hill nearby. I think they were also involved with gold mining. Should be something interesting… I mean, a haunted hotel? Sounds promising."

Julie frowned. Probably mad that she hadn't thought of Mokelumne Hill before I did.

I packed an overnight bag, made a reservation at the vintage Hotel Leger and headed east into the Sierra foothills.

Entering Mokelumne Hill city limits, I was surprised to find the town had only one main street with small businesses on each side and a number of older homes scattered about.

Apparently, Halloween was a seasonal high point for tourism, and this year, even more so, if they'd heard about the full moon phenomenon. I was impressed by the witches and goblins, pumpkins, and ghouls decorating front yards and store windows. Dried cornstalks lined the streets. Jack-o-lanterns hung from each lamp post. Shopkeepers dressed in witch, warlock, ghost, and vampire costumes hawked holiday-themed merchandise on the sidewalks. Every shop window displayed witches and cauldrons, spirits and ghouls. Tourists clambered atop horse-drawn hay wagons and carts.

Coming here was a good choice. Writing this story was going to be a piece of cake, since the local businesses took advantage of the tourists' interest in the merry-making, and the Leger Hotel took advantage of the tourism. Like our editor, the Mokelumne Hill city fathers thought their citizens had grieved the 9/11 tragedy long enough, and should get their minds back on spending money, where they belonged. Let the nation grieve if it must. Mokelumne Hill merchants would strike while the moon was full!

I ate lunch at the hotel dining room and delighted in the attentions of a charming waitress with long black hair, sparkling gold eyes, and fluttering lashes. With a glance, Jenny Moore, according to the nametag attached to her ample bosom, churned up feelings of…dare I say…lust? The same feelings I often had for Julie, but never acted upon, being a widower well past middle-age, and an almost-regular churchgoer. Imagine my surprise when Jenny handed me a folded napkin with a message scrawled inside. *Meet me outside the bar tonight. 11:45 P.m. Come alone.*

I left my lunch half-eaten and stumbled outside to ponder the situation. With her charms, and the number of young men in town she could have chosen, what could she possibly want with an old gray-headed guy like me?

The afternoon dragged by as I interviewed shopkeepers, gathered a few local ghost stories, and snapped photos until well past sundown.

Back in my room, I tried to ignore Jenny's invitation. Several stories I'd heard that afternoon were possibilities for my contest submission. I couldn't help checking the time again every few minutes.

Finally, at 11:25 P.M, I was drawn back to the hotel bar like a demented moth to a flame.

Tourists packed the bar and the loud music made normal conversation impossible. I could see Jenny weaving back and forth through the crowd, taking drink orders, but she never glanced my way. She was even prettier than Julie, her dark complexion and long black hair a stark contrast to my blonde coworker. My first impression was correct; she had played an old guy for a fool, just for the fun of it. She had no intentions of meeting me at 11:45 P.m. I walked out onto the sidewalk for another look at the stars before I planned to return to my room.

At 11:35 P.m. Jenny slipped out the back door. For weeks she had scoured the tourists, sure she would find the middle-aged man with silver-white hair and mustache she needed, but as the days grew shorter, she had nearly given up hope. On nearly the last possible evening before Halloween, just such a man had walked into the bar. He could change her destiny.

Jenny wrapped her red cape around her shoulders and circled the building. There stood her savior! She had always been blessed with the ability to sense the future, knew when the kettle was about to boil or a visitor to knock on her door. An oppressive spirit had even settled on her the morning of September 11th. But, on this night, the moon overhead nearly full, her fate was in the hands of a stranger. Without his coop-eration, she would not escape the family curse.

Jenny moved from the shadows into the light where the older man stood beside the entrance to the bar. "Hello. You came!" She placed her small hand on his arm, glanced shyly down and then gazed into his eyes, intent on bending his will to her own. If ever she needed to ply her skills, it was now. "I'm Jenny. Thank you for coming. You're the only one who can help me."

"I'm pleased to meet you, Jenny. I'm Clive. But, I don't understand. Surely you have family or friends better able to help you. What is troubling you, my dear?" Clive patted the hand she had placed on his arm.

Jenny lowered her head again, brushing her lashes against her pale face. Her lips trembled as a practiced tear trickled down her cheek. A curl of white hair tumbled to her forehead, displaced from the top of her black curls.

"Here, here, now. None of that." Clive brushed the lock off her forehead and tucked it behind her ear. "I'll help if I can. Don't cry." He tipped up her chin, pulled his handkerchief from his pocket, and dabbed the tear from her cheek. "Now, give me a smile and tell me all about it. What can Clive do to dry up those tears?"

"I fear you'll think me crazy, sir, but I swear what I'm about to tell you is the truth." Jenny took his arm and pulled him to a bench farther into the shadows. Amongst occasional sighs, gulps, and tears, she began her tale. "Years ago, during the gold rush, a miner was unjustly hanged, falsely accused of theft, right here in Mokelumne Hill. His name was Herman Moore, and he's buried in the graveyard up yonder." She nodded toward the crooked trees surrounding the dark cemetery. "Sometimes his ghost is seen walking among the headstones. Since Herman's death, his female descendants have suffered a terrible curse."

"No! What do you mean?"

"It seems Herman came from Europe, descended from and connected to a family of magicians and sorcerers. Some even say he was related to vampires. I'm one of his descendants. About four or five times each century, during the week when the moon is full on All-Hollow's Eve, any of his unmarried female descendants between the age of eighteen and twenty-nine are in grave danger unless..." A single tear slid from Jenny's eye.

Clive sucked in his breath and placed his arm protectively around her shoulder. "Go on. Unless...what?"

"For the first time in twenty-seven years, the moon will be full on Halloween, and to avoid the curse, I need the aid of an older man with long silver-white hair, who resembles the judge who sentenced poor Herman to death. Before the stroke of midnight, if I place a drop of this man's blood on Herman's gravestone, the curse will be broken and I'll be safe." Jenny's pale lips trembled. She dropped her gaze to her clasped hands in her lap. "I only need a single drop. It's the only thing that will save me."

Clive raised perplexed eyebrows. His hand dropped lower over her shoulder. "What will happen if you fail to comply?"

"It's so terrible I dare not speak it aloud." Whispering these words, Jenny clung to Clive's shoulder and wept piteously. Had she convinced him to go with her to the headstone? And, once there, could she muster the courage to do what she must to stave off the curse that would alter her life forever?

I was speechless. In my fifteen years as a newspaper reporter, I've met a lot of women, but never had I encountered such a stunning creature that so captivated my heart within moments of meeting. Never had such a ridiculous tale so captured my imagination. I was inclined to leap from the bench, take her by the hand, and race to the cemetery. Only with great difficulty did I pummel my rash impulses into submission, sit back on the bench, and stare into the starry sky to consider her request.

Overhead, the moon was only a sliver away from being a perfect circle. It hung blood-red over the city, casting an orange glow across the sidewalks still churning with costumed tourists, jostling and laughing, their joyous songs of nonsense carried on the night wind into the sky. A goblin and a witch passed nearby and turned into the bar, raucous with drink and merriment.

The young woman stirred in my arms, her sobs finally ceasing. She dashed tears from her cheeks and looked up at me. "You will help me, won't you? I'm so desperate. We only need a teeny weeny drop of blood, really. I'd be so grateful."

If she truly believed her outrageous tale, considering the unusual request, even a gentleman such as I, couldn't help wondering…how grateful? Wicked thoughts I never allowed myself to think about Julie swirled through my head. On the other hand, just exactly how much was a *teeny weeny* drop of blood, and just how crazy was this charming waif of a girl?

I shivered. A gust of wind rustled the cornstalks tied to the lamp posts. The moon seemed to be sliced in half as a thin cloud crept across its center.

I glanced at my watch. 11:47 P.m. I decided to humor the dear child and see where all this would lead. "Well, let's get on with it. Can we walk to the cemetery?" My hand rested around the small penknife I always carried in my pocket. If a teeny weeny drop of blood was all it took to satisfy her fantasy and win her gratitude, I could do that. The naughty images I'd banished from my mind resurfaced.

Jenny took my arm and hustled me toward the cemetery. She squealed as a man dressed as a vampire loomed from the bushes. I took her ice-cold hand and pulled her closer as we entered the graveyard lit only by moonlight. Here and there, costumed tourists edged amongst the headstones, talking and laughing. Jenny seemed like a charming girl despite her fantasies, and my heart stirred. I wanted so to calm her fears and win her affection. Perhaps I'd bring her coffee in bed tomorrow morning…

"Here it is." Herman Moore's gravestone gleamed in the moonlight. Jenny danced toward the stone and ran her fingers over the grooves forming the letters:

Herman Moore 1810 -1854

"Poor Herman." Jenny glanced at her watch. "Are you ready? We don't have much time. It needs to be done before midnight." Jenny's beautiful smile, holding so much promise only moments before, faded, replaced by a fiendish leer. Her lips parted and instead of dainty white teeth, the four canine teeth appeared so much longer than I remembered. "I'm sorry, Clive. Really, I am."

I cringed at the sight of Jenny's wild eyes, gleaming in the moonlight. The thrill of a moonlight adventure with the lovely lady faded and common sense returned. Jenny had no intention of settling for a pricked finger and a teeny weeny drop of blood. For whatever reason, it seemed only my blood splashed across the accursed headstone would bring back her sweet smile.

"Hold on there, young lady." I backed away, glanced left and right, saw no one near. Where had all the costumed tourists gone? The witches and ghosts and even the vampire had disappeared. The Leger Hotel and all the tourists seemed miles away.

In the distance, the town clock began to strike. Twelve o'clock…the witching hour. *Bong…bong…bong.*

The hour that a vampire, if there was such a thing, might easily assault a stranger to thwart her twisted notion of an imagined family curse.

Bong…bong…bong.

My dull life back home suddenly held a great deal more appeal. How I wished I was back in Sacramento, eating tuna sandwiches and playing gin rummy with a neighbor, and had never heard of Mokelumne Hill.

Bong…bong…bong.

Bong! Midnight. *Bong…bong…*

Jenny shrieked and rushed at me, her sharp teeth bared…

Nearly paralyzed with fear, I put up my hands, closed my

eyes and held my breath, as Jenny's teeth sank into my throat. The news reporter in me had always wondered what it was like to be dead. I guessed I'd soon know…

Time ticked by. I awoke, lying on the ground. I ran my hands up and down my chest and over my neck. A trickle of blood dripped from my fingers onto my jacket. "I'm still alive?" I opened my eyes. Herman Moore's gravestone gleamed in the moonlight.

Somehow, I struggled to my feet. Jenny's red cape lay on the ground, but…where was Jenny?

Still dizzy, I stumbled out of the graveyard, down the street, to the Leger Hotel. Maybe Jenny had slipped away and gone back to town. The hotel bar was still noisy with rowdy tourists when I went inside. I worked my way through the crowd and slid onto the only empty seat at the end of the bar. I needed a drink to clear my head.

The bartender swiped down the bar in front of me. "What'll it be, friend?"

"What's good for a shock? I've just had…" I touched my neck and wiped away a tiny smear of blood. Best not tell the bartender what had happened. Who would believe Jenny thought she was a vampire, and I'd barely escaped with my life.

"Whiskey? Say…You okay? You're bleeding." He handed me a cocktail napkin and I dabbed my neck.

"Thanks. I'm not much of a drinker. I'll just have a beer."

The bartender drew a glass of local ale and slapped it on the counter. "That'll be seven bucks."

"Seven bucks! This afternoon, your waitress only charged me five." I reached for the glass and took a long swallow.

"What waitress? We didn't have a waitress this afternoon. Bill Duckworth and I worked the afternoon shift. Who you talkin' about?"

"You know. Jenny Moore, long black hair, a white streak in front? Tall, big booz—*um*... personality?"

Color faded from the bartender's face. He backed away from the bar. "The last time anyone named Jenny Moore worked here was in 1854, when they hanged her father. Folks have reported seeing her ghost walk the halls, mostly during the full moon." He turned to another man behind the counter pulling a glass of beer. "Hey, Bill. When was the last time a guest reported seeing Jenny Moore?"

"I don't know. Maybe, around Halloween, last year?" He shook his head and turned away.

I finished my beer in two gulps, tossed a ten dollar bill on the bar, then pushed my way through the crowd, went outside, and stumbled down the wooden sidewalk. My hands shook as I plopped onto the bench where Jenny and I had talked.

A small black cat hunched beside the bench, tail whipping around its four black feet. A white blaze of fur over one ear, past one gold-colored eye, ended beside its nose. The kitten stared up at me, a look of terror in its eyes, such as to soften the hardest heart.

I picked up the kitten, stroked its back, and peered into its eyes. Tiny prickles crept up the back of my neck as I tried to erase an impossible thought from my mind. I shook my head. "Couldn't be," I whispered. The kitten mewed piteously and blinked its golden eyes. I held the kitten to my cheek and heard the rumble of a purr. The kitten gently licked a spot of the blood from my neck, and then nuzzled my collarbone. "Don't worry, honey," I said. "I'll take you home with me. I think I'll call you...Jenny. I hope you like tuna sandwiches and gin rummy." I tucked the kitten inside my coat and straightened my jacket over its barely discernible bulge. We made our way through the crowded bar and up to my room.

While little Jenny slept on my pillow, I wrote a 700-word newspaper story about the first Halloween full moon in twenty-seven years, about the miners buried on boot hill, how Herman Moore was unjustly hanged, and how his daughter's ghost is sometimes seen in and around the Leger Hotel when the moon is full.

The story turned out to be poignant and colorful and I figured it might even win the editor's contest for the best Halloween story. At the very least, when the *Sacramento Daily Sun* subscribers read my piece, for a few minutes, they'd forget the tragedy that took almost 3,000 lives on September 11th. But I didn't write a word about meeting a lovely girl with long black hair who lured me into a graveyard, seconds too late to fend off an old family curse.

I didn't write why I returned home from my weekend excursion with a small black kitten with gold eyes and a white blaze on her forehead that resembled a lock of hair, who had a taste for blood. Who would believe it?

Nameless

Kim Keeline

In Colma, California, known as "the City of Souls," the dead outnumber the living a thousand to one. You'd think one more body wouldn't matter.

The tombstone read:

*Norton I - Emperor of the United States and Protector of Mexico
Joshua A. Norton 1819-1880*

But that wasn't who was dead.

I mean, Emperor Norton *was* dead—in a coffin six feet under. His body had been moved to Colma in 1934, during the great San Francisco cemetery eviction, to make way for development.

A woman's body lay on top of his grave, sprawled like a doll dropped from a child's hand.

I hadn't meant to find her. Once I did, I had to discover who she was.

My name is Margaret, but everyone calls me Daisy because "Margarita" is the flower's name in Spanish. I'm fifteen and a sophomore at El Camino, the city's only high school because the dead don't do homework.

Mom is second generation in the funeral business. She met my dad when she started at Woodlawn Memorial Cemetery, where they both still work.

We live directly across the street from Woodlawn, so their commute is less than a minute walk. It's not like you are ever far from a cemetery when you live in Colma. When there are seventeen major cemeteries, every street has at least one entrance to a graveyard. You get used to it.

Heck, there are history walks and annual events connected to our cemeteries. We get a lot of tourists. Wyatt Earp's grave is one of the most popular, but at Woodlawn, the favorite is Emperor Norton.

Joshua Norton was an eccentric old man in Gold Rush San Francisco. Sort of homeless, possibly a bit crazy, he declared himself Emperor in 1859. He printed his own money, made proclamations, and became sort of a legend. He has both a tombstone and a nearby stone circle plaque. People still leave cards and flowers on his grave.

The next tombstone over is the Empress Norton. It's for Jose Julio Sarria who wasn't even born until more than forty years after the Emperor's death. He was an activist and the first openly gay person to run for public office in the United States. He performed a drag act as "The Grand Mere, Absolute Empress I de San Francisco, and the Widow Norton" and was buried next to the Emperor in 2013. I think the two graves are San Francisco all over—history, eccentricity, gay culture, politics, everything.

Both tombstones are visible from our condo's dining room window, if you know where to look. I also take peaceful walks in Woodlawn a lot. Few people are around in the mornings—living people at least.

I wouldn't have gone out that morning if it weren't for my brother, Nick. He's six years older and goes to UC Santa Cruz. He hadn't been around much lately the last few years.

I didn't mind.

He showed up Friday, as we were starting dinner, and announced he'd be spending his spring break with us. Nick hardly spoke and spent all evening texting on his phone. When I went to bed, he kept insisting to my parents that everything was fine. Sure, whatever.

***

"Hey, Gerber." Nick brushed past me in the hall outside our bedrooms Saturday morning, his cell phone getting most of his attention. He has a habit of calling me types of daisies to rile me.

"Dad says *'hay* is for horses,' but I'd say this *hey* is coming from an ass," I replied.

He snorted but didn't stop his shamble to his bedroom, so I went on to get my breakfast.

A few minutes later, my folks entered the kitchen talking in the same low, tense tone they'd been using since Nick's arrival. My shoulders started to tighten as I tried to finish my cereal. The talking stopped abruptly when I walked in the kitchen to put my bowl in the dishwasher. Typical—*Nothing happening here.* Meanwhile, underneath, all sorts of drama.

My dad leaned against the counter drinking coffee. "Sleep well, princess?"

I tried not to roll my eyes at the baby nickname, I swear. "Yeah, okay. You guys?"

"Finer than frog hair." Normal morning exchange. My parents followed me into the living room. Nick was now sprawled there texting, his feet over the side of the armchair.

"Guys," my mom said with fake cheeriness, "what about a picnic later? Or do you have plans, Nick?"

My brother glanced up. "I think I'm meeting some friends. I'll let you know."

My parents exchanged glances.

Suddenly I just wanted to get away. "I'm going for a quick walk."

Another exchange of glances, then a nod from Dad. "It's foggy though."

That was okay—I liked fog. I grabbed a light sweater from the peg by the door. Behind me, I could hear my mother's voice rise in complaint to Nick. I headed down the stairs out of the building. Maybe they'd be done arguing by the time I got back.

As I stepped outside and crossed the street to the gates of Woodlawn, I could breathe again.

The Castle mortuary building rose eerily ahead of me, above the empty paths and silent graves. My feet carried me on my usual route. Sounds are amplified in the fog, but I heard nothing beyond the distant buzz of traffic.

I stopped, unsure of what I saw ahead. Maybe it was because the fog made things a bit indistinct. Or maybe I couldn't believe my eyes. Just a pile of clothes, right? No, there was an arm. Was she okay? As I got closer, it became clear she wasn't.

I glanced around and pulled out my phone. In the fog, anyone could be just out of view. Call my parents or the police? I'm not a little kid, but at that moment all I wanted was my mom and dad.

Dad appeared at my side before I could put away my cell phone. He put his arm around my shoulder and we stared at the body from a short distance away until the cops arrived and moved us farther back.

Soon crime scene tape was strung up. It was like a cop show, right down to the uniformed officer asking me questions. I had nothing helpful to tell.

I spent the rest of the day reading, music turned up high in my earphones. My folks left me alone for the most part, sneaking down the hall to check on me occasionally. Mom made my favorite meal of spaghetti for dinner.

***

The morning TV news didn't mention my name, stating only that a local teenager found the body of an unidentified woman. Cause of death was unknown, but an overdose was suspected. No identification or other possessions. From the condition of her clothing, the news anchor stated that the police thought she might be homeless.

I had a vague recollection of dew-covered baggy clothes, brown and blue, and a pale arm. Her long brown hair hid most of her face, which was pressed into the grass. I was glad I hadn't seen if her eyes were open.

Sunday passed in a daze. The cops called with more questions, hoping I'd remember something new, but I didn't. They still didn't know who she was. Dad said Woodlawn offered to bury her if nobody came to claim the body.

That night I dreamed she was lying on Norton's grave, which had sprouted a new tombstone that read: UNKNOWN WOMAN.

***

"Daisy, wait up." Stan rushed down the hall toward me. He was new to the school but we both played flute in band, so we'd been talking a lot. "You live near where the body was found, don't you?"

The very thing I wanted to avoid. "Woodlawn?"

"Do you have a view of the cemetery?"

"Yeah. Why?"

"It's a real mystery in your backyard—aren't you interested?" I'd never seen Stan so enthusiastic.

I shrugged, trying to keep my tone neutral. "You like mysteries?"

"Sure. True crime podcasts, forensic shows. As a kid I read the Hardy Boys series. Don't you like mysteries?"

"Sure. I mean, I read some mysteries. I don't have anything to tell you though."

"But a teen found the body. Maybe somebody we know." He elbowed me. "You aren't normally so quiet."

Stan was funny and usually good company, but I just wanted this conversation to end. "I have nothing to say."

He sighed, then pulled his backpack up. "Ok, see you at band."

I nodded and he took off down the hall. I tried to push the sight of her body out of my mind.

"We okay?" Stan slid up to me after band. I'd managed to avoid him before practice.

I shrugged. "Why wouldn't we be?"

"Seems like you've been avoiding me since this morning."

I shook my head and gathered my things to head home.

Stan trailed along beside me. "I get a little intense. Sorry if it creeped you out. I–I want to be friends."

I glanced at him. He looked like a puppy who'd been scolded. A wave of guilt and embarrassment hit me. "It's just…" I struggled to find the words. "Difficult." I hesitated for a second and then it all poured out, from leaving for a walk to get away from my brother to the police calls over the weekend.

By the time I finished, we'd come to a stop under a tree, a few blocks away from school. Stan stood openmouthed, taking in every word.

"I wonder who she was and why she ended up there," he said.

"Me too." I'd been worrying about it a lot. "Why the Emperor's grave? There are plenty of other graves closer to the gates. Why would a homeless woman go there? The guards opened the gates less than an hour before my walk."

"And where'd she come from?" Stan gnawed at the corner of his thumbnail.

I leaned against the tree. "If she's not local, she might have come by BART."

Stan's face lit up. Thankfully he stopped chewing his nail. "There's a lot of homeless in San Francisco, so it'd be harder for police to identify her." He slapped his knee. "Maybe she had mental problems and thought the grave was important. Maybe believed she was his Empress or something."

"He already has an Empress," I answered.

"Huh?"

"Never mind. Whatever this woman's reason was, she might have left a clue between the BART and the cemetery."

"Like what?"

"She didn't have anything on her. Even a homeless woman should have some possessions."

Stan looked around thoughtfully. "So you think she left her stuff somewhere on the way to the cemetery?"

"No harm in looking."

Stan started to nod but then turned doubtful. "Shouldn't that be the job of the police?"

"A homeless woman isn't their highest priority. She doesn't deserve to be buried nameless."

Stan hummed briefly and then appeared to come to a decision. "If you're gonna look, I'm coming too."

"Sure," I said. "Safety in numbers, right?"

Stan's smile outshone the sun.

We walked around the BART station and then took a direct route to the grave, hardly talking. Was it a relief not to have to explain myself or did I need to break the silence?

Stan looked at Norton's monument and then glanced over at the Empress's headstone. "I see what you mean. But the Empress is modern."

"That's San Francisco for you," I said. "But we didn't find any clues."

"We took the most direct route here. If she wasn't a local, could she have wandered around, lost?"

I shook my head, frustrated. "Any phone navigation would have led her that way."

"Maybe she didn't have a phone."

I tried thinking like her. A homeless woman rides the BART to Colma, early in the morning. She doesn't know the area or have a GPS system to guide her. "I have an idea."

We were soon in a back alley near a garden center. There was a small exit from the BART station that led this way. It wasn't the most direct route, but it was secluded if you were looking for privacy. My eyes swept the alley, looking for something the woman might have stashed.

We found nothing but disappointment.

Stan groaned and rubbed his face. "Maybe another direction?"

I pulled out my phone and checked the time. I needed to get home soon. "I think this is a waste of time."

"It's nice you wanted to find out who she was."

We were almost to the main street when a bit of blue fabric caught my eye. I paused to look closer. A small drainage ditch ran parallel to the alley, choked with weeds and covered in graffiti. Whatever I had seen was underneath a bush on the far edge of the ditch.

Stan peered into the ditch. "You see something?"

"Hang on, I'm going closer." I hopped down, and walked over to the blue item, now about waist high from my vantage point. It was a small duffel bag. I took some photos, in case the police questioned me later. Maybe Stan wasn't the only one who had read too many mysteries.

"Is it hers?" Stan called.

Dirt and leaves rained down as I pulled the bag out from under the bush, scratching my hand on its branches. "Hard to tell."

Holding it by a dirty strap, I climbed back to Stan. He put out his hand to steady my progress up the embankment, quickly dropping my hand when I reached the top. My face flushed, I brushed at the dirt from my arms and then slowly opened the bag. The main compartment had two T-shirts, a pack of gum, a water bottle, a pair of rolled up blue socks, and a bag of nuts. Nothing to show the duffel belonged to our mystery woman. An interior pocket contained tissue paper, plastic utensils, and a couple of hard candies.

Only one exterior pocket left to search. I found a large envelope, Saturday's date and COLMA scribbled on its front. My hands shook as I opened the envelope. This was our last chance to prove the bag was hers and maybe gain a clue to her identity.

Inside were several pieces of paper and some stiff cardboard, presumably to protect them. I drew out the papers and fanned through them.

My heart sped up. "Emperor Norton had certificates like these printed and people let him pay for things with them, like they were money, with the understanding that they'd be paid back with interest years later." Stan leaned over to look but tucked his hands behind him. My hands were clammy as I carefully held the certificates out. "Although he died before he repaid any. Still, this may be paper held by Joshua Norton himself. Nowadays, people collect things like this."

I carefully slipped the papers back in the envelope.

Stan did a search on his phone. "Norton dollars might be worth more than $20,000 each!"

"And there are five of them. If these belonged to the dead woman, maybe the police can use them to track her identity. Her family will want them back."

"But we aren't even sure this is the woman's bag."

"There's the Norton connection and the date on the envelope." I turned over the envelope in my hand. There was a faint pencil scrawl on the bottom edge. "Does this say, 'Rebecca Center'? Could that be her name?"

Stan frowned. "It could be, but my mom donates to a homeless shelter and I think she calls it 'Rebecca Shelter' or 'Center' after the founder."

"Could you find out?"

Stan called his mom and verified the name of "The Rebecca Center."

"Maybe they can identify her." A clue.

***

"Did you see the newspaper?" Stan slid the front page out of his backpack as soon as he found me at school the next day. "It's got a drawing of the woman and the police are asking for info. What did they say about the bag?"

"They aren't sure it's connected. But they—and my parents—did not like that I was investigating." I pushed my hair out of my face, flushed with remembered anger. "Apparently, I'm supposed to leave things to the professionals." I looked at the simple drawing of the woman's face. She still didn't have a name.

Stan looked around to see if anyone was listening. "What about the Rebecca Center?"

"It didn't convince the cops, but hopefully they'll ask around."

"We could do that."

"What?"

"I've arranged to take some donations there after school. It's a short BART trip. Maybe someone will recognize her, and we can tell the police."

My parents would never know, if I got home before their work ended. "I'm in."

The Rebecca Center was located in a nondescript building in a warehouse district. Stan's donations were quickly processed by a lady at reception. She didn't recognize the drawing but directed us to someone else. That woman studied the newspaper, then asked us why we wanted to know.

I stammered out an answer. "I found her body and want to find her family. She shouldn't be nameless."

The woman stared again at the drawing of the dead woman, her brow wrinkled. With a sigh, she sat down, tossing the paper on her desk. "Tricia DeLongean used to be a client here but now she's a weekend volunteer. She got off drugs, had a place to live, and a job. I can't believe she's dead."

"What about family?"

The woman frowned. "A sister, I think, although they weren't close. I got the impression the family were long-time San Franciscans. She said her sister was really into family history."

We searched our phones as we walked back to the BART station, hoping to trace Tricia's sister.

"If she was married, she might not have the same last name." Stan kept scrolling on his phone.

I clicked on a link, my mouth dry. "Here's a Portia DeLongean with a small home-run business nearby."

"What do you want to do?"

"Let's go."

We nervously walked up to the chipped green door and I pushed the doorbell.

The door cracked open. "I'm not buying anything."

"We're not selling, ma'am," Stan piped up.

I held up the newspaper article. "Do you know this woman?"

The door inched wider. A pale face peered out. A sharp intake of breath and the door swung open. The woman who stood in front of us looked a lot like the drawing. Her long brown hair escaped from a knot at the base of her neck and she wore a frilly red and yellow blouse with blue slacks.

"That's my sister, Patricia," she said, studying the sketch. "What happened?"

"I'm so sorry for your loss." I swallowed hard. "I found her body, but nobody knew who she was. So we went looking for family."

Portia's blue eyes scanned us as if verifying we were alone. "Come tell me more."

Stan was already following the woman down the dim hallway, so I trailed reluctantly behind. Photos of stiffly dressed people from other eras lined the walls, mixed with old photos of the city.

In the living room, I was drawn to two items that hung prominently on the wall across from us. The woman eyed me warily as I went to take a closer look.

"Is this an actual Emperor Norton note?" I pointed to the framed item at the bottom. It looked like the certificates I had handled the day before.

She beamed. "Nice to see a young person recognize something important. It's the Emperor's scrip. The plaque above shows that my family's bar was patronized by the great man himself."

The brass inscription was a bit worn but it clearly stated that the establishment was under the patronage of the Emperor. "I didn't know any of those signs still existed."

"It's the treasure of my family. Few have seen it. I don't have many visitors." She gestured to a nearby chair. "Tell me about my sister."

I sat down and explained about my walk and finding the body on Norton's grave. She sat very still, watching my face, drinking in my story. "We were able to track you down after we found her bag."

"I thought you said the police didn't find anything on her."

Stan and I took turns explaining what led to the bag's discovery. The finding of the Emperor's notes appeared to excite, but not surprise, her.

"So the police have her bag then." She pulled at the frilled cuffs of her blouse. It was as if her voice came from a great distance. "My sister and I haven't been close for years. She… got into drugs, you know—and had mental issues. There was nothing I could do." Portia sighed and looked around. "I was afraid she sold the Norton scrip long ago. Those certificates were our inheritance…one of the few things besides the family home."

She stood, almost knocking over the small table next to her, leaving us to scramble to our feet as she headed to the front door. We were apparently dismissed.

"Woodlawn cemetery offered to bury her," I said, catching up to her. "My parents work there."

Portia nodded. Seconds later the door was shut in our faces with a quick, "Thank you for telling me."

The woman was now identified, her family notified. Portia said she would talk to the police and get her sister's belongings returned to her. I should have been proud.

"That woman was odd," Stan said as we walked back to the BART, "But it's still cool. We got to see Emperor Norton stuff and help the woman's family."

He was right, but I felt something was missing.

***

"Hurry up, Nick. I want to get there early."

"Almost done, Shasta." He came down the hall, combing his hair.

My parents were putting on their coats by the door.

"I'll be right back." Nick disappeared down the hall.

Rather than pace, I went to the dining room window. It wasn't foggy. A good day for a memorial, if there ever was a good day.

Below our window, Portia DeLongean stood at the gates of Woodlawn. She looked around quickly and then strode into the empty cemetery, heading directly down the path toward Emperor Norton. She must have been here before, considering her family's history. Her sister must have also considered the grave significant, to visit and die there.

Patricia had been off drugs, according to the shelter volunteer. Did she want to say goodbye to the Emperor and then commit suicide?

At least she wasn't a Jane Doe any longer.

"You're the one holding us up now," Nick said, behind me, "standing in the window like a store mannequin."

I swatted at him and followed my parents out the front door. Nick was already tapping on his phone as he followed behind me. I thought I heard him swear under his breath, but who knows? Probably trying to figure out where to go with friends later.

Our solemn group soon arrived at the chapel. Woodlawn had arranged for a short memorial, followed by a scattering of ashes in their garden of eternity.

I was pleased to see Stan at the chapel entrance. After introducing him to my family, we joined the small knot of people inside. I was pretty sure a couple of the people were cops. I recognized a few employees from Woodlawn. Living in Colma makes most of us see these ceremonies as important for the family, to help them with their grief.

Not that Portia looked particularly grieved. Aggrieved was more like it, but I guess some people behave strangely when loss is fresh. We paid our respects, murmuring the normal condolences to the scowling, fidgeting mourner. Even for those involved in the business, there isn't anything better to say. My folks are merely smoother saying the normal phrases we all fall back on.

The ceremony didn't take long. When Portia was asked to speak, she waved away the microphone, swallowing hard. She kept clawing at her sleeves, a nervous habit that spoke to greater emotion than her stony face.

At the end, Portia told the staff the scattering of the ashes would be private. Then she nodded to me and Stan and trotted up the aisle. My family and Stan followed her out of the Castle, headed for home. Ahead, Portia paused at the turn for Emperor Norton's grave.

My mom gently pointed toward the grave. "Her body was found over there, if you haven't been before."

"I've never been here," came the quick reply.

Loud voices rang out. A short distance ahead, Nick was arguing with some young Asian guy I didn't recognize. What was that about? My parents excused themselves to go over to Nick, leaving Stan and me standing with Portia, who was still staring off at the Norton gravesite.

There was nothing to it but to try to fill the awkward silence.

"Did the police give you Patricia's belongings?" I asked.

"What there was. I also went through her apartment. She didn't have much." Her eyes remained locked on the Emperor's grave.

I hadn't thought about it before, but the shelter lady did say Tricia had a place to live. Why didn't she have keys on her or in her bag?

"I'm glad we found the Norton certificates. I believe they are valuable—but you know that." Now I was babbling.

Her sharp eyes struck me. "They're my inheritance. They mean everything to me."

Stan and I nodded, mute from the force behind her words. What about her sister?

She again pushed at her sleeves, and the lifting fabric revealed numerous marks, sores, and bruises on her arm. Was this a sign that she used drugs? Or of a struggle? "Is your arm bothering you?"

She tugged on her sleeve. "You should mind your own business. Patricia never could, either." Surprised by the growing anger in her voice, I took a step back and bumped into Stan.

My family were still talking with Nick and the young man. They weren't watching me nor this strange woman.

Portia, almost as an afterthought, muttered, "But she learned."

My mind began racing. I took a stab in the dark. "Did you ask her to meet you here because of the Norton money?"

"I've never been here." Her face told me otherwise, eyes darting, searching for escape. Her fingers flew to her sleeve again.

Stan put a hand on my shoulder, but I continued. "I think you have," trying to sound like I was sure. "She wrote down

Colma and the date, as a reminder to meet you here. But then she hid her belongings before she arrived."

"She didn't..." Her voice pitched high with anger. "She wouldn't—"

"Wouldn't give you the Norton certificates?"

"They were mine," came a strangled hiss. "She took them out of the safe deposit box to donate them to some shelter. Even though I needed them. Grandpa was supposed to leave them to me."

At the fury in her voice, Stan looked around for support, but nobody had noticed. "Did you kill her?" he blurted.

She practically spit the words "prove it" and sprinted down a side aisle. Stan and I ran toward the others, calling to the police.

Later, while the police questioned Portia, my family sat on a bench nearby, getting to know Dave, Nick's boyfriend. Nick's unexpected visit to us was because they'd had a fight. They had apparently made up, as they were now holding hands.

Nick was blushing—he'd been working up the nerve to tell us he was gay, then Dave spilled the beans.

Stan and I left my family to talk and took a seat on the next bench over.

"You solved a murder." His voice was embarrassingly warm with admiration.

"Things just started bothering me. Where were her sister's keys? Why would Patricia have a note with Colma and the date unless it was to remind herself of an appointment? Then there was Portia's interest in the Norton certificates and how she lied about being here before. Plus the marks on her arm and weird behavior."

"Portia arranged a meeting, then made the death seem like an overdose? But she couldn't find the Norton money."

Stan shook his head in disbelief.

"I suspect both sisters had drug problems over the years. Patricia got her life together—and wanted to repay the Rebecca Center. Maybe she told Portia, hoping her sister would also turn to them for help. But the family inheritance meant too much to Portia, both sentimentally and financially…" I shrugged.

"I thought Colma would be deadly dull when we moved here." Stan gestured vaguely around the cemetery. Then he leaned over and quickly kissed my cheek, "But you make it feel pretty lively." He gave a shy grin. "See you tomorrow?"

My heart was pounding. I didn't know what to do, but managed to croak out, "Definitely."

Stan took off down the walkway, with only a quick wave back. Colma didn't look that dead to me right now, either.

A few minutes later, Dave walked with my family back to our condo. Glancing over my shoulder, I was amused to see my red-faced brother walking hand in hand with his boyfriend.

All my life, he had been so brave and self-assured. So perfect. I'd resented that. Maybe I hadn't really known him.

I scowled back at him, my hands on my hips. "You could have told us. You should've known Mom and Dad would love you no matter what."

Nick grinned. "What about you, Gerber?"

I tried to remain stern. "What about me?"

"Do *you* love me, no matter what?"

The nerve. "You know I do, you ass."

He reached out and ruffled my hair. My scowl broke.

Maybe it was our laughter, but there may have been a tear or two.

Over Me

Terry Shepherd

It was closing time at the Sacramento Bank and Trust, the Thursday before payday. My six tellers were loading the tills with the extra cash for the expected onslaught of customers who instantly transformed their compensation into currency. As the head cashier, it was a reminder how most people live from paycheck to paycheck.

I thought about how Michelle and I were barely getting by on *two* salaries. My cop wife was meeting me here in fifteen minutes to make a special trip to the cemetery to visit her parents and celebrate her late father's birthday. I had come to enjoy these weekly pilgrimages. It was often the only time she talked about her job.

My thoughts distracted me. I couldn't see the weapons until they were in our faces. My finger hit the silent alarm button as I took the emotional temperature of the other tellers.

Four bad guys, dressed in identical black outfits that included Kevlar vests and full-coverage facemasks that obscured all but the dark eyes behind them. Their body language spoke of methamphetamines, a drug of choice for weak men who needed the fortitude to rob a bank.

Michelle had warned me that bad guys often modified their AR15s, transforming them into fully automatic weapons that could spit out ten deadly hollow-point rounds per second.

The quartet positioned themselves to cover the entire row of tellers. The one who appeared to be their leader fired a burst into the ceiling tiles.

"Okay, friends," his gravelly voice barked. "We know it's payday. Fill my buddy's sack and nobody gets hurt. If I see any of you try to slip us an ink bomb, everyone dies."

Our bank was one of the few where bulletproof glass didn't separate the help from the patrons. The leader nodded to one of his colleagues holding an empty laundry bag and the man vaulted over the wall and into our workspace.

The cops were alerted. Help was on the way. Now we just had to follow directions and try to stay alive.

My team reflexively watched my reaction. I slid the cash drawer free and turned to face the bad guy.

"Follow the boss' lead everyone," he snarled. "All together. Do it now."

He put the cold steel barrel of the AK against my temple. "Tell your people to follow directions."

"Give them what they want," I said to my team, surprised at how calm I sounded. Death pressed inches from my brain, and I didn't seem to care. "Point that thing somewhere else. You don't want to make a mistake and fry for murder."

"Fry for murder?" Where did that come from? Perhaps a line from one of the many old-time cop shows Michelle and I watched.

"Okay, brave boy. Perhaps losing your package is more motivating than losing your life."

The perp chuckled and lowered the weapon, and now my jewels were in the crosshairs. He was right. After six years of marriage, Michelle and I were finally trying for a baby. She wouldn't be happy if someone damaged the mechanism.

That was when I heard the shots—three in rapid succession, followed by the voice I knew best.

"Freeze! Drop the weapons or you'll all roll out of here in a meat wagon."

The bad guys didn't comply, swinging their ARs in Michelle's direction. She pinged two of the four perps in the back of the head with her Glock. The pair dropped to the tile floor, dead on arrival.

Damn, I loved that woman!

The leader fired as he turned. Another explosive blast from Michelle's service weapon split his skull. The last electric impulses in his brain kept a death grip on the trigger of his AR as he went down. Bullets continued to spray from its white-hot barrel.

The commotion gave me an opening to make my move. I swept a forearm upward, pressing the remaining assailant's weapon away from me. I jabbed a fist hammer against his windpipe. The bad guy let go of his gun and grabbed for his throat.

The AR15 felt at home in my grasp. I pressed the firearm against his forehead. "Move and you're dead."

The building was suddenly awash in blue uniforms. I recognized the shift commander's voice from a half dozen barbeques Michelle and I attended at his place.

"Shots fired. Officer down."

My wife.

***

Seven Years Earlier

Her eyes told the story—incalculable loss and a broken heart that all the king's horses and all the king's men couldn't put back together again.

But beneath the veil of sadness and shame was something else.

I scanned the barista on the other side of the counter at the coffee shop within walking distance of the bank where I worked.

Her body carried the luggage of someone addicted to the products she sold. But her auburn hair and carefully crafted makeup spoke of a person who still had a modicum of self-image.

What caught my attention was the necklace. My female co-workers spoke of how keys were becoming a part of many ensembles. Hers was shiny and small and golden, dangling from a chain in the direction that most men's eyes eventually go.

Her smile seemed genuine enough. The rescuer in me wanted to know what was behind it. It had taken me six months to spin up the courage to ask her out. I hoped that today would be the day I could actually do it.

"Your usual, Mr. McCarthy? Glad to expedite it so you have time to digest before returning to the world of high finance."

She was good. She knew her customers' tastes. And she knew enough about us that we became more than just transactions.

I flushed and nodded. "I'm embarrassed. You know so much more about me than I know about you."

Her head dipped, revealing delightful, red, self-conscious cheeks, "There's not much to tell. What you see is pretty much it."

I pointed to the necklace. "I'd love to know more about the key."

Her eyes searched mine. The speed with which they danced back and forth told me she was deciding. "I'm on break in five. I'll bring your Frappuccino and bear claw to your table and we can talk."

I was usually focused on my phone when gobbling sustenance at the coffee shop. But today, my gaze followed the fluid movements of her body as she made my drink and selected the largest bear claw in the display case with a plastic-gloved hand. There was something elegant in her sway as she brought the treasures to my booth.

"What made you ask me about my necklace?"

"Something about the key is familiar. Is there a story to go with it?"

I could see her body tense. "Perhaps when we know one another a little better."

"I'd like that. Are you up for some quality time when we're both off the clock?"

She was.

She glanced around, as if she didn't want anyone else to hear, finally holding out a hand. "I'm Michelle Merrick. I guess if I'm going to go out with you, we should know one another's names."

I grinned, returning the firm handshake. "Logan McCarthy. Bank Teller. Grad student in finance. Recovering Minecraft addict."

She laughed. "We're always reducing life stories into three sentences when there's so much more hiding in the spaces between the words. I've watched you, Logan McCarthy. You're kind to everybody. And a good listener. I have trust issues. Your job is to earn mine."

I was up to the challenge.

My supervisor rolled her eyes when I recounted the encounter. "You're a painful introvert. How you engage effectively with our customers is a mystery." She tapped her temple. "Your left brain is your comfort zone. Your biggest joy is when the cash drawer balances at the end of the workday. And you immerse yourself in grad school at night, so you don't have to socialize with anyone." My boss took a deep breath. "It'll never work."

***

In time, it did. There was something about Michelle that drew me out. I learned how her mother was the abuser and how her father couldn't stand up to it. She revealed how that darkness welded a self-perception as someone who "wasn't good enough" into the deepest recesses of her brain, how a half dozen therapists couldn't crack the code to unpack it, and how a once-athletic body had atrophied into lethargy.

When the dam finally burst, the story came out like a flood. "I'm twenty-two. My Dad left Mom and me when I was thirteen," she had said. "After years of therapy, I've accepted that they probably never should have married. They fought like the star-crossed lovers they were. He was my alpha, and I loved him to death. He traveled a lot for work and always brought me puzzles to solve when he came home. I have a closet full of Rubik's Cubes, Sudoku books and every brainteaser you could imagine. 'Your brain is a goldmine,' he used to say, and, 'There's enough untapped potential inside to make any dream come true.'"

The attention to detail, her incredible memory, how she could read customers all made sense. This girl could be a detective.

"But the one dream I really wanted to keep real didn't happen. I wanted a normal family. The dream was one puzzle I could never solve.

"The night he left us, he came to my room and apologized. 'I'm not meant to be your mother's soulmate,' he said. 'You were the one good thing we created together, snuggle bug.' He always called me his snuggle bug. 'I've got to go my own way, baby. I will never forget you. I pray that in time you'll both get over me.' He said those last two words with an emphasis that cut me to the core."

Michelle let the incongruity of the story sink in. "I never did. It's his fault. He signed each birthday card from then on, 'To my Snuggle Bug. Love, Dad. Over me?' Maybe it was supposed to be a joke. Talk about two visceral sides of an emotional coin. I cried my eyes out every year."

Another pause. Michelle fingered the key. Her eyes welled with tears. "He died three years ago. I guess my mother wasn't the only woman in his life. There were a half dozen female faces I didn't recognize who showed up to hear the reading of his will. For a man who worked as hard as he did, there was virtually nothing left. His insurance paid off our house, but beyond that, the only other thing the attorney handed to me was an envelope."

Michelle palmed the key, lifting it so I could inspect it. "This was inside, along with a single sheet of paper. 'To My Snuggle Bug. Over me? Love, Dad.' He wrote the same words but in a different order."

"That did it. I've never been over him. And except for polishing this key and cleaning the chain, it's always around my neck."

I squinted. The thing looked familiar, but her aura was intoxicating, and I couldn't place it. "Does the key unlock anything?"

"Not that I know of. Keys were part of the puzzles we solved. He ran a locksmith business for a while, and I built a collection of the dud keys he cut that didn't work. I still have every one. But this," she twisted the metal in her fingers, "is the most special to me."

She let me examine the treasure. I turned it over, studying it with a detective's eyes, looking for anything that might be a clue to its meaning. "What did your mother think about this special gift and the drama surrounding it?"

Michelle shrugged. "She dismissed it as another of his pranks. He may have had other lovers, but I think he always carried the torch for her. The headstone he had carved was for the two of them. Maybe that was his one swipe back at my mother. On one hand, I think in her heart she still loved him. On the other, she was livid at the prospect of lying beside him for eternity."

"That's strange. Wonder why he did that?"

The hint of a smile cleaved Michelle's face. "I think he knew that if they were together, I would come to visit them. I see him every Sunday. The East Lawn Memorial Park is my church, and his grave is my confessional."

"Do you ever talk with him about your dreams for the future?"

Michelle turned her palms upward, framing her body. "What have I got to offer? A high school education. About fifty more pounds than I need and a pretty plain face."

I wanted to dispute it. Michelle was growing on me.

She sighed. "At least the coffee shop has health insurance. I thrive on routine." Her eyebrows rose an almost imperceptible centimeter. "And working there brought you into my life, Logan."

I could sense that she was taking a risk with that last statement. Our connection was still being formed. Her heart had already been broken. Would I stomp the pieces to bits?

Michelle didn't seem worried about that. "What's your story?"

"Not much more than the short version. My family's expectations are higher than my motivation. They want me to be a CEO when I'm just as happy cashing people's paychecks. It's put distance between us. I rarely talk with my parents."

Michelle darkened. "You gotta work on that one, Logan. How does that old Joni Mitchell song go? 'You don't know what you've got till it's gone.'"

I didn't want to go there. I had my own set of issues and ignoring them had become my Olympic sport. "You're wrong about a few things," I said. "You have a lot to offer, and my gut tells me your father loved you much more than he could communicate. I'm grateful that you're taking a chance on another guy who can't possibly measure up to the best man you've ever known."

Michelle's laugh was like the water that stumbled and danced in the American River rapids. It bubbled with delight, touching the place in my soul where a dozen failed romances had begun. "Yes." Hearing that one word made my heart beat faster. "And Daddy was far from perfect. But you're right. I've never been able to let any other man get close enough to see if I could finally get over him. 'Over me' has been my blessing and my curse. I suppose visiting his grave every week reinforces that obsession."

I realized this was her unhealthy comfort zone. Her dad's annual "Over me?" birthday cards didn't help. Michelle could not move on.

And yet, our friendship grew into romance. As we tentatively explored intimacy, the necklace was always there. I grew to despise it. "That key dangles between us like an unwelcome chaperone," I told her late one night.

She hovered over me, swaying her shoulders back and forth so the key tickled my nose. "It's part of who I am," she said with a genuine smile I had not seen before. Michelle bent down to kiss me. The sensation felt familiar, exciting, empowering. "You are part of who I am, too, Logan. And I like it. I think the three of us can coexist just fine."

***

I began falling in love with Michelle Merrick. So, I did my research on her father to see if I could help her find closure and peace. Everyone in town knew about him.

"After the key shop," a mutual friend told me, "Michael Merrick became a serial entrepreneur. He was an idea man who could turn just about anything into money. We shared the same accountant. After a few too many martinis one night, the guy admitted that Michael grossed over sixty million dollars during his lifetime. But while his customers were loyal and his investors always came out ahead, the man himself never seemed to have any wealth when all was said and done."

One of Michael Merrick's drinking buddies shed light on his troubles with women. "Like the abused spouse he was, he hooked up with one loser after another. We all suspected that this was where the cash went."

I asked Michelle about this one night after an emotional love-making session.

"It was odd," she confessed. "When they all showed up at the attorney's office, it surprised no one that he was broke. 'Over me?' was a straightforward question for them to answer. They were."

Meeting Michelle's mother was a further confirmation. She dismissed our relationship. "The man of the hour," she called me, perhaps comparing me to her late husband, Michelle's "Over me" father. And it wasn't a compliment. Michelle told me later that it meant, "He won't be around for much more than an hour."

Her mother's experience with men reinforced that belief.

I intended to prove her wrong.

***

As our relationship progressed, I gently pressed my barista to explore junior college. Michelle found she had a knack for law enforcement. Preparing herself—physically and mentally—for the academy, she shed the extra weight and focused her analytical brain on becoming a cop.

That turned out to be her life's passion. As I remained in my own uncomfortable comfort zone at the bank, Michelle earned her detective stripes.

***

Our love continued to bloom, and her mother put one last curse on our shoulders when she announced she had terminal cancer on the day I proposed.

"Logan and I are engaged," Michelle told her, displaying the huge rock I couldn't afford on her left ring finger.

"I'm dying," was her mom's response.

By then, Michelle had mastered a cop's compartmentalization. My fiancée just looked at me and shook her head. "Well, Mom," she said, hiding the emotion I knew she wanted to express, "we can either get married tomorrow so you can witness it. Or we can wait till you croak and savor the moment without you."

Her mother's tone echoed disgust. "Happiness doesn't last."

"Over me?" Michelle said as we drove home. "I look forward to being 'over her.'"

Michelle's mother accommodated us by succumbing quickly. The cancer spread like a stain and took her in six months.

As the pastor concluded the burial service, I focused on the ornate headstone for the first time. The elaborate frieze above the two names reminded me of an Egyptian temple. The artistry was a hieroglyphic mixture of sculpture and symbology, much too opulent for the simple people who slept at its feet.

When the pastor intoned, "Ashes to ashes, dust to dust," my fiancée couldn't suppress a laugh. This one went beyond the American River rapids, billowing into a full-blown howl.

"Did I say something wrong?" the stunned preacher wondered.

"No, sir," Michelle said, still trying to catch her breath. "I was just thinking. They are stuck together forever... And she can't argue with him."

***

I won't say our union was without acrimony. Michelle was damaged goods, and I was an underachiever. The drive she now felt to surpass her dead parents' expectations was the polar opposite of my sloth-like approach to life. Our personalities were perfect for our chosen professions. But proving her mother's prophecy wrong became the central glue that held us together through the rough patches.

Our relationship grew into an understanding of the challenges we each brought to the union and a celebration of the things we loved about one another that kept the fires burning.

I joined Michelle in her regular pilgrimages to the cemetery and listened as she talked with the spirits of her father and mother about the things she always wished she could have shared with more-engaged parents. Their silence seemed to refresh her. Answers to her questions came, and with them, an uneasy peace.

"I sure grew up to be something totally different from what they expected," she whispered one spring Sunday afternoon. The blue sky was dotted with puffs of cotton. Green buds on the trees spoke of the renewal that comes with each passing year. Michelle turned toward me. "How about your expectations, Logan. Did you ever in your wildest dreams think you would marry a cop?"

"I married my best friend," I answered, a finger sliding under her top to massage the key that was still the only jewelry—besides her wedding ring—that Michelle wore.

"You and this key are the two greatest things to have happened to me." Michelle nodded toward the headstone. "Over him? At last, I think I am." She squeezed my hand. "Over you? Never."

Somewhere in the breeze, I thought I could hear her mother's voice say, "Happiness doesn't last."

***

Present Day

I don't remember running from the teller cages to her side. I don't remember the clump of other officers who tried to pull me off of her. I do remember the upward swath of bullets that painted a line across Michelle's bulletproof vest, and the one that had nicked her carotid artery. I remember pressing my palm against the stream of red that spurted with each of her heartbeats.

And I will never forget Michelle's gaze as the essence of all she was slowly slipped toward the darkness.

"Mom was right," she said in a voice I didn't recognize. A bloody hand reached up toward the top buttons of her uniform shirt. Surprisingly strong crimson fingers ripped it open and felt for the necklace.

"Hang on, baby," I said, my vision wavering from tears I couldn't control. "Help is on the way."

Her voice was now a whisper. "Mom was right," she repeated, pressing her fingers against my cheek. "Happiness doesn't last. But oh, what a happy life you gave me."

"No, baby," I pleaded. "Don't leave me. Please don't leave me."

Michelle squeezed the key, the color draining from her face. "It's okay, babe. Get over me and love again. Promise me that."

"No! Not now. God, please. Not now!"

The hands of the one woman I had truly loved relaxed and fell to her chest. The spurting crimson slowed. Her breathing softened.

"Over me," she gurgled. Michelle's eyes closed.

I was certain the love of my life was dead.

The medics arrived seconds later. I recognized Donna, a friend Michelle had made when their paths often aligned at crime scenes. She and her partner eased me aside and instantly began trying to save my wife's life.

When they closed the doors of the ambulance, Donna opened a fist. "Hold on to these. You can give them to her yourself when she wakes up."

She placed Michelle's wedding ring and the golden key necklace into my hands.

Donna touched my shoulder. "It's up to her now."

***

The surgeons worked on Michelle for three hours. They filled her with nearly four liters of blood and warned me that losing so much of the body's most elemental liquid might have deprived her brain of oxygen for too long to sustain function.

But they didn't know my girl.

The chief resident appeared in the waiting room, where Michelle's paramedic friend sat with me. "She's still with us. Her EEG shows brain function, but it will be a while before we know what we've got. Is there anything you can bring that could help determine what her level of cognition might be? A memento? Something important?"

I thought about the three most important icons in Michelle's life. I showed the doc her wedding ring and the key I had been clutching nonstop in my hand, as if letting go of them would rip Michelle's spirit from my grasp. I would have to figure out how to bring her the third one.

***

Donna held the gossamer-thin sheet of vellum against the headstone. I used a piece of charcoal to emboss the ornate frieze and the chiseled names of Michelle's parents on it, carefully rolling the poster-sized paper into a protective cardboard tube.

"What does it mean?" Donna asked. "That artwork on the top of the headstone? I've never seen anything like it."

"That's the mystery," I answered. "One of many about Michelle's dad that he took with him to the grave."

Donna exhaled. "It's beautiful… and cryptic. And Michelle never decoded it?"

I shook my head. "She's the puzzle queen. None of us can. Hopefully, this will help the docs help her."

***

Two weeks later, I got the call. The nurse's voice sounded excited but cautious. "She's waking up. Can you come?"

Even without makeup my girl was as stunning as ever. But the gray pallor of death still haunted her. Did the woman I fell in love with still exist? Doctors surrounded her. Their faces spoke volumes, none of it good.

"Talk to her," the nurse whispered. "See if she knows you."

"Baby?" I was so afraid that I barely recognized my voice. "Can you hear me?"

Michelle smiled. Her eyelids flickered open to reveal dilated pupils. "I *saw* him, Logan. My dad. On the other side. I asked him what all those birthday cards meant. He just grinned and said, 'The answer is right in front of you." An IV-connected hand felt for the necklace. "My key?"

"I have it right here, baby. Get better so I can put it around your neck and get us out of here."

She squinted at the cardboard tube tucked under my arm. "What's in the tube?"

"It's Sunday," I said. "You can't go to your parents, so I brought them to you."

The nurse helped me unfurl the vellum.

Michelle's eyes focused. They seemed to see the etching in a new way. "MMMCMXCIX–MMCLXXVI? What does *that* mean?"

What neither one of us had recognized was suddenly as clear as day.

"3999–2176." It was the nurse's voice. "Roman numerals. Are those numbers significant?"

My teller's brain reflexively spat out the answer. "It's a safe deposit box at our bank. I'm certain of it." Although that part of the business was something I never handled, I knew the number sequencing by heart.

Michelle closed her eyes. Life, hope and our future were surging back into her. "So that's what Dad meant. Well, Mr. Detective. Let me get some sleep. Go check it out."

"That can wait, sugarplum," I whispered, planting a kiss on my wife's forehead. "Get well, and we'll investigate that one together."

***

Michelle was in the hospital for another month. It took six more weeks of physical therapy before she felt confident enough to leave our house. That day finally came. I took her to a bed and breakfast by the ocean. Her near-death experience only strengthened our love for one another. We took long walks on the beach and re-discovered the physical attraction that years of focus on careers and cash flow had dimmed.

We had been given a second life together and vowed to be grateful for every single day.

Michelle's strength slowly returned. She insisted I return to work and began going to her regular check-ups without me.

One memorable morning, I saw the sparkle return to her eyes. "I'm ready to decode my father's final puzzle."

My supervisor matched Michelle's key with her own. Even from inside the private viewing cubical at the bank, I could hear the click as box 3999–2176 popped open. My boss brought the long, thin steel container to us.

"This one is heavy," she said. "Let me know when you're done."

Michelle nodded to me, as if touching the box might make it vanish, like the man who had deserted her so many years before. I raised the lid. The afternoon sun illuminated its contents.

Stunned to a shocked silence, I inventoried the piles of stocks and bonds, the collection of valuable silver certificates and the solid gold krugerrands that her father had carefully inserted into half a dozen quarter rolls. The haul totaled to just over six million dollars. He had saved one of every ten dollars he earned for the daughter he abandoned.

The one thing left for Michelle to open was an envelope in her name, written in her father's hand.

She did it with a halting precision. I could sense the duality she felt, desperately wanting to read the message but terrified of what it might reveal. Her eyes darted from the folded paper to me. "I wish he was here. There is so much I want to tell him."

I pointed to the treasure she held. "He is here. He's watching you right now. Let's see what he has to say."

Dear Michelle,

You figured out my riddle! Bravo!

I'm sorry I couldn't be there to witness the important moments in your life, snuggle bug. I've made many mistakes, but you are my one great triumph. There was no way I was going to let my past damage your future. So, I created a trail that only you could follow. I hope the contents of this box provide the security for you that I never could.

Let the pain of the past go, my beautiful baby girl. Tomorrow is always your story to write. Make every chapter a good one. I always knew that wherever I was, you were watching "over me." Know that wherever I am now, I will always watch over you.

Love,

Dad

We were both quiet on the ride home. But Michelle's smile and her far-away look finally piqued my curiosity. I wanted to ask her how she felt about the letter. What did the doctor say? Would she have the courage to return to work?

But all that came out was, "I love you, baby."

I slowed to a stop at a red light. My wife turned to me and wrapped a hand around my own. A radiant glow surrounded her. She never looked so beautiful. She leaned in close and whispered two words into my ear.

"I'm pregnant."

One Tossed Match

Joseph S. Walker

It was a rare quiet day at Wolf's, the joint near the Oakland docks where I tend bar. Seafront joints are a shade more civilized than they used to be. The monster cargo ships hauling cell phones and sneakers are at sea for weeks rather than months, and the sailors can lounge in their bunks browsing Facebook and streaming porn, just like real people. Still, a certain number feel it's not their right but their God-given obligation to go wild when they have solid ground under their feet for a few days. We keep a couple of truncheons under the bar and the cops on speed dial.

I was an hour from punching out, and I hadn't had to bust anybody's head or clean up any blood or vomit. All I was thinking about was picking up a pizza and heading home. That's when Russ Leopold walked in. I hadn't seen him in five years. He was carrying a few more pounds and a lot less hair, not that I'm anybody to talk. He went to the corner of the bar farthest from the door and sat down, five stools away from anybody else.

I finished drying the glass I was working on. I was tempted to ignore him, but I could hardly stand there for an hour pretending I'd gone blind. I drew a beer and set it in front of him. "Afternoon, Russ."

"Abe." He picked up the glass and drained half of it. "How you been?"

I leaned against the bar. "Had a colonoscopy a couple months ago. Want to hear about it?"

"Christ, no."

"Then I guess you're caught up with me. What brings you in?"

"Heard anything about any old friends lately?"

I shook my head. "I don't like guessing games. You got something to tell me, tell me."

His lip twisted. "Don't you get paid to listen to people talk?"

"If I enjoyed it, they wouldn't have to pay me."

"Whatever." Russ pulled a folded sheet of paper from his hip pocket and dropped it on the bar. "Have a look at this."

It was a printout of an obituary page from some publication called the *Redding Record Searchlight*. There were three or four big pieces about people who'd kicked off, but a small blurb at the bottom was circled in red. It read:

Gabriel Fitzgerald Booth, aged 83, of Pershing, has passed away after a brief illness, leaving no known family. Interment will be at Evergreen Woods Cemetery on Monday at 9:00 a.m.

I dropped the page on the bar. "You've got to be kidding."

"Age matches. Middle name matches."

"Where in the hell is Pershing?"

"Shasta County. North end of the Sacramento Valley. It's a ranching town, I think. About four hundred people."

"Three hundred and ninety-nine now. Even if it's him, so what?"

Russ tapped the paper with his finger. "Says no family. I'm thinking any little trinkets Gabe might have had are still there."

I laughed out loud. The crane operators at the other end of the bar looked up in surprise. "You're dreaming. You think you're gonna walk in his house and find your cut giftwrapped under his bed?"

"It ended up somewhere," Russ said.

I nodded at the sheet. "How'd you get this, anyway? What do you do, read every obituary column in the country?"

Russ folded the paper and stuck in his back pocket. "I have an alert on my phone. Tells me when certain names pop up on the web."

None of that meant much to me. I'm about the only person I know anymore who doesn't have a cellphone. I never got the appeal of people being able to bug me whenever they want. Before I could say anything about it, a woman down the bar started tapping her ring sharply against her empty glass. I made a just-a-minute gesture at Russ and went to draw her a refill.

Forty years ago, in 1976, Russ and Gabe Booth and I were on a crew, and I don't mean we rowed for Stanford. Russ and I were just kids, big and scary enough to keep people quiet during a job. Gabe was the planner. There was a driver named Ace, and a lock man who called himself Smith. We had a pretty good run, working up and down the west coast. Then Gabe came up with the big score, a diamond delivery at a San Francisco jewelry exchange. The job was going fine until a couple of security guards who'd seen one too many John Wayne movies decided to make a play, and bullets started flying. Three minutes later, a guard, a jeweler, Ace and Smith were dead. Russ and I and the other guard were wounded. Gabe was gone. So were three million dollars' worth of uncut diamonds.

Waking up chained to a hospital bed, with a D.A. looking at you the way a butcher looks at a side of beef, is a hell of a way to celebrate the bicentennial. The public defenders Russ and I ended up with made it clear that the only way we would ever breathe outside air again was to flip on Gabe. The cops caught up with him a couple of days later. We testified at his trial, and all would have been right with the world except for one little detail. The diamonds. The cops couldn't find them, and Gabe refused to say where they were, even when threatened with a heavier sentence.

In the end Russ and I were inside for seven years. They gave Gabe thirty to life.

Russ's last visit to Wolf's, five years back, had been to tell me Gabe got released. *"I have no idea where he is, but I'm sure he ain't happy with us,"* he had said. *"Watch yourself."* I jumped at shadows for a few weeks after that, but nothing ever came of it. As far as I was concerned Gabe Booth was ancient history, and I was happy to leave him that way.

Russ waggled his empty glass at me when I got back. I refilled it while I asked him what exactly he had in mind.

"I got the address of his house from tax records," he said. "If there's no heir the state will eventually reclaim the property, but that'll take time. I say we go search it first."

"You're nuts. Look, he bought his place, right? He had cash, meaning those diamonds are long gone."

"Not all of them." He leaned closer and dropped his voice. "You know what they'd be worth today, Abe? Twelve million. You could buy the entire town of Pershing for a tenth of that. He didn't spend it all. I can feel it."

Once a thief, always a thief. I hadn't so much as jaywalked since the day I walked out of prison, but the number twelve million would catch anybody's interest. "Say you're right. You really think you can walk in and just put your hands on it? Gabe had years to come up with hiding places."

"That's why I'm here," Russ said. "We've got double the chance of finding it if we search together. And we're both owed. When's your next day off?"

"Tomorrow. But I'm not sold yet. This is a hell of a long shot."

"What? You've never bought a lottery ticket?"

***

Russ picked me up outside my apartment the next morning in a black SUV that looked like every other car on the road. He had a bag of doughnuts and a thermos of coffee. "It's a four-hour trip," he said. "I figure I'll drive the first half. Something in the glove box for you."

I opened the glove compartment, saw a revolver with a two-inch barrel, and shut it again. "No thanks."

He glanced over in surprise, then returned his attention to the road. "You used to have a rule about never going anyplace unarmed."

"Turned out great for me, didn't it? I haven't touched a piece since I got out. If you're expecting somebody to shoot at us, you can drop me here."

"Just a precaution," Russ said. "So, what, you're really just a bartender? I figured you were dealing, at least."

"Why? Are you?"

He hit the air conditioning. "Let's say I dabble. I've got some money on the street, do a deal every now and again."

"You're gonna end up in another small gray room, brother."

"I'm careful." He sniffed. "Anyway, you're no saint. Minimum today we're talking a B&E fall. If things go wrong."

"Let's not let things go wrong."

It's been a while since I've driven that far. The interstate rolled endlessly through dry brown hills with occasional patches of dusty pines and trees I couldn't name. Tourists hear *California* and picture beaches, maybe the Hollywood sign or the Golden Gate Bridge. They don't know how much of the state is one tossed match from burning up and blowing away. Russ and I chatted a little, but there wasn't a hell of a lot to talk about since almost everyone we both knew was dead. Once upon a time we killed long drives between jobs talking about women, but I guess we were both past that. I certainly wasn't going to brag about the very occasional company I had to pay for.

We switched seats at a gas station in some little town I never noticed the name of. Russ reclined the passenger seat, got a ball cap out of the back and pulled it down over his eyes. I thought he went to sleep, but I'd been driving twenty minutes when he suddenly spoke. "You ever want kids, Abe?"

"No. You?"

He didn't answer.

We got off the Interstate in Redding and followed a two-lane road east through dry hills. There were more trees at first, but they had a desperate, parched look about them. Russ consulted his GPS. "We're gonna go through downtown Pershing, such as it is," he said. "Gabe's place is a couple miles the other side."

The country got flatter and emptier and I thought sure every little town up ahead was it, but it wasn't. Until it was. I was happy to finally see the WELCOME TO PERSHING sign, but there wasn't even a stoplight. The road just rolled right past a few dozen homes, a feed store and a couple of gas stations. We were putting the town in the rearview when Russ looked up from his phone and pointed to the right. "Pull over here."

It was a cemetery across the street from a mobile home park. There was no real lot, just a wide paved area running alongside the road for a couple hundred yards. I put it in park and looked around, confused. "He lived in a mobile home?"

"No," Russ said. "This is where he's supposed to be buried. I thought we might stop and see."

I gave him a look.

"Come on," he said. "Been a long drive. I wanna stretch my legs before we hit his place."

He got out of the car. I shrugged and followed.

There was a brick wall a foot and a half high around the graveyard. The grass inside was brown, and the wind made our clothes ripple and snap. Way off in the distance were the Cascades, but everything around us was flat and tired and empty. Russ pointed at a little mound of fresh dirt near the rear wall. He walked directly toward it. I followed, trying to go between the graves instead of straight over them.

Gabe's headstone was about the size of a prison cafeteria tray and set flush with the ground. They can mow right over them that way, not that this dried-out grass needed much mowing. There was nothing on the stone marker except his name and the years 1933 and 2016.

"I saw Billy the Kid's grave once, in New Mexico," Russ said. "They've got a cage built around it to keep people from vandalizing it, I guess. It's a big rock that says what an outlaw he was."

"Yeah, well. Gabe was no Billy the Kid." Nothing about this spot had any connection I could sense to the man I had known. Gabe Booth was a tough, cocky little bastard who was maybe three quarters as smart as he thought he was. His eyes, when I sat in the witness stand describing how he'd planned our jobs, were colder than the stone his name was carved on.

I wandered a couple of feet away and rolled my shoulders, trying to shed the stiffness of the long drive. A semi rumbled down the road, back toward Pershing. Coming right behind it was a black and white sheriff's cruiser. It was hard to be sure from this distance, but I thought I saw the driver's head turn toward us. I looked over at Russ and he had his phone out, taking a picture of Gabe's headstone.

"Planning a photo album?" I asked.

"Let me ask you something," he said. "It ever strike you funny that you're Abraham and Gabe's name was Booth?"

"Never thought about it."

"That popped into my head one day inside. Abe and Booth. Like to laugh my ass off. One of the guards thought I was making fun of him and gave me a nasty rap."

"First Billy the Kid, now Lincoln. Who needs the History Channel with you around? Let's get out of here. A cop just rolled by and I'd rather not be around for his next pass."

Russ put the phone away, stuck his hands in his pockets and stared down at the stone. For a second, I saw him the way somebody who'd never met him would see him. Somebody who hadn't been there in 1974, when he got into fistfights in three different bars in one night, or 1975, when the two of us went to Vegas and blew through ten grand from a bank heist in one weekend. I saw an old man.

Gabe's house sat on a little knoll another mile and a half down the road, casting a long shadow in the afternoon sun. A gravel driveway a tenth of a mile long went through an unpainted wooden fence and a dusty yard up to the one-story brown structure. There was no garage and no car. Before we got out, Russ took an automatic tucked in a leather holster out of the center console and clipped it to his belt.

"Sure you don't want yours?" he asked.

"I'm sure. Let's just do this."

We walked around the house. Assuming the fence was the boundary line, the property was a couple of acres. I kicked at the dirt. "You remember that pouch? It was no bigger than a paperback book. If he picked some random spot out here and buried it, we could spend a month with a backhoe and never find it."

"Jesus, you're a pessimistic bastard. Let's just deal with the house."

The back door window had nine small panes. Russ took off his ball cap, held it against the pane closest to the doorknob, and punched it out. He shook pebbles of glass off the hat as I reached in to unlock the door. Teamwork.

We went through a cramped kitchen into the living room. All the shades had been drawn and we pulled them open to get light to work with. There was a bedroom, a bathroom, and a spare room that was completely empty. There wasn't much furniture, and most of it was particle board, a lot like the things in my apartment. The sparse, anonymous feeling of the place was familiar, too. Some of us are like that after a long stretch inside. We've spent so much time looking at bare walls that we can't think of anything to hang on them.

We ended up back in the living room. "The fruits of a life of crime," I said. "I think he modeled it off Cary Grant's place in *To Catch a Thief.*"

"At least there's not that much to search."

"Unless he put it behind some drywall. Or in the ceiling. Or the crawlspace. We can take the TV, though. It might just pay for our gas."

"I'll start in the kitchen," Russ said. "Hell, maybe he just shoved the diamonds in the flour bag. You can start out here."

There was a coffee table with two drawers. The first was crammed full of a year's worth of junk mail. I flipped through some of it until I realized I had no idea what I was hoping to find. A bill from a gemstone storage service? I dropped the pile on the floor.

The second drawer had three boxes of Girl Scout cookies. Thin Mints. I opened the boxes to make sure they really contained cookies, then ate a couple to make sure Gabe hadn't cunningly concealed diamonds in them. He hadn't. He also hadn't taped them to the bottoms of the drawers, nor to the underside of the table itself. I was about to tackle the couch when movement caught my eye. I looked out the front window, cursed, and called for Russ. We stood back in the dim passage to the kitchen and watched a sheriff's cruiser coming slowly up the drive, the sunlight bouncing off the windshield.

"We should have parked around back," I said.

"You should have brought the gun. Maybe Gabe has one in the bedroom."

"No time now." The cruiser stopped, the front bumper a few inches from Russ's car. Both doors opened and two deputies got out. The passenger had to work some at unfolding himself from his seat. He was a big guy to begin with, and his arms bulged with muscle, but he had a paunch that looked like a bowling ball shoved under his uniform. The female driver was younger and might have been the smallest cop I'd ever seen, but she came around the car with a quick, confident step and stood a little in front of her partner as they surveyed the front of the house.

Both of them had their hands resting, not so casually, on their guns.

"Stay out of sight," I told Russ. Before he could respond I opened the front door and stepped out onto the concrete slab that served as a porch. I raised my hand and grinned in what I hoped was a convincingly idiotic way. "Afternoon, officers. Can I help you with anything?"

"I hope so, sir," the woman said. "I'm Deputy Sidwell. This is Deputy Hardwick. May we ask what you're doing at this residence?"

"Here?" I looked at the house as though I'd just noticed it for the first time. "Why, this is my cousin Gabe's place. He passed away a few days back and I'm just here to put things in order. It's kind of you to stop and check on me."

"Well, here's the thing, sir," the woman said. She and her partner had drifted a little closer to the porch. Her eyes kept moving between me and the windows and I hoped Russ had the sense to hang back. "I knew Mr. Booth pretty well. Had many occasions to speak with the man. He was always adamant about saying he didn't have any family."

"Isn't that a shame." I raised my hands in a helpless gesture. "There was a feud, years back, and he said he didn't want anything to do with us again. We always hoped to bring poor Gabe back into the fold."

"Uh huh," Sidwell said. I was starting to wonder if Hardwick could talk. Maybe he was just struck dumb by the wonder of creation. "May I ask your name, sir?"

"Billy," I said. "Billy Redding."

"It's a hell of a thing, Billy Redding. You're a dead ringer for the old mug shots of Abraham Ritter."

I opened my mouth but couldn't think of anything to say to that.

"Is Russell Leopold inside? Gabe always said that if you turned up the two of you would be together."

"I don't know who that is," I said. I wanted to reassert my claimed identity, but I couldn't remember the name I'd pulled out of thin air twenty seconds ago.

"Let me explain your problem, Mr. Ritter." Sidwell was only a few feet away now, her shoulders squared. "My partner and I had a very lucrative understanding with Gabe Booth. He wanted to be left alone, and he wanted to feel safe. He paid us very well for his privacy and for protection. And there was one other thing he paid for, in advance, in case you or Russell Leopold ever showed up."

"What's that?" I asked.

"Revenge," she said. She started to pull her gun, and Russ opened fire from inside the house.

I don't know if he'd heard any of the conversation or was just reacting to Sidwell drawing. I dove for the ground so hard that I knocked the wind out of myself as deafening flat cracks came from both sides. I rolled over broken glass and put my back against the wall under the window, fighting for oxygen.

Hardwick was down, stretched out on his back with his limbs flung out wide. Sidwell was on one knee, firing through the windows. She bounced to her feet and charged the door, slamming through. I heard Russ running back deeper in the house.

I couldn't get any air. I looked down and the whole right side of my shirt was dark with blood. I hadn't knocked my breath out. I'd caught a round. From the looks of it, not far from the scar I carried around from 1976. Collapsed lung? No time to think about it.

I couldn't stand. I half crawled and half dragged myself across the slab and down onto the dirt, over to Hardwick. He was done, a neat red hole punched in his forehead. Russ had evidently judged him the main threat. I had a feeling he was wrong about that.

There were yells from the house, two different voices, and then three more gunshots. I picked up Hardwick's piece from the dirt next to his hand. The pain was coming now, like a freight train around a corner. I heard myself wheezing and tasted blood as I managed to lever myself into a seated position with my back against the SUV.

This is why I don't buy lottery tickets, I thought. I would have laughed if I'd had any air for it. The house was silent. My hand was shaking, but I raised the gun and pointed it at the door and waited to see who would come out.

Cranes in the Cemetery

Jennifer K. Morita

A body lay in the old, historic Sacramento cemetery—
and it was fresh.

Living and breathing less than an hour ago, she
rested under the shade of a crepe myrtle, exposed to the open
air unlike the other residents housed in foreboding crypts or
lying beneath worn tombstones stained by lichen.

We backed away wordlessly, careful not to tread on the
tiny paper cranes littering the path.

The trouble began with sushi at two a.m.

***

Preparations for the annual bazaar were in full swing at
the Buddhist Church, and this year Baachan recruited me to
join her cronies making hundreds of sushi rolls to sell during
the two-day event.

"We need young arms, Maya," my eighty-four-year-old
grandma said. "We can't carry those heavy trays anymore."

I was in Sacramento visiting my grandparents, affec-
tionately called Baachan and Jiichan, for the first time since
moving back home over a year ago. Born and raised on Oahu,
my parents had shipped me and my sister off to California
every July to spend time with our dad's side of the family.

In those days, it wasn't summer unless we were at Baachan's church, playing bazaar booth games, dancing *obon* in our pink, crinkly cotton *yukatas* or slurping shave ice to stave off the dry valley heat.

It had been years since I'd been to the bazaar.

Now, Baachan and I walked past the church's security gate into the parking lot, temporarily transformed for the bazaar. A white awning stretched across the lot and over the wooden tower in the center. By noon, it would shelter more than 35,000 eating, drinking, and dancing visitors from the hot Sacramento sun.

But at two o'clock in the morning all was serene.

The courtyard—lined with empty game and food booths—was silent except for the occasional rustling of multi-colored paper lanterns glowing hazily in the cool air.

The action was in the *kaikan*.

We could hear the well-oiled sushi-making operation even before entering the large hall which alternately served as the temple's cafeteria, gymnasium and performing arts stage.

Long folding tables filled half the kaikan. Older men— clad in hair nets, aprons and rubber gloves—occupied the corner closest to the kitchen where they carried vats of cooked rice to be scooped onto plastic-lined tabletops. Oscillating fans cooled the grains while two men carefully mixed in seasoned vinegar using large wooden paddles.

Someone made the rounds filling empty bins of rice at tables where volunteers busily rolled *kappa maki* sushi. In another corner, chattering women used plastic molds to shape rice into rectangles for Spam musubi.

My nose twitched as Baachan and I made our way into the kaikan past the smokey sweet smell of soy sauce and Spam sizzling on the kitchen gridle and into the pungent cloud of vinegared rice.

"Over here." A gray-haired woman with a round face beckoned us with a friendly smile as she peered at us through spectacles perched on the tip of her nose. "I saved a place for you and Maya."

Auntie Kay, short for Kaoru, and my baachan had been best friends since camp. I'd known her my whole life, and even though I was over 30, she still snuck Japanese candies into my hand every time I saw her.

"Still writing, Maya?" she asked. "You know, my son works for the state. He's looking for a public information officer. Good pay, good benefits."

I suppressed a sigh. I'm blessed to come from a long line of well-intentioned relatives—Chinese and Japanese—for whom freelance writer is not a real job. No less than three generations of kin are always giving me career advice. Ever since the newspaper I once worked for folded, their friends were, too.

"Thanks Auntie, but the writing is going fine."

Baachan reached into the quilted tote dangling from her arm and produced two aprons, souvenirs from past bazaars judging by the logos. I'd already secured my wavy, shoulder-length black hair, so once we donned aprons and gloves, we took our spots next to Auntie Kay.

All the *futomaki* essentials were laid out like place settings at a dinner party. We each had a bamboo rolling mat covered in cling film, a bowl of water and rice paddle. Communal plates piled with fillings—red pickled ginger, kampyo, tamagoyaki and shiitake mushrooms—were strategically located along the table.

Someone had already placed a sheet of roasted *nori* on my mat. I plopped a generous scoop of rice on the seaweed paper and began to spread the sticky grains, using my paddle like a bread knife when I heard a disapproving cluck.

Mrs. Oda, the Jedi Master of sushi, hovered behind me.

She was about Baachan's age, a worn, navy blue, cotton smock covered her thin frame. Standing beside me, her short, spiky white hair barely reached my shoulder.

Mrs. Oda had been in charge of sushi-making for the bazaar ever since I could remember, overseeing everything from simmering the dried gourd to arranging the rolls in their plastic, to-go bento boxes.

"Use your fingers to gently separate the rice," Mrs. Oda said, dipping her digits into the water bowl and demonstrating. She stood by and watched me add ingredients in a neat line across the bed of rice, reminding me to overlap the shiitakes.

"Like they're shaking hands," she said. "Not too much ginger. It's there for color and a little heat, but too much will throw off the balance and overpower everything else."

Using fingers to hold in the fillings, I tucked my thumbs under the mat and started rolling. When I reached the end, I held my breath and unfurled the mat, cognizant of Mrs. Oda's watchful gaze.

My futomaki came out lumpy, the nori wrinkled and shriveled.

Mrs. Oda shook her head and tsked. "*Umeboshi* lips," she said gravely, referring to pickled Japanese plums sour enough to pucker lips. "You either didn't use enough rice or there were gaps. Don't worry. I can fix it."

And with that, she whisked my sushi away to another table where wizened experts surgically repaired all the futomaki fiascos. Even the ones beyond saving found new life, the insides scraped into a bin for *chirashi*, a mix of rice and veggies.

"Maybe I should stick to *musubi*," I said, glancing over my shoulder at the group a few tables away.

"Musubi is too easy. Challenge yourself. You need to learn how to make sushi, Maya," Baachan said. "How else will your generation take over for us when we're gone?"

"You're not going anywhere, Baachan. Not for a very long time. Points for effective blend of pep talk and Asian guilt, though."

She grinned and patted my hand. I reached for another nori sheet and started over.

Four hours and several rolls later, a woman about my age breezed into the kaikan, the latest iPhone pressed to her ear. I glanced up at the clock above the stage. Who could she be talking to at six o'clock on a Saturday morning?

Dressed in black leggings, an oversized black sweater and white Adidas sneakers, her ensemble was surprisingly chic considering the time of day. Even her hair and makeup were flawless.

She hung up and said something to Mrs. Oda before they both went out to the hallway where I could see them having an animated discussion.

"Who is that?" I whispered to Baachan.

She glanced up, pursing her lips. "Victoria Shima."

Her vaguely disapproving tone raised my reporter's antenna. I was dying for gossipy scoop, and Auntie Kay was happy to oblige.

"It's Victoria Johnson, now," Auntie corrected in a low voice. "She isn't too popular around here. She's Tom Pits' chief of staff."

I knew the conservative U.S. Congressman, who represented the district just east of Sacramento, was a vocal proponent of migrant detention camps. These overcrowded, substandard government prisons separated children from their families as they were caught trying to cross the border in search of better lives.

As a policy, it didn't sit well among *Niseis*—Japanese American citizens—who were forced to spend a chunk of their childhood behind barbed wire in concentration camps during World War II.

They had long memories—and so did their loved ones. Most of them, anyway.

"Her grandmother lived two barracks down from ours. You remember Reiko, don't you? She was a few years younger than us, and we used to walk around camp with her so people would give us candy."

Baachan and Auntie Kay met as young schoolgirls when their families were uprooted from their Bay Area homes and sent to Topaz, a crowded, dusty camp in the middle of a Utah desert.

Auntie Kay spread the rice so roughly the nori tore. "Her own grandmother …" she muttered, shaking her head.

"Never mind that," Baachan said. "I found some beautiful *origami* paper for the Girl Scout fold-in. Can you come, Maya?"

I was never a Girl Scout. "What's a fold-in?"

"We're folding 120,000 origami cranes to send to Washington to protest the detention camps—one for every Japanese American incarcerated during World War II," Baachan explained.

How could I refuse? I'd been in the fourth grade before I realized my grandmother's innocuous "camp" stories weren't fun summer activities. Although appalled by what the U.S. government had done to its own citizens simply because they were Japanese, I'd grown up safe in the knowledge it could never happen again.

I was wrong.

"There's a demonstration downtown next week too, but you'll be back in Hawaii by then," Auntie Kay said.

I smiled at the image of the two little baachans—well into their eighties and barely five feet tall—waving signs and marching on the Capitol steps.

Amusement was replaced with admiration for these grandmas turned activists.

My back and feet ached by the end of my first sushi shift, but I managed to avoid umeboshi lips, even earning a nod of approval from Mrs. Oda. Baachan and I left just as the sun made its appearance.

I'd parked in the alley that ran between the church and a Chinese restaurant. As I opened the door for my baachan, I noticed a well-dressed, middle-aged, platinum blonde woman walking toward a little red car in the restaurant parking lot. She paused to pour what looked like the remains of coffee into nearby bushes before tossing the blue cup into a dumpster, getting in her car and speeding away.

A little early for dim sum, I thought, easing away from the curb.

I turned onto Riverside Boulevard toward my grandparents' Land Park neighborhood, when Baachan gasped beside me. "Is that Victoria's car? What on earth is she doing at the old cemetery?"

Following her gaze, I spotted a silver Mercedes SUV illegally parked along the wrought iron gate to the Historic City Cemetery.

"Pull over, Maya. Something's wrong."

The last thirty-four years taught me it was pointless to argue with Baachan, a retired schoolteacher who'd never lost the knack for bringing unruly children to heel.

No sooner had I turned off the motor than she sprang from the car, moving surprisingly fast for a great-grandmother of four. By the time I caught up to her, she was peering at something on the sidewalk.

"So strange …," she muttered to herself.

It was an origami *tsuru*.

The lopsided, blue paper crane, measuring about three inches, lay on its side, one angular wing jutting into the sky.

I started to reach for it until a single, sharp cry from the cemetery stopped me. Baachan clutched my arm and pulled me toward the entrance.

"Come on," she said.

My friend would've told me to get back in the car and call 911. But Koa was home in Honolulu, so I ignored his voice in my head.

Flanked on either side by high stone pillars, the imposing black iron gate was open just enough for us to slip through.

Another crane led us up a hill along a crumbling asphalt path. The dim, early morning light cast shadows over the terraced gravesites, and I felt the watchful stares of the stone statues as we crept by.

Baachan and I continued to follow the origami trail.

I might have missed it, hidden among the shrubbery and marble edifices, if it weren't for the bright pink tsuru lying next to the contorted body of Victoria Shima Johnson.

She lay face up beneath a statue of a kneeling, handless angel, whose stony gaze seemed to be pleading to the heavens for mercy.

We gaped, frozen in horror. This time I was the one who grasped Baachan's arm, and we backed away wordlessly, careful not to tread on the tiny paper cranes littering the path.

It wasn't until we reached the safety of the cemetery gates that I fumbled for my phone.

***

I'd been awake for more than twenty-four hours by the time we finished giving our statements to the police.

I collapsed on my bed and slept through lunch, waking only when a persistent fly buzzed in my ear.

Blearily, I realized it was my phone.

"Your plant is dying," Koa said when I answered.

"Isn't that what you're supposed to be taking care of while I'm gone?" I said groggily, the last word ending in a yawn.

"It was dying before you left. I'm a cop, not Miracle Grow."

"So, arrest me."

I swear I could hear his lips curling in a reluctant grin.

"I found someone to fix that lock on your sliding door. He should be done by the time you get back."

"You didn't have to do that. The building manager was going to get to it."

"It's okay. I know a guy."

"Of course, you do."

I'd grown up with Koa, now a homicide detective with the Honolulu Police Department, who was on a first name basis with everyone from the mayor to the parking valet at the Hilton Hawaiian Village. He lost his mother when we were twelve and had to help his dad get dinner on the table, do the laundry, and take care of his little brother. All these years later, he was still watching over people. Even from a distance.

I sat up, glancing at the clock on the nightstand. It was nearly seven o'clock, and Baachan and I were due back at the church for another late-night sushi shift. That's when I remembered.

As if reading my mind, Koa said, "I heard you found a body."

"How…?"

"I know a guy."

Koa lived a thousand miles away on the other side of the Pacific Ocean. Who could he possibly know in Sacramento?

"...So, what happened?" he interrupted my musings.

I rolled my eyes and told him. When I was finished, he sighed. Loudly.

"Be careful, ya? Trouble tends to find you," he warned.

"I'm making sushi with baachans. What could go wrong?"

He grunted disapprovingly.

"Look, if you run into ... problems, I know a guy ..."

"I'll be fine," I said, firmly.

After a light meal of grilled mackerel, rice and pickled vegetables from Oto's Market, Baachan and I headed back to the church, expecting to find crowds of people spilling into the alley and milling around Broadway and Riverside as they tried to cross the busy intersection.

But the alley was empty except for a few stragglers and a police car haphazardly parked across the parking lot entrance.

We found some familiar faces in the courtyard. I recognized Reverend Kenji and the Betsuin President huddled at a picnic table with other temple leaders.

"What's going on?" my grandmother asked Auntie Kay.

"The bazaar's been cancelled."

Every year since 1947, the neighborhood once known as Japantown fills with the sound of taiko drums, the smell of teriyaki chicken sizzling on rows of grills and the cacophony of thousands of people laughing and talking and having fun. It's a beloved annual tradition that started as a way to rebuild a community torn apart by racism and war.

And just like that, a seventy-two-year tradition had been cancelled, the racks of neatly-rolled futomaki now destined for the trash bin.

"The police say Victoria was *poisoned*, and they think it happened when she was here last night. They have to test all the food. The police are in the kaikan now, talking to Mrs.

Oda and some of the other ladies that worked in the kitchen last night."

Auntie Kay stopped short of voicing what we were all thinking: if the police were right, the killer had to be a member of the temple. Someone we all knew.

Suddenly the tsuru—usually a symbol of peace—took on an ominous meaning. Baachan and I glanced at each other, silently wondering if the police had already connected those paper cranes with the *Betsuin* and the upcoming fold-in.

"Why was Victoria here, anyway?" I asked. "Does she attend services?"

Auntie Kay huffed. "She did as a child and used to put in a few appearances here and there to keep the family happy, but not lately for obvious reasons. Reiko said Victoria promised her mother she'd deliver supplies for sushi."

The church doors parted, and Mrs. Oda emerged surrounded by men in suits and a uniformed officer who towered over her. Bringing up the rear were two crime scene investigators, distinguishable by rubber gloves, white, billowing plastic body suits and bulky tool kits.

One of them, a dark-haired man who seemed to know the reverend, carried a box of takeout containers filled with Spam musubi, sushi and chirashi.

I thought of all the hours volunteers spent prepping ingredients—simmering the dried gourd and mushrooms, making and slicing rolled omelets, not to mention cooking hundreds of pounds of rice—all for nothing.

But the wasted food was quickly forgotten when we saw Mrs. Oda being whisked away in a patrol car.

While Baachan and I gaped in horror, Auntie Kay marched up to the crime scene investigator talking to Reverend Ken.

"What do you think you're doing?" she demanded.

"Auntie Kay…," I began, hurrying over.

"It's all right," the man said in a soothing tone aimed at calming Auntie Kay. "They're just going to ask Mrs. Oda a few more questions since she was in charge of the kitchen. She's not under arrest."

But Auntie was already picking up her phone, no doubt calling her daughter, a prominent Sacramento attorney.

Dark, intelligent eyes followed Auntie Kay before settling on me. He removed his rubber gloves with a snap, exposing well-muscled hands and blunt fingers with clean, neatly manicured nails and a simple, gold, wedding band.

The metal nametag on his lapel read: SGT. EDWARD HASEGAWA.

"I don't think I've seen you here before. Are you a church member?" he asked.

"I'm just visiting my grandmother. I live in Hawaii," I said, jerking my chin toward my baachan, who was huddled in deep conversation with Auntie Kay.

His brows arched. "Hawaii, huh? I was there last year for a conference. Stayed with my cousin in Kaimuki. Met some really nice people."

Reaching into his back pocket, he took out a business card and handed it to me. "I gotta get these samples back to the lab. If you run into any trouble, or think of anything, don't hesitate to give me a call, okay, Maya?"

Trouble? Who was this guy, and what exactly had my grandmother been saying about me?

"Uh, sure. Thanks." I took the card and stuck it in my tote.

Baachan was quiet during the ride home. She'd insisted on driving, and at first, I thought she was concentrating on the road. Until she almost blew through a stop sign.

"There's something wrong with the tsuru," she said, frowning. "They're not ours."

"What are you talking about?"

"The tsuru at the cemetery… It was the wrong kind of paper. No one uses construction paper—it's too thick, especially for cranes."

"Maybe whoever made them ran out…"

"No. They were sloppy, uneven…like a child made them."

Or someone unfamiliar with origami.

An idea began forming in my tired brain, but Baachan beat me to it.

"You should call your new friend," she said.

"Who?"

"That detective I saw you talking to at church."

"I don't think he's a detective… Don't *you* know him?"

She shook her head. "No matter. Call him. Tell him the killer is trying to frame Mrs. Oda."

Although I'd been thinking along the same lines, I wasn't sure the police would see it our way, so I persuaded Baachan to wait.

***

That night, instead of going to the bazaar, I met my cousin at her home in the tony East Sac neighborhood. Julie, a family law attorney, was a few months younger than me and happily married to another lawyer. Their remodeled house on 34th Street was Fab Forties adjacent, a few short blocks from the famed row of stately old mansions.

After greeting Mike and her two daughters, we decided to walk to a nearby restaurant for a quiet girls' night out. Cooled by a breeze wafting off the Delta between the Sacramento and San Joaquin rivers, we strolled along tree lined streets past small, but charming, Craftsman bungalows dating back to the 1920s.

"So, what's up?" Julie asked after a waitress seated us outside. "Not that I don't love hanging out, but I'm guessing you and Baachan are up to something."

She was right. Our wily grandmother let slip one of the partners at Julie's downtown law firm was none other than Victoria's husband.

"Steve? Nice guy, great attorney. If you're ever in need of a divorce lawyer, he's the one you want," Julie said, sipping her Chablis. "Ironic, since I hear their marriage was on the rocks."

Luckily, I'm not married. "You ever meet her?"

She emitted a wry laugh. "This is Sacramento. It's grown a lot, but it's still a small town at heart. I've known Vicky since we were kids. I see her at all my firm's functions. She and Steve used to live a few blocks from here, across from McKinley Park before they moved to Granite Bay. Bigger house, more land, gated community."

Tom Pits territory.

We were about to dig into our *risotto primaveras* when a car horn blared, and we looked up to see a woman tossing a Louis Vuitton tote over her shoulder as she dodged J Street traffic.

Recognition flashed across Julie's face. Her brief, but friendly wave was reciprocated as the woman hurried inside the restaurant, Tory Burch sandals slapping against the pavement.

Something about the way sunlight glinted off salon-straightened, platinum blonde locks reminded me of something, but I couldn't quite put my finger on it.

"Elise Miller," Julie said before I could ask. "She's an attorney at my firm. Come to think of it, her husband works… worked…with Vicky. Some sort of political consultant, I think. Our kids have played on the same soccer team for years."

She chuckled at my raised brows, before sipping her wine. "I told you. Small town."

I was still contemplating the various players when Elise exited the restaurant carrying plastic food containers. I watched as she crossed the street and got into a red Mini Cooper, pulling away from the curb with a squeal of tires.

And just like that, the elusive memory jarred loose.

I dropped my fork with a clatter. Rooting around in my purse, I unearthed a business card, grabbed my phone and dialed the number printed on the front

"Sergeant Hasegawa, this is Maya Wong. You gave me your card when we met earlier today. You need to search the dumpster in the alley for a blue coffee cup. You might also want to test the soil in the bush next to it." I paused, quickly adding, "Can you get fingerprints off construction paper?"

***

Preparations for the annual Buddhist Church bazaar were in full swing once again. With only hours to go before the first visitors arrived, the activity spilled outdoors, where volunteers hastily set up rows of tables and chairs and men with tongs hovered over teriyaki charring on the bank of grills.

Elise Miller's arrest was the talk of the kaikan.

"It's the oldest story in the book," Baachan said sagely as she rolled futomaki. "Victoria fooled around with the wrong woman's husband."

Auntie Kay clucked angrily, accidentally tearing a sheet of nori. "To think that *hakujin* woman tried to frame Mrs. Oda of all people—and with tsuru."

As if on cue, Mrs. Oda emerged from the kitchen, eventually making her way to our table just as I was finishing my first roll. Silently, she inspected the sushi.

"*Yoku dekimashita,*" she said with a slight bow. "Good job. You're coming back next year, right?"

Even out of the corner of my eye, I could see Baachan's triumphant grin.

"Maybe you could work for the police," Auntie Kay suggested after Mrs. Oda left. "I bet Sergeant Hasegawa would put in a good word for you."

"I'll think about it," I lied.

But something clicked at the mention of the crime scene analyst who recently spent time in Hawaii.

Small world indeed.

After a full day at the bazaar with my belly full of teriyaki and shave ice, I sat on Baachan's porch and called my old friend.

"Lemme guess," I said when Koa answered. "You know a guy in Sacramento, ya?"

The One

Eve Elliot

Amanda Stack stepped from the cab outside Sacramento's Calvary Catholic Cemetery and pushed her oversize Chanel sunglasses farther up her nose. The sun melted into the horizon after another sweltering day, streaks of salmon and coral bleeding into the darkening sky.

The driver retrieved her rolling carry-on case from the trunk, and she held out a hundred dollar bill folded between two manicured fingertips. He took it and scowled. The meter read $99.85, which she thought was already highway robbery. She was damned if she was going to cough up a tip, too.

The driver muttered under his breath as he dug in his pockets and fished out a nickel and a dime for the change, slapping each into her palm with grubby fingers. She smirked and thanked him, sweet as cherry pie. It stung, of course, to hand over that hundred, but not as much as it usually would have.

Tonight was different.

Tonight she had six hundred more of them, crisp and sharp and smelling like heaven, nestled safely in the lining of her Gucci bag.

She telescoped up the handle of her case and began to walk through the cemetery, glancing around to see if she had company. She liked this graveyard, it was peaceful and quiet, and not so large that it took her forever to do what she needed to do. Her high heels clicked on the paved walkway and the wheels of her case rumbled behind as she turned to her right and strode briskly up the familiar pathway, toward the section she knew so well.

Maybe she shouldn't have taken the time to come here, she thought. Maybe her first impulse to head right to the airport had been the right one. But when the driver had turned down Verner and the broad brick entrance had come into view, she'd tapped on the grimy partition and told him to stop.

You'll be glad you did this, she assured herself. *It's just an extra ten minutes, then you can grab another cab and head for the airport.*

As she walked, she glanced down at the smooth, flat gravestones embedded in the earth, her eyes flicking past the names of grandparents sharing eternity together, husbands and fathers gone too soon, wives and mothers remembered with fresh flowers even decades later. *Beloved husband of Catherine,* one read. Another remembered *Louisa, Loving Mother of Jeremy and John.*

She slowed her pace as she approached Amelia's plot, the one she'd found herself tending to sporadically over the last year. Not often, she had to admit, but enough to make sure the crispy brown bouquets were cleared away at least once in a while and the raised letters on the memorial stone were brushed free of dirt and debris.

She stopped in front of it now and let herself remember. A year ago, almost to the day. She'd been standing in front of this plot, her attention snagged by something, she couldn't remember what, when she'd noticed Ted for the first time.

Well, more like noticed him noticing her, a skill she had carefully cultivated ever since she'd graduated out of training bras. It was always good to notice when a man was noticing you. And with this man in particular—Ted Merrion, nothing to look at, a little stoop-shouldered from age, his remaining hair more of a suggestion than anything, but sporting a genuine Rolex Submariner and a kind smile—it had been *very* good that she'd noticed him noticing.

A widower, he'd said. Ten years his wife Doris had been gone, God rest her soul. No children, just his wife's greatniece somewhere and an elderly mother in Alturas. And after a moment of uncomfortable silence, he'd asked her, in that mild, gentle way of his, which loved one she was visiting. She'd looked down fondly at this very grave and told him.

In Memory of a
Dear Sister, Mother and Wife
Amelia Louise Powers
January 30, 1981 – August 11, 2017
Never Forgotten, Always Missed

He'd been easy to talk to, which wasn't always the case with these older guys. And he hadn't been hitting on her, that was the other thing. This was a cemetery, for God's sake, who in their right mind would hit on someone in a graveyard? No, he'd simply noticed her looking so sad, he'd told her later, and thought she could have used someone to talk to.

At first she flat out hadn't believed him. She'd grown up grindingly poor with a single mother and a series of "uncles" and "friends" and even a new Dad once, who had stayed longer than the rest but cleared out all the same without a look back. She'd learned early and well that men could be charming, could be flattering, could even pretend to care, but at the end of the day they only wanted one thing from a pretty young thing with a cute smile and an even cuter body. She'd learned not to trust their come-ons, their flirtations, their fake interest in anything other than the cleavage that kept drawing their eyes.

But Ted had been different. She looked for his angle, but never found one. She waited for him to make a pass, but he never did. When he took her to dinner he dropped her home afterward without even so much as a wistful glance up at her apartment window or a sloppy goodnight kiss.

He was a gentleman. An honest-to-God gentleman, and when he'd told her he loved her, well…she knew that she had found the man she'd been waiting for. She had found The One.

It hadn't taken long from there. Within a month she'd moved in, and within three he'd proposed, pushing a large, clunky diamond ring up over her knuckle, trembling hands and tears in his eyes. He'd never thought he'd be lucky enough to find love twice, he'd said. And she'd been genuinely touched by it all, in spite of herself. Despite everything, despite the age difference, despite how mild-mannered he was, how soft and wistful he looked when he reached for her at night, she knew they could make each other happy.

It was hard not to think of that first day, standing here as she was, looking down at the polished marble stone and the fanciful script carved into it. But she had a plan, and not much time left to see it through. Amelia had been good to her, no doubt, but she didn't have time for this, she needed to get going…

"Amanda?"

She whirled around, a startled cry escaping her lips.

"Teddy! Jesus, you—"

"Oh my God, Amanda," Ted sobbed, his whole body crumpling with relief as he came towards her. He was wearing the same windbreaker he'd been wearing the day they'd first met, those same chinos. It was like she was right back there, like the last year with him hadn't happened.

Except now he collided with her, wrapping her in his arms and sobbing into her hair, holding her so tight she could hardly breathe. He hadn't done *that* the first time they'd met.

"Ted…Teddy, honey, you're hurting me," she gasped, and he finally released her, stepping back. His eyes were wet and rimmed red, his nose running a little.

"I'm sorry, I'm sorry," he blubbered, his voice thick with snotty tears. "I'm just so relieved to see you."

"What are you doing here?" She tried not to sound too irritated, going instead for rattled surprise. "You're supposed to be in Alturas, helping your mother move to the nursing home."

He'd started nodding before she'd even finished speaking. "Yes, yes, right, but when I got there the administrator called to say there was a delay, something to do with the first payment not going through. So we couldn't move her in this weekend after all."

"Oh, that's such a shame," she said. "You should have called me, maybe I could have helped straighten it out."

"I tried calling you, but the number's been disconnected," he said, looking at her with imploring eyes, mutely begging for an explanation. "I called over and over, got the same message every time. I got so worried, I came home this afternoon but you weren't there. Your clothes were gone, everything… oh, sweetheart…" He dissolved into tears again, burying his face in his hands. When he spoke, his voice was thin and high. "I've been here for an hour, just hoping you might show up here, and thank God you did, I've been so worried."

"Honey, I'm so sorry," she soothed. She glanced over at the bench they'd shared last year, and gently guided him towards it, pulling her case along with her. "Come and sit down with me."

He sat down heavily and wiped at his eyes with the tissue she offered him from her purse. "I got so scared when

I couldn't reach you, and when all your things were gone… What's going on, Amanda?"

She hesitated and reached up to stroke his hair. "You're exaggerating, Teddy honey, I didn't take *all* my things with me. Come on now, don't you think you're overreacting, just a little?"

He shrugged helplessly and opened his mouth to say something, but nothing came out.

"I can explain everything, but I need you to take a deep breath for me, can you do that?"

He nodded and closed his eyes as he inhaled deeply. A couple of errant tears squeezed from beneath his lids and rolled down his face. She wiped them away with gentle fingers.

He noticed my clothes were gone, she thought, watching his face as he began to calm down. *But the question is…*

Has he noticed the money is gone?

She tried to think quickly, another necessary skill she'd developed in middle school. *What should I tell him?* If he knew the money was gone, she'd have to come up with something spectacular. If he didn't know it was gone…well, she could still salvage this, then, couldn't she?

"There now, that's better," she soothed, her voice low and gentle.

"Tell me what's happening, Amanda," he said, sounding like he was on the very edge of bursting into full-on tears. "Tell me the truth…are you…*leaving me*? Is that what this is about?"

"Oh, honey," she said. "You don't seriously think…Oh, Teddy, the ideas you get sometimes."

"But you've packed your bags, and you're…you're… here," he said, looking up and around, as if only realizing where they were. His gaze landed on Amelia's grave.

"I thought if you really were leaving me, you might stop by to say goodbye to your sister…and it looks like I was right."

His lip began to quiver, and she hurried to stave off another crying jag. "Sweetie, listen to me, you're working yourself up over nothing, I promise you." She hesitated, looking at him for some sort of guidance as to whether she should say more. His soft, pained gaze helped her decide.

She let out a heavy sigh. "Okay, look, I really didn't want to tell you this. But I hate to see you so upset, so here goes. I've been planning something for you. A very, very big surprise."

He stared at her, his mild eyes watery with tears and confusion. "A surprise?"

"A surprise," she echoed, nodding. "I thought you'd be away all weekend, so I thought I could pull it off, but I guess not." She smiled indulgently at him, like he was a naughty child who had misbehaved but was too cute to scold. "You're just too hard to sneak on, Mr. Merrion."

"What surprise?" he asked. He didn't sound excited. He sounded like he could have finished that sentence with "…*requires you to cancel your phone and pack all your things?*"

"Well, I guess I have to tell you now," she said, a teasing note to her voice. "Unless you trust me enough to let me keep it a surprise until I get back."

His lip quivered a bit, and she could see he wanted both. He wanted to show her he trusted her, but he wanted to know what was going on more. And honestly, she couldn't blame him.

"All right," she said, stroking the soft white hair at his temple. "Remember when we went to Baja, and we met up with Jim and Lucy? The couple who ran that fishing charter business?"

His eyes drifted to the right, searching for the memory. His gaze returned to her, wider now.

"In Cabo San Lucas," he said, nodding. "What about it?"

"And you said," she nodded as well, prompting the memory, easing him into remembering it the way she hoped he would. "Your lifelong dream had been to retire to Mexico and start a fishing charter business yourself?"

His eyes flickered and brightened just a little bit.

"Well…" she drew out the word, coquettishly. "You know my friend Helen? I found out her boss is selling his fishing boat. It's moored down in Cabo, as it happens, and well…" she scoffed theatrically, like what she was about to say was obvious. "I didn't want to buy it for you sight unseen."

He stared at her.

"So that's why I was going away," she said, gesturing to her case. "I thought I could pop down there while you were with your mom and get it all taken care of before you came back. I honestly thought I'd be back by tomorrow and could surprise you with the good news when you got back."

Speechless. Dumbstruck. Only his eyes moved, roaming over her face.

"And as for the phone, I dropped it yesterday, damn thing, you know how I'm always doing that," she said. "They're just so slippery, and you know me, I'm so clumsy with them. Well yesterday, I was taking it out of my purse and whoops!" She made a flinging gesture with her hand and laughed. "There it went, flying into the street, and before I could grab it, someone ran right over it. I just haven't had time to get a new one, I'm sorry, honey. I should have known you'd be trying to reach me, I'm so sorry."

His eyes were following her every gesture. They'd even followed the imaginary phone being launched into the air.

"You…you were going to buy me a boat?" he finally asked.

She squeezed his arm. "Yes! For your birthday, in fact. I'm just sorry this had to happen to ruin the surprise."

"So…" His pale eyes appeared eager to find comfort in hers. "Is that why you took the money?"

So he knows about the money. Damn.

Oh well. The story was out now, there was no reason not to keep going.

"Are you mad?" She bit her lip and felt her brow crease as she met his eyes without flinching. "I don't blame you if you're mad, but honestly, honey, Helen said her boss had another buyer interested and was only going to hold it for me over the weekend. It's a…Damn, I had pictures the guy sent me, but they were all in my phone. Let me try to remember, it was a…" She searched her memory for the details the guy had mentioned, his way of sweetening the deal. "It's a thirty-three foot Skipjack, with a big double berth down below, too. And some fancy fish finder thing on board, he said. It sounds really good, at least to me."

She watched Teddy's eyes, which had grown rounder with every detail she mentioned. But double beds and fish finders alone weren't going to convince him.

"I just thought, if we don't go for this now, we might lose the chance. And it's your dream, baby. I just didn't think we could pass this up."

He had talked about it constantly in Mexico. At the time, she'd thought maybe he'd just been overexcited, feeling youthful and full of vigor, the way vacations always made him feel. Resort stays in particular always made him randy and bright-eyed. There was just something about hotel sex, he'd said. It made him feel like an illicit lover, forty years younger and ready to romance his sexy young girlfriend, even if he did have to pop a colorful little pill to do it.

He looked down now, his expression bewildered and searching, as if he could find answers at his feet.

"I guess I did the wrong thing, huh?" she finally probed tentatively.

He looked up quickly and turned so he was facing her. "No, no, sweetheart, it's just that…well, like I said, the nursing home tried to process the payment and it came back NSF. When I came back home and you weren't there, well," he faltered, looking a little guilty, "I began to wonder, and so I called the bank and they said you'd made a large withdrawal. That's when I began to think…"

"Oh, I'm so sorry, sweetie," she said, wrapping her arms around his neck and squeezing tight. "Wow, I couldn't have messed this up worse if I'd tried. Look, I have all the cash, right here," she said, opening her purse and slipping her hand underneath the lining. She opened the bag wider so he could peer in and see all the crisp new hundreds bound and stacked together in neat rows. "We can just take it all back to the bank on Monday and forget this ever happened."

His eyes moved from the money back up to her face, and then back down to the money again. She was about to take out some bills and offer them to him when he looked up at her, a weepy smile spreading across his face. She, too, smiled with relief.

"I'm sorry I doubted you, angel," he said then, and reached to hug her again, burying his face in her neck and breathing out, like a balloon deflating. "I should have known it would be something like this."

"Yes, you should have," she needled him gently, and made to stand up. "So what do you say we head for ho—"

"Just…one thing, sweetheart," he asked, grasping her wrist to stop her from standing. "If you're supposed to be at the airport…what on earth are you doing here?"

She pursed her lips and sat back down, gazing out towards the setting sun as the last shimmering rays speared out across the sky. She took a deep breath and turned back to him with a smile.

"I was on my way to the airport, and I just had this sudden need to see Amelia again," she said. Tears welled in her own eyes, and she dabbed at them delicately so as not to ruin her makeup. "I don't know what came over me, but I've been thinking about her so much lately, I felt this crazy need to come see her before I left. She and I used to talk so often, I just...I just really miss her sometimes. It probably sounds nuts, I know, but it's the truth."

He took her hand in his and entwined their fingers. "I understand, honey. I was like that with Doris, for many years after her death."

Amanda nodded, warming to the subject. "See, I knew you'd understand. Sometimes you just need to...I don't know, share the same space with them for a while. As crazy as that sounds. And honestly, honey, I started thinking that if I *were* to buy this boat for you...well, that would mean we'd probably be moving. Down to Baja, where you wanted to start the fishing charters. I thought..." she faltered, her voice catching on a jagged breath. "As much as I want to do that with you, it would mean leaving Amelia behind. Does that sound stupid?"

"Not at all, honey," he said, kissing her softly on the cheek. "I think you're the sweetest thing alive, you know that?"

She shied away from the praise, smiling at him with bashful delight. "Oh stop, you big softie. You're the sweet one."

He glowed from her praise, and for the first time since she'd whirled around to see him there, she felt like everything might actually be all right.

"In fact, baby," she said, tilting her head to the side in thought. "I don't know, maybe you'll think it's crazy, but..."

"But what, sweetheart?"

She scrunched up her nose, the way he'd said he found adorable. "Is there any harm in the two of us going down there, just to look at the boat? I've booked my ticket, you could just buy a ticket on the same flight. We could go down together, make a fun weekend out of it."

Ted paused, considering. "I don't know—"

"Just to look," she said. "There's no harm in that, is there? Helen's boss said he'd take me out for a spin, and if you were there too maybe you could do some fishing, see if he knows anything about running a charter business. From my phone calls with him, he sounds like a very nice guy."

Ted began to shake his head, though without conviction.

"Look, maybe this is the chance you've been waiting for all your life. Maybe you'll take one look at it and fall in love, and you'll be glad we went."

"It's just that my mother is going to need a lot of expensive care in the next few—"

"Of course, of course. But don't you still have that other account? That one with the proceeds from your wife's estate?"

He straightened up and grimaced. "Oh, no, I couldn't use that money for Mom. It's not even really my money, I told you that. I promised Doris I'd invest it until her great-niece grows up."

"I know," she soothed, "and you've done a wonderful job growing those funds. You took it from, what, five hundred thousand or something, to over a million?"

"From four fifty to one point two million," he said, a tinge of pride in his voice.

"Exactly! Look at how much you made that money grow for your great-niece. I don't think Doris ever had any idea you'd be able to grow it that much so fast. You're a genius, Teddy."

"Well, I don't know about that," he scoffed, coloring under her praise.

"And that's just my point," she squeezed his arm again. "I think you've earned the right to spend some of your own money on your dream, don't you? You can always just borrow a bit from the other account to settle up with the nursing home, and then pay it back later. The girl is only, what, fifteen? You've got at least three years to pay that account back."

She could see him thinking about it, working out how he could, in fact, very likely pay it back before he was supposed to turn it over to the girl. But she also saw doubt in his eyes, and the last thing she wanted to do was worry him.

If I push him too hard...

"It was just a thought, honey," she said, offhandedly. "Whatever happens, I think we should take this chance just to have a nice weekend together." She squeezed his hand. "My flight's already paid for, it would be a shame to waste it. And then of course, there's the hotel..."

Ted's eyes gleamed at the mention of the hotel. She figured the hotel would seal it.

And she was right.

"What the heck, let's do it," he said. He kissed her again. "What time's the flight? Do we have time for me to go home and pack a few things?"

She twisted her watch around on her wrist and frowned. "Hmm...the plane leaves in two hours, but I did want to stay and visit with Amelia for a bit."

"Tell you what," he said, rising to his feet. "I'll dash home and grab some things, you stay here and visit with your sister. I'll swing back and pick you up, it's only about thirty minutes to the airport from here."

She frowned up at him. "Are you sure? Maybe we should just head right to the airport, you can always get a toothbrush and whatnot at the hotel."

"No, no, I want to make sure I have everything I need," he said, winking at her.

His colorful little pills, she thought. Of course.

"Do you want to take the money with you?" she offered, holding out her purse. This was the hard part, but she did it offhandedly, with casual ease. "I do feel kind of weird carrying around this much money, but the guy said he'd give me twenty thousand off for cash under the table."

Another gleam in Ted's eyes. And then doubt again, clouding his expression.

"I mean…we *are* just looking," she assured him. "But…if you really love it, it would be nice to be able to jump on such a great deal."

Ted hesitated, then snapped his fingers. "You're right, let's take it with us, just in case. You've got it all safe and sound in that purse, so just hang onto it. I'll be back before you know it, sweetheart."

She stood and hugged him tightly, kissing him three times in a row on his grizzled cheek. "This is going to be great, honey," she said. "This is so much better than my plan."

"I love you, Amanda," he said earnestly, his eyes shining.

"I love you too, Teddy." She kissed him and patted his rump playfully. "Now go so you can get back here quick and we can start our weekend."

She watched as he hurried towards the parking lot and smiled and waved as he turned just at the point where his next steps would take him out of sight. He threw his hand up in the air in a jaunty wave and disappeared.

She remained still for a moment, waiting to see if something might make him turn around and come back. But after a few minutes of silence, the twilight sky settling around her like fog, she turned and walked over to Amelia's grave.

She looked down at it for a few moments. Just a few. And then she turned and walked on.

She moved quickly, almost dragging the case along behind her, feeling it bump and bang as if it were a little dog that couldn't keep up. Not much time, she thought, thanks to this little interruption. Still, if she were lucky, she'd be able to make it with time to spare.

She rounded a corner and slowed down, taking off her sunglasses to peer closely at the row of tiny, neat gravestones lining both sides of the walkway. Balloons and spinners, stuffed animals and toy trucks, streamers and ribbons and fresh bouquets crowded every small grave. She walked slowly, reading each grave, passing by the ones that didn't interest her.

Eventually she stopped at one that did.

> *Our Beautiful Angel*
> *Phoebe Marie Livingston*
> *Daughter of Dave and Caroline*
> *Born May 18, 1986*
> *Mercy Hospital, Folsom*
> *Called Home to Jesus*
> *June 25, 1987*

Amanda quickly did the math. Only fourteen months younger than herself.

Perfect.

She withdrew her new phone and snapped a picture of the tombstone, checking it to make sure the details could be clearly seen. She had lucked out, finding one with so many details committed to stone like this.

Yes, it had definitely been worth stopping here.

There were so many rich American men in Cabo, after all. She needed to make sure she could get back across the border with one of them.

Once she was done with the boat guy she'd met on that cheater's website, once she'd lined up someone who wasn't already married, she'd go to the consulate in Mexico and explain, through tears, that all her ID had been stolen, including her passport and birth certificate, and she needed new credentials to get back home.

It had worked before, in the Dominican Republic. It would work again.

All she'd have to do once she got back across the border was slip back up here and tell her sad story to the County Records Office. A few tears, maybe a story about a cheating husband who dumped her in Mexico, and she'd walk out with a new birth certificate and a whole new life.

Phoebe Marie Livingston. She tried out the name as she turned to go, thumbing through her taxi app to book a new pick up.

Phoebe Marie Livingston.

It wouldn't be that hard to get used to, she thought, passing by the grave of Amelia Powers, whoever she was. No harder to get used to than Amanda Stack had been.

Or Maisie Bellamy before that. Or Josephine Paget, the name engraved on the passport she was about to use, the name she'd used to book her private jet and would have to burn once she left the country.

But she didn't mind losing Josephine, or Amanda for that matter, now that she had Phoebe. With Teddy's sixty grand tucked safely in her purse, and his one point two million in her chic little rolling suitcase, she could be a lot pickier this time. She could live well for years before starting her search for The One all over again.

The Plot Thickens

Kenneth Gwin

The roof was slippery from heavy dew. He sniffed along the edges, careful not to fall. He checked under the eaves where pigeons sometimes nest and lay their eggs. His favorite spot was a place where the roof hung over a bit of porch, giving the pigeons a protected shelter from the rain.

There was a rustle of feathers and frightened calls as two birds took flight, leaving a pair of eggs tucked among some sticks and grass. He was able to grab one egg, but the other rolled out of reach, wobbling over bumps and shingles to tumble helplessly over the edge.

Undisturbed, he took his time to enjoy his small dinner and ignore the scolding of indignant birds watching from the safety of nearby telephone lines.

He tested the air for other treats. Without promise, he slid down from the roof to explore the area around the porch. Stupid people leave food anywhere.

The porch was cluttered with human stuff. Sniffing around, he found a trace of something tempting in the air. The trail led him to a small door that opened easily as he pushed inside.

More scraps were scattered here and there. Pausing to enjoy each morsel, he sensed something off; a different smell lingered in the room.

Creeping over the slippery floor, he could see a dark shape sprawled in the doorway, its eyes barely visible in the darkness. It tried to move. Maybe it was asleep. Then it made a sound—a wounded animal sound. And there was something wrong with its face. Strange. An unknown creature. He backed away, unsure.

There must be safer places to look for food.

Outside, he continued over fences to search the neighborhood trash for any snacks that could be found.

***

The man was helpless, hearing tentative scraping coming from across the room. He listened, frightened. He didn't want to die.

He felt his life slipping.

What could be worse than getting shot?

Maybe it was better this should end.

Then a movement, just over there.

Slowly, the sound came closer. He could see it. A shadow crept toward him—just inches away.

Now face to face with an animal in the darkness, he tried to scream, shout, back up, stand, anything to get away.

The animal's mask and beady eyes—

Man to beast, sharing fear and curiosity.

He could hear himself breathing.

A moment forever.

The animal moved away.

Leaving fear.

And desperation.

And sorrow.

All alone—

He didn't want to die like this.

***

Larry woke up, rolled over, not sure where he was, his throat dry as dust and his tongue so fat he could hardly breathe. Opening one eye, he could see a nightstand smudged with white powder and an ashtray full of butts.

The woman was still asleep.

What was her name? He couldn't remember.

He eased out of bed, careful not to wake little Sleeping Beauty. His head hammered in protest from the slightest movement. He parted the curtain to peer outside. The morning was a blurry smear of glaring light blasting through the window.

Shit! What have I done? He wasn't sure. He sat back on the edge and tried to sort through scattered memories.

He looked down—Lizzie, something…maybe that was her name. Her breathing came out in gentle, gasping wheezes.

Standing up—whoa!—way too fast. He ran for the toilet, found the door, stumbled through, nearly choking on dry heaves, wretches, and uncontrolled spasms. He washed his face in the sink, slushed some water around in his mouth and looked in the mirror long enough to recognize himself in the yellow light.

Shit!

He found his shirt and pants at the foot of the bed. His shoes had been tossed across the room. He grabbed his jacket as he headed for the door, checking to make sure his drugs were still safe in his pocket.

He looked back at Sleeping Beauty. She was a good enough lay.

At least she didn't try to rip him off.

Someone had left his front door unlocked. *Him or me?* Larry wondered.

"Dad! You okay?"

Messed up as the Old Man was, he should be awake by now.

No answer came from inside the house, so he figured his dad was probably sound asleep. The Old Man spent most of his time asleep—in bed or sitting in his chair, watching TV, or babbling about some mindless crap.

Inside the Old Man's bedroom, the shades were down, and the room had that look and smell of neglect and failing health. Larry nudged the motionless body.

The Old Man stirred, mumbled something.

"Dad? You want breakfast? I could scramble you an egg. I'm making coffee."

"Aliens…"

"What?" Larry bent closer to hear what the Old Man was trying to say.

"Bastards." His voice was a raspy croak. "You gotta watch out for those things. We got little green monsters creeping around at night."

Larry wasn't sure what he was talking about. Most of the Old Man's brain had been left somewhere in the weeds. "What you talking about?"

"They came right in, so I shot him. You know I keep a gun under my pillow."

"How'd you get a gun?"

"You don't know the half what goes on. A man's gotta protect himself."

"What the hell you talkin' about?"

"I told you. Space people been coming around at night. I seen 'em. You gotta be prepared. I don't wanna be no ab-duck-tee. They do all kinds a strange shit to a person."

Larry never responded to most of the Old Man's fantasies. "So, where's the gun? I thought I'd put any guns away where you couldn't hurt yourself. I can't leave you alone for a minute. You're worse than a goddamn kid."

"I heard them landing—"

"Where your glasses?"

The Old Man pulled an ancient revolver out from under the covers.

"Fuck, Pops, you could shoot yourself." Larry reached for the gun. "Gimme that thing before we both get hurt."

The Old Man had a tight grip but was too weak to offer much resistance and soon let go.

"Cut the crap, Dad. I'm gonna make breakfast."

That's when Larry found the dead body stretched out on the kitchen floor.

"Space aliens, my ass! You shot some dude and he's crawled into the kitchen. He's dead!" Larry was worried the neighbors had heard the gun go off. Then he realized the dead guy must have been looking for drugs and cash.

"Space people—I told you." The Old Man announced from the bedroom in a voice that declared, *I told you so.*

"Shit! Shit! Shit! What a goddamn mess! We gotta get this guy outta here. We don't want the cops in here." No way he'd want his little business being exposed. He quickly checked the stash he'd hidden in a toolbox in the closet. Then he checked the body. He couldn't find any weapons or drugs, and only five bucks in his wallet.

The Old Man stumbled to the doorway wearing a saggy T-shirt and yellowed underpants.

Larry looked up. "So, what happened?"

"I told you. One of those aliens came in my room, made a bunch a scary noises, so I shot him."

Larry stepped over the body. "You stay back. I'm gonna clean this up so I can make us breakfast. I gotta figure something out. You still want coffee? I'm gonna be hungry after this."

Larry moved his car to the back of the house and dragged the body, wrapped in blankets like a mummy, down the back steps. But a corpse can be uncooperative, and he soon found out there was no way he could fold it into a shape he could stuff into the trunk. He needed something else. A truck. A van. A better plan. The Old Man's pickup hadn't been driven for months and the battery was deader than that guy on the ground. This wasn't going to work. And the thought of cutting the body into manageable chunks nearly made him puke.

So, he struggled, hoisting the body onto the back seat, then went to the other side to drag it across the upholstery and roll it over, headfirst onto the floor, trying to move things as fast as he could, and not look suspicious if anyone came looking. He propped its feet up so he could close the door.

Now what?

He tried to think of a likely place to stash the body. He drove around the neighborhood. A dumpster looked promising, but when he looked inside it was almost empty. There wasn't enough trash to cover things up. And he wasn't sure he was strong enough lift the guy all by himself and heave him over. Then he thought about finding someplace in the woods, but he didn't have a shovel and didn't like the idea of leaving evidence under a tree or along the side of a country road.

Still, what to do?

Could he leave it in an abandoned building?

Someone would eventually find it.

A lake? A river?

He heard you have to poke a body full of holes, so it doesn't bloat and float to the surface. Jesus! He can't blame the Old Man for taking care of business, but this is getting sicker by the minute. He needed help—a friend. A real friend would help him hide a body. He needed a friend; someone he could trust.

Or owed him.

Big time.

There was one regular on his list of clients, someone with a major dependency and plenty of habits he'd want to hide—

Bob the Gravedigger.

He had a shovel.

A big one.

He dealt with bodies every day. His was a dying business. And his place of business wasn't that far away.

"Can't help you, buddy. You think I'm crazy?"

Bob turned the motor off on his little cart and lit a cigarette. That probably meant he was thinking it over. Larry gave him time to ponder the pluses and the minuses. The suggestion of easy drugs should be tempting bait.

"Well..."

Skinny and fidgety—anything involving drugs would get Bob's attention.

"Listen, I'm in a bind here. The Old Man shot this guy trying to rob us. See? I'm part of your supply chain. You don't wanna go looking for another supplier. I'm your man. Your secret's safe with me. We depend on each other. You don't want to lose your job if anyone found out about your little problem. We're a team."

Bob listened, waiting.

"I'm in a bind here. I could really use your help."

Bob listened some more.

"I need someone I can trust."

Larry could see the idea of trust running around inside Bob's little head. Nothing like a bit of praise and validation to prime the pump of a drug abuser.

"We have to rely on each other. You've always been a good customer—and a friend—don't forget."

"You don't see me running around with dead bodies that don't belong. I got a job and a reputation to uphold."

Reputation? My ass! Word was, Bob wasn't above robbing bodies, or anything else, to pay for drugs.

"Hey, this is new to me too. It's a problem."

"No shit."

"So, can you help me here?" Larry slipped his hand into his pocket. "First installment—I got it right here." He lifted the bag to give him a peek. "And more next week. And the week after that. You get the drift?"

Larry could sense Bob's brain whir into action.

"What do you want me to do?"

"Maybe open one of those things," Larry looked across the field of headstones to the stately structures that could offer plenty of places to hide these unfortunate, earthly remains. "Or bury him. Proper. Probably he didn't deserve to die, but those are the risks when you break into a man's house."

Bob looked away. "We can't do this during the day. And you can't leave that thing here—people walkin' around, mournful and all. I'll leave the south gate unlocked tonight. Meet me at 10:00 over at my maintenance shed. Over there." He pointed. "We'll figure this out."

***

Larry drove around with the dead body as a passenger as he made his rounds. He couldn't leave it unattended, worried that someone would start snooping and mess things up. So, it was business as usual as he tried to pretend there was nothing suspicious about the tidy bundle laid out across the backseat of his car. But he wished the air conditioner worked better. By the afternoon things were starting to smell like a bad piece of meat.

A dense fog had settled in with the night, bringing in hints of salt air from the coast. The trees were dripping from the cold and wet.

Bob the Gravedigger explained that most of these private mausoleums were over a hundred years old. The locks were seldom used and some only had gates or bars and not solid doors to keep the curious away.

"It's not like a movie. These aren't crypts with squeaky doors where vampires slip in and out at night. These are condos for the dead, and when you're dead, you're dead. Know what I mean?"

"Yeah." Larry looked warily at the surrounding mist and dark. "I get the idea. I got a deader in the back seat—hasn't moved an inch all day. Now what?"

"Well, I thought about digging a grave a little deeper, you know, before a funeral, then covering him up below the liner, so when they lower the casket, he's down there, underneath everything. Let's just say, out of sight, out of mind, and no one's the wiser."

"Sounds like a plan to me. So, what's the problem?"

"No funerals till Friday. We can't leave your friend here stewin' in the sun for the next three days."

"Can't you store him somewhere in the meantime?"

"This is long-term parking. I can't take him inside and we don't have refrigerators out here to chill your dearly departed before he takes his final flight."

"You're not making this easy. How 'bout digging up one of the recent ones? Maybe nobody will notice if there's already fresh sod on top."

"Could. But I've been thinking—kind of a compromise. We've been doing some landscaping under the eucalyptus out back. We've put in new pipes, sprinklers, curbs, stuff like that. We can just slip him in with the plantings. Easy-peasy. The backhoe's already there, ready to go."

"I don't know…"

"It's the best I can do." Bob crossed his arms.

"Well…"

"It's good for the roses we're planting too. Think of the comfort it will bring to those bereaved folks walkin' by."

Larry thought for a moment. "Okay. And don't forget our little deal. Drugs enough to keep you going in exchange for help and silence."

"A deal's a deal. I'm a professional grave digger." Bob spoke smugly. "I'll be the last person to let you down."

That was reassuring.

They loaded the body on the maintenance cart and drove together to the far end of the lot. Larry watched as Bob cleared a spot behind the roses, then fired up the backhoe, and started to dig. He soon made a suitable grave.

"That didn't take long."

Bob climbed down to examine his handywork. "I told you. I'm a professional."

"Are you sure this is a good spot?"

"Don't worry. The guys doing the landscaping are friends of mine. Nobody cares. All we have to do is cover things up and then go home like it never happened."

"I guess…"

"Just gimme a hand here and we'll be done with this."

Together they lifted the body off the cart and eased the bundle into the gaping hole.

"See? Easy-peasy. Now, I'll just fill this up and smooth some dirt over the top. No one's gonna notice."

"I see."

When Bob turned toward the backhoe, Larry pulled a shovel from the maintenance cart and hit him soundly across the back of the head. Bob crumpled to his knees.

"Wha…?"

Larry hit him again, just to make sure.

Bob fell in a heap.

"Sorry to be the one to let you down. You should know you can't trust a drug dealer *or* a druggie. If you could hear me, I'm sure you'd understand."

Larry rolled the lifeless body over and watched as it dropped into the waiting grave.

Intemperance

Rick Schneider

"Okay," I said. "I'll be right there."

I hung up and checked the clock on the night-stand. Midnight. I turned to my wife, Stasia, who looked at me bleary-eyed.

"Hon," I said. "Sorry. Trouble at Bidwell Acres."

"The cemetery?" she asked, more awake now.

"Yes. I'll call you and let you know when I'll be home."

She snorted. "No, you won't," she said, and fell back to sleep.

I pulled on my Sherriff windbreaker as I walked to the cruiser parked in my driveway. The temperature hovered around 55 degrees. About right for a mid-October night in Temperance, California.

I drove the five miles from my house to the cemetery, Bidwell Acres, named after John Bidwell, California Guber-natorial candidate for the Prohibition Party in 1880. He ran for President of the United States a few years later. Lost both elections but won the hearts of the people in this part of Cali-fornia. He founded a town, Chico, just a few miles from here. People from this town honored him by renaming their town Temperance. He was so pleased by the honor he donated the property that became Bidwell Acres. Legend has it he's buried there in an unmarked grave. Local entrepreneurs say he haunts the town and has done so since the repeal of Prohibition in 1933. The tale makes little sense, but brings in tourists and helps the local economy. There are even two cemetery ghost tours you can take starting at eleven o'clock Friday and Saturday nights. The fee is reasonable at $10 a head. Tips encouraged.

It was on one such tour that the trouble started.

Police tape sealed the entrance to Bidwell Acres, which meant I had to get out of my cruiser and rip the silly stuff down before approaching the scene. The handiwork of my easily excitable night-shift deputy, Hector Guillo, no doubt. He loves that yellow tape.

I saw the flashing blue and white light bar from Guillo's cruiser and headed that way. I nosed my car close to Guillo's and shut off the engine. I checked my sidearm to be sure I had it secured in my holster.

"Chief, good to see you. Sorry for rousting you out of bed."

I'm the Sherriff of Temperance, not Chief of Police, but Guillo never got it right. I let it pass. "No problem, Hec. Talk to me."

He pointed. "This is where the victim died," he said. "EMTs took him away just before you arrived. You can see their tire marks. I told them to be careful, but they didn't listen." He shook his head. "He was DOA. Dead on Arrival."

"Yes, I know what DOA means, Hec."

"Of course, Chief."

I bit my tongue and counted to three. "Are the witnesses secured?" One of the more frustrating things about law enforcement is rounding up witnesses before they scatter. Given this took place amongst a group of mostly out-of-town tourists, after dark, on a Saturday night, in a cemetery upped the odds in favor of witnesses who wanted to get the hell out of town rather than spend the night talking with the police.

As if to validate my fears, Hec spit on the ground in disgust. "Most of them got away. But we took down three statements. Plus Shylock."

Shylock Broadback—his actual name, I swear—ran one of the ghost tours. He stood a few feet away, stovepipe hat adorning his ancient head, arguing with someone. Probably a tourist asking for his ten dollars back.

"Can't Shylock give us the names of the witnesses that scampered?"

"No, Chief. He takes cash most times. Sometimes he asks their names, as part of his schtick, but mostly only if they're cute young ladies, and then I suppose he gets fake names as often as not."

"Yes, I suppose he does," I said. "Where are the eyewitness reports?"

Deputy Guillo tapped his head. "Right up here," he said seriously, immediately causing me a headache of epic proportions. "Haven't written them up yet," he explained.

"I thought you just said you took down three statements. And you used 'we'. As in someone helped you."

"Oh. I meant me. Nobody else is on duty this late."

"Don't you have a phone?"

"Yep. That's how I called you."

This was going nowhere. "Did you use your phone to record the statements?"

His eyes lit up. "Yes, sir, Chief. Want to hear them?"

I nodded. "Tell Shylock to stick around. I want to talk with him after I listen to the statements."

The statements captured on Hec's phone in a surprisingly professional manner, all told the same basic story, though as is typical they varied on many of the details. Their cemetery ghost tour started at eleven PM sharp with Shylock giving his spiel about John Bidwell's history of anti-alcohol crusades and the "verified sightings" of his ghost starting the year the 21st Amendment repealed Prohibition. As the flow of beer, wine and liquor resumed, Shylock had explained, strange things began happening in and around the cemetery that bears Bidwell's name.

I've heard Shylock do his schtick a couple of times, and, in the darkness with his skeletal features accentuated by the stove-pipe hat and his theatrically hushed tones, it can get pretty creepy. Two of the three witnesses had admitted as much, while a third—Samuel Peppers—scoffed at the notion. Turns out Samuel was there with his wife Altria, one of the other witnesses and a staunch believer in the occult.

Just as Shylock got to the point where he raised his voice to add to the ambience a wail erupted from behind one tombstone and a "ghost" came rushing directly at them. At this point, one of the tour participants clutched his chest and dropped to the ground. The paramedics confirmed him dead upon their arrival (hence Hec's "DOA" reference).

The dead man, a Mr. Sylvester Coates, attended the tour alone according to all three witnesses, though two of them said he was wearing a green jacket and the third—Sam Peppers—insisted he was in shirtsleeves.

Two of the witnesses said the "ghost" floated on air, while the third (yep, Peppers again) insisted he saw black sneakers underneath a ghost costume. All three agreed the ghost wore all black except for the eyes, which were iridescent yellow orange.

When Guillo asked them about the voice of the ghost, each witness gave a different answer. Peppers said it was clearly a male voice, deep and resonant. His wife said she heard the voice crack mid-wail as if it belonged to a teenage boy. The third witness, an elderly woman named Tante Freeman, said she heard a deep woman's voice. When Hec pressed her as to why she thought the voice was female, she couldn't answer.

"Let's get Shylock over here, Hec," I said. He immediately barked at the old man to come over. By this time, Shylock's disgruntled customer, who turned out to be Peppers, had gone.

"Shylock," I said and nodded as he approached. He returned the nod.

"When can I expect an arrest of those damn kids?" he said in a voice that contained equal measures of fury, embarrassment and respect for my badge.

"You saw kids?" I asked.

"Just one this time, but I seen all four before. Always thinking it's funny to scare the tourists."

"Which kids, Shylock?" Guillo cut in, irritating me.

"You know which kids. I don't need to tell you, and I'm not going to. Last thing I need is to get my permit revoked to run these tours. These tours is all I got left, you know."

I in fact knew that Shylock Broadback had socked away millions over the years. He'd had a cousin that clued him in on an investment in a website that sold books way back in the late '90s.

"Shylock," I said, trying to keep my voice even. "Just tell us who the kids are."

I could see he didn't want to speak the names.

I tried a fresh track, determined to circle back to the kids' names. "What about the victim?"

Shylock nodded. "A loner. Most of the folks interested in ghosts come in groups. Determined to scare or dare each other, I suspect. This guy showed up last minute, out of breath like he'd been running."

"Pay in cash?" I asked.

"Yes," he answered. "Funny thing, though. He didn't have a tenner. He had to search his pockets for a fiver and five ones."

"How did he act on the tour?" I asked.

Shylock screwed up his face in an attempt to look pensive. "He hung to the back. Didn't ask any questions."

"Did you see his reaction to the kid that jumped out?"

Another face scrunch. "That's the funny thing. It looked like the ghost targeted him."

"Targeted him? How?"

He spit on the ground. "He was silent at first, just sorta gliding up at us. I admired his technique, really. Looked like a legit ghost. Then, when he got close to the victim, he let out one hell of a wail. Shook *me* to the bone, it did."

"And?"

"And the guy clutched at his chest and fell down, and the ghost got the hell outta there."

I processed that for a moment.

"The names, Shy," Guillo kicked in, beating me to it. "The names of the kids."

"Okay, dammit," he said, looking over both shoulders before continuing to speak. "Jaimie Hammond is the ringleader. And his girlfriend, Maria Rachel Flacco, is never far from his side. Alonzo and Alzello Beamer are part of it, too. Those are the ones I seen over the years."

He'd just named the son of the mayor (Hammond), daughter of a selectman (Flacco) and the twin sons of the richest man in town (Beamer). Beamer owned half of the stores downtown, having wisely invested the money he'd earned from a six-year journeyman NBA career.

I would have to tread lightly.

I sent Guillo back to the office to write up the report after we finished with Shylock and headed home to grab an hour of sleep.

It was 4:30 when I trundled back into bed. Stasia stirred long enough to acknowledge my presence and sniff the air. Satisfied, she went back to sleep. The gesture was involuntary on her part and was a holdover from my drinking days. My face turned red, also involuntarily, guilt surrounding me instantaneously as though I'd just come from the bar. I hadn't. It had been four years since my last drink.

At least she didn't ding me for failing to call.

By six o'clock, I had showered, shaved and driven my cruiser to the station house. I poured myself a cup of coffee, black, and nodded at Truelook, the newest recruit. In Temperance, the newbie gets to show up early for the day shift and make the coffee. Truelook and I shared an ancestor two generations back, and I felt like a heel treating him like crap, but that's the way we do it in Temperance.

"True," I said, after taking my first grateful sip. "Get Singalong and meet me in my office in five."

"Singalong's not in yet," he said, gesturing at the obviously empty room.

I took another sip of coffee. Then one more.

"Did you do the handshake with Guillo?"

"Yeah," he said. "He told me about the dead guy on Shylock's cemetery tour. Accident, though, right?"

I considered that. "Maybe yes, maybe no. Either way, a contributing factor is some dumbass kid jumping out and scaring the shit out of an out-of-towner."

"Who was he?"

"Hope to find out more this morning." I turned to go. "As soon as Sarah gets here, bring her in."

Truelook nodded.

I knew it wouldn't be long. Sarah "Singalong" Master hadn't missed a shift since I couldn't remember when. We called her Singalong because she always hummed to whatever music happened to be playing. Just hummed, never sang the words. Turns out she has a mental block about remembering song lyrics. Damn near perfect recall for names, faces and facts, but can't even remember the words to "Mary Had a Little Lamb." One day, before any of us knew of her issue with lyrics, one of us—I don't remember who—shouted at her, "Dammit, Sarah! Sing along!" The name stuck. I asked her if it bothered her, told her I'd make the guys stop.

"Nah," she said. "Singalong is cool. Better than anything else you pervs would come up with."

She was probably right.

Ten minutes later, Truelook and Singalong trooped into my office and took the two empty chairs opposite my desk.

"Morning," I said, nodding at Sarah. "Thanks," I said to Truelook, who had brought the coffeepot in with him and was now holding it out toward my cup, offering a refill.

I went through the details from the previous night and then made assignments.

"All the kids we're talking about being involved are still technically minors, so we'll need to notify their folks. That makes sense in this case, anyway, since the parents are all so, well…" My voice trailed off.

"Rich?" Singalong offered. "Powerful? Both?"

"Let's just say they're important to the town. The mayor will ask for an update, regardless. So, Sing, you take Beamer."

"Yes!" she said, executing a fist pump. She'd made no secret of her hero worship of Rayley "Big" Beamer, modest though his career had been.

"True, you take Selectman Flacco. That leaves Mayor Hammond for me. Let's contact the parents ASAP and set up the interviews with the kids. We'll do the kids here at the station in the interview room. Let's shoot for late afternoon."

I decided to start with the mayor at his office and let him decide when and how to pull in his wife Jennifer. There were two primary reasons for this. First, as soon as the meeting in my office adjourned, I got a text from the mayor asking for an update, so I had to see him anyway. Second, his wife Jennifer scared me. She stood six feet tall and oozed sex appeal. Part of it was her looks: she had a nice body and a pretty face. But mostly it was her attitude. She came on to a lot of guys, including me. Once, in the midst of a fairly bad drunken binge, I'd kissed her. That was as far as it went, but since that day I've avoided her when possible.

I gave myself an hour before seeing Hammond because I wanted as much information about the victim as possible. If I was going in there to accuse his son of being the ghostly catalyst of a man's death, I'd damn well better have my shit together. That turned out to be a wise choice.

While going over Hec's report and mulling over Shylock's statement, I got an email alert. The subject line contained the victim's name. I opened the email and read a synopsis of the attachments, of which there were several.

Sylvester Coates was a man of means who lived in Silicon Valley. At 45 years of age, he held several patents dealing with the manufacture of computer components. He lived in Los Altos, the richest city in California. He had graduated from Berkeley with an undergraduate degree in computer science. He'd added a master's degree from Stanford.

What was he doing at a cemetery ghost tour in Temperance? We're located three hours north of Silicon Valley. Was he looking for an "off the grid" getaway? Maybe he was looking to invest his considerable wealth some place other than the overpriced Bay Area. I called Truelook and told him to find out in which hotel Coates had stayed last night, then I closed my email and prepared to visit Mayor William "Billy" Hammond.

"Sit, Sherriff," Hammond growled, back turned to me, head buried in his phone.

I obeyed like a well-trained dog, though I expected no treats for my effort.

"Your text surprised me this morning," I said to his back. "Thought you were out of town."

He grunted, head still bent over his phone. "Came back early."

I waited for him to finish whatever the hell he was doing with his phone. Maybe he was playing solitaire. Finally, with a substantial sigh, he turned to me.

"What have you got? This Coates guy have a bad heart or something?"

I did a double-take. How did he know the victim's name?

He laughed and answered my unexpressed question. "It's my business to know when dignitaries are visiting Temperance, especially when they drop dead in the middle of the cemetery. I've already had calls from his people, wanting to know all the details. So, what are the details?"

I relayed what I knew about the scene, edging up to the part about the teens Shylock fingered as probable miscreants.

"Some jackass jumped out at the guy and he dropped dead?" His words conveyed astonishment, but I had the feeling he already knew everything I'd told him. Did he have an "in" with Guillo?

"Yes, sir," I said. "Should get the official word from the coroner today, but that's what fits the data best."

"Any idea who the jackass is?" he asked. Again, I got the feeling he knew more than he was telling. Did he know about his son's ghoulish hobby?

"Well, sir," I began. "Shylock says there's a group of kids that has disrupted his tours in the past, jumping out at his group trying to scare them."

"Mm hmm," he said, rolling his wrist to get me to continue.

"Shylock says Jaimie is one of the kids."

He reacted in what appeared to be genuine surprise. "Jaimie?"

"Yes, sir."

"My son?"

"Yes. That Jaimie."

"What the hell has that idiot got himself into now?" he thundered.

"Sir, Shylock says he's the ringleader." I hated to keep dragging Shylock into this, but the mayor needed to hear it all. I expected an outburst but didn't get one.

"Shylock would know," he said, pensive now. "I suppose you want to talk with Jaimie? I'll need to be there. And our lawyer."

I swallowed. "What about Jennifer?" I asked.

He shook his head derisively. "I'll deal with Jennifer."

"Four o'clock today? At the station?"

"We'll be there. Jaimie may not be able to sit by then, but we'll be there."

After leaving Hammond, I returned to the office and sat at my desk mulling over the interview. In the midst of my reverie, my cell rang. Truelook.

"True," I said by way of greeting.

"Boss," he replied. "Got the Flacco parents to agree to a 4:30 meeting at the station. Maria Rachel will be there, too." He pronounced Rachel as "Raquel" and rolled the "R" slightly.

"Lawyer?"

"Nope. Didn't want one."

"What about Coates?"

161

"Didn't stay anywhere in Temperance last night. No reservations, no check in, no nothing."

I stored that away for later processing.

"Okay, thanks. See you this afternoon."

"Boss," he answered, then disconnected.

Sarah had worse luck with Beamer. He'd blown up all over her and she'd failed to get an agreement for an afternoon meeting involving his twin sons. Instead, he promised his lawyer would call me. I didn't look forward to that conversation.

"Sherriff," Mayor Hammond began, "please address all your questions to Mr. Laughton."

Mr. Laughton, dressed in a navy suit and a solid red tie, represented the Hammonds. I'd locked horns with him before. He was good, especially at shutting down the flow of information from his clients.

We'd had our pow-wow at 2:30 and determined that Jaimie Hammond was indeed the ringleader of the group, based on discussions Truelook and Singalong had had with various members of the Temperance school system, adding additional import to this interview.

Now we sat in the interrogation room, Sarah and I on one side of the table, facing the mayor, Mr. Laughton and Jamie on the other. Jennifer Hammond was not in attendance. Each of us wore grim expressions.

"With all due respect to Mr. Laughton, I'll address my questions to Jaimie directly," I said, looking at the kid as I said it. "Jaimie," I began, not waiting for Laughton or Hammond to protest, "where were you last night between eleven o'clock and midnight?"

"He was at home," the mayor broke in. "I saw his car when I pulled into the driveway."

I shot Hammond a glance. "Jaimie can answer for himself. But I will note for the record that, based on your interruption, you did not actually see your son at home last night during the time in question."

That earned me a dirty look from the Mayor. There could be hell to pay if I didn't back off.

"Mayor Hammond isn't under investigation here," Laughton said.

"Good, then we can focus on Jaimie," I said. "Jaimie, please answer the question about your whereabouts."

Jaimie looked defiant. "I was at home, just like dad says."

"Alone?"

He continued to meet my gaze. "Yes."

"What time did your dad get home?"

"Again," Laughton interrupted. "Mayor Hammond isn't the subject of this discussion."

I smiled at Laughton. "Just trying to ascertain the strength of Jaimie's alibi."

He threw up his hands in disgust. "Alibi? We're not even talking about a crime here! Someone jumps out and yells "Boo" in a cemetery. Please educate me on what law or ordinance that violates."

"A person is dead because of a malicious prank. At a minimum, as the Sheriff of Temperance, I need to find the person who did it and make sure they understand the gravity and thoughtlessness and stupidity of their actions. That's at a minimum. According to the little bit of research I've been able to do thus far, it very well may be a crime."

"I'll answer the question," Jaimie said. "He came in just before eleven. I knew because I watched his car swerve into the driveway, followed by him stumbling out of the car. And no, I wasn't actually in the house. I was in my car across the street."

"Alone?"

"No. I was with Maria."

"Maria Rachel Flacco?"

"Yes."

"What were you doing?"

He smiled and chose not to answer.

"That still left you time to get to the cemetery."

"I had better things to do." The smile again.

"Will Maria back you up?"

He nodded. "Yep."

Maria did back him up. She was less smug and more demure about the session in the back of Jaimie's car, especially in front of her parents. But the stories matched. Her parents corroborated her story in that they heard Jaimie dropping her off at their house around eleven thirty. The Flaccos live almost half an hour from the cemetery, so it would have been impossible for either Jaimie or Maria to have been the "ghost." After the interviews, we regrouped and decided it couldn't have been the Beamer twins, either. First, there was only one ghost. Second, the Beamer kids were both around 6' 6" tall and our ghoul wasn't.

When Beamer's lawyer called, I told him we no longer needed to talk with Alonzo and Alzello. He sounded disappointed, as though he had geared up for a good fight and I'd taken that pleasure from him.

I got in the cruiser, determined to go over the scene at the cemetery one more time. On my way through town, I saw Jennifer Hammond duck into the liquor store. Much as I wanted to avoid her, I was curious as to why she hadn't attended her son's interview. I found a parking space and parked the cruiser. I sat for a moment, screwing up my resolve. I hadn't gone into a liquor store in a long time.

I contemplated the ridiculousness of it all. An alcoholic sheriff in a town called Temperance, named for a man who extolled the virtues of tee-totaling and the evils of drink, then I got out of the cruiser and walked toward the store.

I entered and stood in the doorway, hesitant to go farther. The proprietor looked up, saw me, an expression of surprise covering his face. I'd known Charlie really well back then. Really well. I nodded to him. Then Jennifer must have seen me because she shouted out.

"Sheriff! Fancy seeing you here!"

She had a bottle of vodka in her hands. She walked up to where I stood, placing the vodka on the counter by Charlie as she passed.

"This it today, Jennifer?" Charlie asked.

"Yes," she answered, never taking her eyes off mine.

"Did you enjoy the champagne?" Charlie asked.

Jennifer flinched and her eyes clouded for a second. "Yes. Thanks, Charlie."

He took the hint and rang up the vodka without another word.

She reached for my arm, but a sudden tremor that shook the ground stopped her. Earthquake. Not a big one, but big enough to knock bottles off shelves. I saw Charlie duck behind the counter as Jennifer and I were thrown to the ground.

"Holy shit!" she exclaimed.

The smells hit me, overpowering my ability to think. The whiskey aisle was closest to me and that's what I smelled first. Jack Daniels, for sure. And scotch and bourbon. I thought I would drown in the aromas as they enveloped me. Then I could smell gin from the next aisle. The distinctive juniper odor assailed my nostrils, which were open wide and welcoming. Hell, I could even smell Jennifer's vodka, which had fallen off the counter and broken, and vodka doesn't have much of a smell.

"Sheriff? Are you okay?"

It was Jennifer.

I shook my head once. Then twice more. Hard. I looked at my uniform, which had become damp with what smelled like Wild Turkey. Not good.

"I'm fine," I said, a slight tremor in my voice.

"That's the biggest one we've had for a while," she said, meaning the temblor. "Charlie's going to have a lot of paperwork to do for the insurance." Then she looked at me, eyes narrowed as she got to her feet. "What the hell are you doing here, anyway? I thought you'd gone off the bottle."

"I had," I said. Then, more emphatically, "I have. I'm still sober."

I stood up and looked over at the counter, where Charlie was brushing off his shirt sleeves. "Damn, Charlie, why don't you carry only plastic bottles?"

His look of chagrin indicated he'd had the same thought. I looked back at Jennifer.

"I came in here to ask you why you weren't with your son at the interview this afternoon."

She cut her eyes away from me. "My husband didn't want me there," she said.

"Why not?" I asked, and I noticed a bruise on her left cheek she'd tried to cover up with makeup.

"Didn't need me, he said."

"Can we continue this outside?" I asked, moving toward the door. She looked at me and then nodded as realization hit her.

"I'm not paying for that vodka," she yelled at Charlie as she followed me out the door.

Outside, with the setting sun hitting her full in the face, the bruise was more apparent. I pointed at it.

"Is that new?" I asked.

She touched the bruise but said, "What?"

The pieces fell together in my mind, which was blessedly clear of alcoholic fumes. I settled on my approach, hoping she hadn't connected with her husband or son since the interview with Jaimie.

"Jaimie has no alibi for last night. We have video of him on previous occasions harassing cemetery ghost tours. Jennifer, a man died last night. Literally scared to death. Jaimie's life will never be the same."

"It wasn't Jaimie!" she shouted.

"Why did your husband come home last night? He was supposed to be out of town."

"I-I don't know."

"Did he surprise you?"

"N-No."

"It's a shame about Jaimie. He's just a kid."

"It wasn't Jaimie!" she cried again.

"Then tell me what happened. You know the victim, don't you? Sylvester Coates."

"Yes."

"He was at your house when your husband got home, wasn't he?"

"Yes."

I waited.

"He came home early because he wanted to catch me with Sylvester," she said.

"And did he?"

"No. We heard him, and Sylvester got the hell out of the house."

"He ran to the cemetery and joined Shylock's tour," I guessed.

"I told him the tour was just starting and he could blend in. But Billy knew he'd been there."

"The champagne?"

"Yes. I didn't have time to hide the two half-empty glasses. He asked me where Sylvester went and hit me when I wouldn't answer. So, I gave in and told him he was headed for Shylock's tour."

"Did he stop by Jaimie's room on his way out?"

She looked surprised, but nodded. "Yes. How did you know?"

"Because he picked up Jaimie's ghost outfit."

"Oh," she said. "Will Jaimie be in trouble?"

"No. Not if he stops."

"He will," she said, resolute. "And Billy?"

I pondered that for a moment. I could see wrongdoing all around on this.

"Good thing he has a lawyer," I said. "If nothing else, Coates's people will sue the shit out of him."

She put her hand on my arm and stroked it seductively.

"Good," she said, purring.

I removed her hand and strode to my car.

Driving home, I thought of the end of Hammond's political career and the likely financial ruin a lawsuit would bring. Would jail time ensue as well? Probably not. I tried to guess Jennifer's next move and couldn't, though I knew she'd land on her feet, with or without Hammond. Would the kids we'd brought in for questioning be scared straight? At least for a while? Maybe. Maybe not. Only one good thing was certain to come of this: Shylock's ghost tour would be more popular than ever.

I parked in my driveway and walked to my front door, the smell of whiskey from my jacket following my every step. Stasia's nose would work overtime tonight.

Hot Box

Donna Benedict

Summer of 1941

According to the governor's office the riot occurred just before day-break during a regular... several hostages were...two of the three prisoners who escaped have been...The third, nicknamed "the 'Wasp'"...still at large...and may be headed for...

Phil closed his mind to the radio announcer's voice and concentrated on easing the screen door shut. He stepped off the porch, dropped to his knees, and began to crawl under the open kitchen window. The smell of Sunday morning bacon and hot dry waffles baking wafted through the open window alerting the saliva in Phil's mouth. He loved Sunday breakfasts. He could almost taste the syrup.

But, not this morning, he'd decided, and he swallowed the lump in his throat.

Crawling beneath the open window, he sensed rather than saw his mother move from the cupboard to the bleached oak table that looked out over the dusty front yard. He realized he had to hurry when he heard the familiar clatter of pottery plates being laid on the table.

On the other side of the window, he stood and dusted off the knees of his Levis. *Ma must have turned the radio off. She shouldn't be listening to that kind of news anyway.* And lately, Phil thought, most of the news was bad, all about that war in Europe and how there could be a draft here at home.

At the corner of the house, Phil stood to resettle his bulky knapsack securely on his shoulders. He adjusted the straps and patted the canvas where he'd tucked in the two peanut butter and jelly sandwiches he'd made last night. The sandwiches didn't weigh much, and he'd put them on top of the new library books his English teacher, Miss Day, had saved for him so they wouldn't be crushed.

"You'll like the boy in *The Adventures of Huckleberry Finn.* He's about your age," she had told him.

Inside the barn door, he took down the dented bucket from its worn wooden peg and filled it with ground corn, food scraps, some kind of vitamins and water.

Back outside the sun began to filter the early morning mist. Phil liked the way it gathered on top of the purple mountains rimming the valley. *It'll be a hot day, but the culvert will be cool,* Phil promised himself, and with no one around, he could read all day if he wanted to.

They came at the sound Phil's shrill "soweee" call, led, as usual, by the Hampshire-Norfolk boar, his thin skin, black bristles and the white belt around his middle barely visible under a red frosting of dried mud. They squealed and trampled each other in their rush for the trough while Phil stayed well behind the fence. There were no two ways about it, he hated pigs.

Last spring he'd even tried to talk his mother into getting rid of them, but she'd "allowed" that, "Pigs pay for the extras, Son, like that book there," she'd added, pointing to a worn copy of *The Sword and the Stone* tucked under his arm, a used copy she'd bought for him last Christmas.

"Besides," she suggested, "All pigs ain't mean. There's good ones, and bad ones. Why, Old Red is as harmless as a pup."

Old Red is castrated or he wouldn't be so lovable, Phil had wanted to say. But he didn't argue. Although he'd been too young to understand what had happened, he hadn't argued with his mother since the day his father was buried. He understood that keeping the farm had been her goal since his father died, and Phil did what he could to help.

His father's old friend, Pete Harfie, had come by to offer condolences shortly after the funeral, he remembered. Then, as the years went by, he'd come by regularly "to help out," the man had said. Recently Phil noted he'd come for dinner whenever he was in town.

After Phil's tenth birthday, Pete frequently invited him to the train station, where he worked as Head Engineer. He'd even let him board one of the engines in the wheel house. And once he'd taken Phil and his mother on a trip to Sacramento for school supplies where he bought Phil a small electric train set. Gradually Pete became an extra hand helping on the farm and coming by for lunch or dinner when he was in town.

"Sweet on your mother," his aunt Ida had commented when she was at the house a week ago. Phil wasn't sure how he felt about that. Looking out for his mother was *his* job and wasn't he doing that, at least mostly?

We're getting by fine, Phil decided, even if sometimes it seemed like, with school and chores, he didn't have much time of his own. And once when his mother mentioned that Pete Harfie's visits were a "Godsend," Phil suggested that maybe he should skip Sunday school to handle more chores.

But she said, "Learning about the Lord is more important than hiding out in a culvert reading."

She'll be madder than a Banty hen today, Phil thought, as he replaced the feed bucket. It was just too bad he was skipping Sunday school.

Outside the barn again, he headed for the back gate that led past the cemetery, to the railroad tracks. As he walked, he thought about getting the award ribbon. He liked the bible stories they read, and Miss Day had once said they were "fine literature." He'd been secretly proud when he won a purple ribbon at Sunday school for the "best recitation" of the Good Samaritan.

When Deacon Martin gave him the award, his Sunday school teacher told the class the recitation of the narrative had been "sensitive."

While Phil realized it was supposed to be a compliment, some of the guys turned and stared at him. That's when Phil's skin got hot, and he squirmed in his seat. He didn't see how understanding the moral of the story was "sensitive." Weren't folks supposed to help each other? Still, he liked how Ma bragged about the ribbon to Pete Harfie.

But, later, when Pete congratulated him, he admitted to Pete he couldn't see how the Good Samaritan helping the guy in the ditch was such a big deal. "Maybe the people who didn't stop to help, couldn't help, or maybe they were afraid of the guy in the ditch."

And Pete allowed that it was possible, but added, "A lot of people run away from life. They refuse to accept responsibility for others who need help. Sometimes they even blame them for needing help. They forget that it isn't any sin to need help. The guy in the ditch needed it and along came a *selfish* Samaritan."

"Selfish? How was he selfish? Didn't he help the guy?"

"Sure Phil, like you said, maybe some of the people who didn't help were afraid to help. Maybe they thought the thieves who went after the guy in the ditch could still be around. But the Samaritan knew there'd be a pay-off."

Phil shook his head. "Yeah? It doesn't say in the story the guy paid him back."

"No, but the Samaritan was a smart man. He knew if he didn't stop and help the man, he'd feel like a coward for being afraid to help." Pete paused until he knew he had Phil's attention before he finished the story. "The Samaritan knew he'd lose something far more valuable than money."

"What?"

"His self-respect, Phil. For not doing the right thing, for ignoring another human being's need."

By the time he reached the Sunrise cemetery and wrestled the rusty old gate open, Phil still hadn't decided why Pete thought the Samaritan was special. He only did what anyone was supposed to do, didn't he?

Once inside the gated grounds, he headed as usual for the southeast corner.

Stepping carefully, he made his way past crosses and angels and other elaborately carved memorials of lives well-lived or cut short too soon. Over the years, he'd read them all and he didn't pause until he reached a small granite marker carved only with a name, date of birth, 1906 and date of death, 1928.

Reaching for the bandana in his back pocket, he kneeled down and carefully brushed the yellow dust off the stone.

He remembered, as he always did, how tightly his mother held his hand that day. He remembered the rain, too. It didn't rain often in the Valley, but it had that day. "Buckets!" Phil heard the grown-ups say. And, although he looked for them, none of the men were carrying buckets, only a big black box that he heard one of the men say his father was in. But when he asked, no one would tell him how his father got inside the black box they put in the hole.

And when he turned five and started school, he asked his mother, "Why?"

She started to cry and would only say it was because his father was a "Good Samaritan."

He often wondered, did she mean someone like the one in the bible story, or did his father do something a man should do, something Pete would admire?

But she never said why.

He wished he could ask his dad, "Why?" There were lots of things he'd like to ask him, like what he knew about wars? And why were his friends' fathers talking about the war in France, and maybe they'd be "drafted," and what was "draft," anyway?

He pulled the cemetery gate shut and headed back down the road.

Pausing only when he was in sight of the railroad tracks, he reached down to the dusty road and picked up a smooth flat stone. When he threw it, the rock cut through the air in a rare, clean arc, and skipped briskly across the desert to land in The All-American Canal where it sank in the center. He smiled as he watched while the water ripples grew.

"Good shot," he said out loud. Whistling, he walked on until he was above the culvert at Ridges Crossing. He was just about to jump down into the gully that led into the culvert, when he caught sight of something bright in the entrance of the big concrete pipe. *Kind of late in the season for hobos*, but he resettled his knapsack and sat down on the edge of the wash.

Probably a Bo, Phil thought. *No point in startling him. Like Pete said once, "Tramps are a skitterish lot. Some harmless, some not."*

Phil dug the heels of his tennis shoes into the side of the slope and slid to the bottom of the embankment. A man, Phil guessed to be the same age as Pete, about forty, sat slumped just inside the pipe. He was short but powerfully built. His eyes, half closed in the shadows, watched Phil's progress. Wary, hot with fatigue, they stared at Phil, looking hostile and unblinking.

"Hi," Phil said, advancing into the gloom and flinging down his knapsack. "Warm for October," he added, before sitting down on the thin layer of silt that carpeted the bottom of the culvert.

Eyes averted and head down, the stranger grunted a reply. Then reaching into the pocket of the coarse gray cotton shirt he wore, he withdrew a short, ugly knife.

Must be tired, I guess, Phil thought. He watched while the man opened the knife and began to pare his blackened fingernails. Hobos weren't all friendly, Phil knew, but they were all hungry. He dug into his satchel and pulled out one of his sandwiches. "Want one?" he asked. Without answering, the stranger continued to pare his nails. But Phil noticed a thin, bright line of saliva form at the corner of his mouth and trickle into his grimy beard. Again, Phil reached into his bag. "Here," he said, holding out both sandwiches. "They're fresh, peanut butter and strawberry jam. My Ma makes the jam."

With an explosive sigh, the stranger closed the knife and dropped it into his lap. He leaned forward and snatched away both sandwiches. It seemed to Phil they were hardly unwrapped before they were gone and the stranger was wiping his mouth on his sleeve.

Then, without taking his gaze off Phil, he belched, loudly, picked up the knife, leaned back against the wall, and said, "Good jam, kid. Your Ma's a good cook. A man could do worse than live in a house with a good cook. You live around here? Kid?"

Phil wasn't sure he liked the man talking about his mother's cooking. And where he lived was none of the stranger's business. "Not far," he said.

The full, loose mouth of the stranger crawled up at the corners. His gaze slid past Phil to the culvert entrance, then back to Phil.

"Kinda' dull around here, ain't it, kid? Nothin' much to do?"

"Oh, I don't know, mister. There's the fair in June, baseball games at school, and football's starting now. We have a good library in town and Ma says she likes the radio reception. I don't listen to the radio," Phil said.

"That right."

"But once in a while the news on the radio is interesting," Phil added.

The man straightened, turned back to Phil. "Yeah, what kinda' news, kid?"

It was easy to see he was interested and Phil paused a minute to savor the chance to relate important news before adding, "Well...the riot and breakout at Bakersfield."

Instantly, the man's body stiffened. His knuckles whitened as he gripped the handle of the knife. Phil shifted uneasily. Then, in his memory, and as if coming from a great distance, he recalled the barely contained excitement of the radio announcer's voice: *Discovered at the two a.m. bed-check...if the men were armed...one of them, known as "the 'Wasp," a former mosquito weight fighter of about fifty years...he has not...*

From somewhere deep inside of himself Phil's adolescent soprano suddenly erupted, cracking. "You know, my father was at that prison for a while."

The stranger's thick brows furrowed. He looked both puzzled and amused.

"That was right after we moved to the Valley, Ma said."

The man's hand relaxed on the knife handle, and Phil could feel the pressure in his belly escape. The stranger closed the knife.

"Yeah, what was he in for?"

"Don't know, I was a little kid. Nobody says much about him...except..."

"Yeah?"

"A friend of his said he used to teach Shakespeare."

The stranger smirked. "Up at the state prison?"

"I guess." Phil looked away.

"I bet the screws got a laugh out of that. Muggers and murderers reading Shakespeare. So your old man was in prison, not there now." It was a statement not a question.

Phil shook his head. "I heard Deacon Martin say he was a good Christian, though."

The man shifted uneasily. "Don't say."

Phil mumbled, "Said some guard..." he paused, studied his shoes. "There was a riot. My dad liked people, he tried to help some guy...That's what I heard."

"Screws don't care who they're trampling on. Seems to me I heard a story about some sucker, turned out he wasn't guilty—gonna' be released, they said. Got himself killed up there by a screw."

Phil didn't respond. He continued to stare at the water-stained concrete on the wall across from him and listened closely. And the man kept talking.

"A real sucker. There was a riot. Story goes screws told everyone to get, stay away, knew anyone found in that cell block wouldn't make it out alive. They didn't. Couldn't have been your Pa of course. Educated man, didn't you say? He wouldn't be fool enough to go in that cell block to help some snitch who'd been knifed during the riot."

Hot. The heat seemed to have risen in the culvert, and Phil thought he was going to be sick. But he swallowed, and turning he looked straight at the stranger.

"Gonna' hop a freight, mister?"

"What's it to yah, kid?"

Phil glanced casually at the watch Pete Harfie had given him for his twelfth birthday.

"Nothing. Except, it's 'bout 1:05 and the 1:30 that goes by here goes all the way to the Mexican border."

"So?"

"Oh, nothing." Phil concentrated on keeping his voice casual. "I know the engineer. If he sees me he slows down at the corner up there," he added, pointing at a sharp curve about a hundred feet up the track.

"Yeah, well, I just might hang around. Have some more good cooking," he said, grinning. "Getting hot in here, kid?"

Phil looked into the stranger's obsidian eyes and felt like he was suffocating. Then, just as the tension became unbearable, the shriek of the freight's whistle came screaming down the gully and sliced through the culvert. Phil's indecision severed his fear. "Come on, if you're going," he shouted, and without looking back at the stranger, he jumped to his feet and raced up the incline into the sunlight, waving his knapsack.

The train was still several thousand feet down the track. Phil felt the rhythmic vibration of the powerful steel wheels pound the ground and pulsate steadily through him as he ran the last 100 feet toward the tracks as the silver bullet-like engine with its single searching eye advanced quickly.

As he neared the tracks, he heard a scuffling sound that told him the stranger had emerged from the culvert behind him and with legs pounding like pistons, the small figure shot past him. Seconds later Phil glimpsed Pete's flaming red hair behind the dirty windows of the engine. The train was still a thousand feet down the track, but it was slowing rapidly to a cacophonous melody of hissing brakes and shrieking steel abrading the trembling rails.

It was then Phil spotted the sparks in a box car with a half open door—a hot box, exactly what he'd hoped for—and he knew what it meant. The train would be stopping and pulling over as soon as possible, probably at Sitesville, less then fifteen miles ahead.

It was Pete who had taught him how to spot a hot box on a passing freight train. "Axle bearings," he'd said, "are housed in a box that uses oil-soaked rags or cotton, called packing, to reduce friction on train wheels. Friction on a train's wheel causes sparks or a fire. Once the rags are on fire, unless that car is seen and removed, it could destroy that car and possibly cars coupled to it. Worse," he'd added, "sometimes, when the wheels of the train haven't been inspected and properly oiled, the bearing alloy will also melt, and a car riding above one of those wheels will fall onto the steel axle, tilting the car and likely leading to a derailment."

Pete had told him what it all meant. Train workers look for smoke or sparks or fire, and if they don't see any, they report that the train is "All Black." If they do see sparks or fire, they send an audible report they see "Red," then, as quickly as possible the engineer will make an emergency stop.

Phil guessed Pete knew about the hot box, since the train was already slowing. And, as it drew closer he could see Pete inside the engine gesturing a thumbs-up. As it slid by, Phil heard the stranger beside him panting as he worked to keep pace with the train. And when Phil calculated the train had slowed enough, he made an abrupt turn and headed for the car he'd chosen.

The stranger shot past him and flung himself belly down on the moving platform. Then, righting himself, he looked back expectantly.

As the engine cleared the corner and picked up speed, Phil waved and the man's face darkened.

"Hey! You wouldn't like it here anyway, mister. This place is full of pigs."

Although it was moving much slower than its usual 60 to 80 miles an hour, the train was out of sight by the time Phil located his knapsack from where he'd flung it. After checking to be certain his new books were still inside and undamaged, he shrugged into the straps. Soon the train would be pulling into Sitesville, and the hot box would be immediately switched off. A sparking wheel under one of those tinder-dry boxes was bad enough in the desert. But Phil knew that Pete's run also passed through some pretty thirsty forest land. No sane man would choose to be riding through a forest on a train pulling a hot box.

Phil shuddered in the warm October sunlight as he considered the unwelcome passenger on Pete's train. He might or might not be one of the escaped convicts. If he was, or even if he wasn't from the prison, the yard Dicks would arrest him when the hot box was switched off. And Phil realized he understood something he hadn't considered before. *The man will think I tricked him.* He'll be right. But not even the Good Samaritan took the stranger he'd found by the road home with him. And Phil understood something else, the man in the culvert must have been in prison. He must have known his father, known he was a hero.

Also, his Aunt Ida had been right when she told him, "Everyone needs someone they enjoy being with, someone they can depend on."

He knew now his father had been that kind of man. Pete Harfie was that kind of man, too, Phil thought as he scrambled down into the gully and up the other side—someone you could depend on.

At the top of the embankment, Phil paused to brush the dust off his knees, thinking, someday he'd be leaving. Someone should be there for his mother, someday, when he left. Besides, he liked Pete, too.

Afternoon sunlight bounced off the mountains rimming the valley. Phil thought about what he'd learned about his Dad and somehow it reminded him of the rainbows he'd seen in an empty crystal glass in Sacramento, and he'd wondered what would happen to the rainbows when the glass was full. After what he'd learned about what his Dad had done, he was sure he knew.

By the time Phil reached the cemetery, the empty space beneath his ribs was widening. When he'd said goodbye to his father once more, he closed the gate behind him and headed home, wondering if there'd be any bacon left over from breakfast.

Not the Killing Kind

Melissa H. Blaine

T he first time my neighbor, Charlie McGrath, tried to kill me, I was sure I had to be imagining it. After all, I, Abigail Wainwright, was not really the killing kind. I kept my fences mended, my animals from straying and my opinions to myself. And at fifty-five, I was more interested in tending to my modest Christmas tree farm in the foothills of the Sierra Nevada Mountains than doing any house-wrecking or neighbor-riling.

So, when something whizzed right by where my head had been just seconds before, followed right away by a loud crack, I chalked it up to either my over-fifty ears, an errant hunter or Charlie's bad aim. Despite the infernal target practicing that he liked to do almost every Saturday afternoon, my neighbor couldn't hit the broad side of a barn.

I glanced around, but everything was quiet. "Hello?" I called out into the silence.

The blue button I'd stooped to pick up seconds before went in my pocket. I made a mental note to check my work shirts, but I didn't come out to this area of my farm often. Maybe it was mine. Maybe it had fallen off a hiker or a hunter cutting through the field.

Either way, I assumed it had a reasonable explanation, much like the sound of the rifle.

After all, Charlie had been harmless to me up to this point. A little odd? Yes. There was the practice of toting his rifle around with him everywhere, even when checking on his rows of Douglas Firs. There was also the occasional glint of sun off glass from his back deck, but that could have just as easily been from a window or a mirror and not from the high-powered binoculars I'd seen him buy at the sporting goods store a few months back. Either way, it seemed unbelievable that the bullet had been meant for me.

Besides, Charlie had no good reason to wish me harm, although I suppose you could call us rivals, of a sort. For a few short weeks every Christmas season, people from miles around flocked to one of our farms to buy the perfect Christmas tree. But it was the middle of June, and we'd always been helpful and congenial with each other, even during the busiest of holiday seasons. Charlie was focused on the plants in his greenhouse, and I was busy planning for my new flock of sheep.

No, it wasn't until later that I realized Charlie McGrath tried to kill me that day. But that day set everything that was to come into motion.

***

The second time Charlie McGrath tried to kill me, I was saved by a big orange tabby cat, and there was no denying it was him.

Had the two attempts happened closer together, I might have been more prepared. But months had passed with no further bullets and nothing to suggest that the first event had been anything other than a figment of my sometimes too-vivid imagination.

So, when I came inside my small two-bedroom farmhouse that chilly September night and hung my heavy chore jacket, with its ripped pocket, on the hook by the door, my thoughts were preoccupied with getting a bowl of soup and starting a fire in the large stone fireplace that took up an entire wall in the living room. The sheep had settled into the back pasture and the barn with ease but having them also meant that my already long chore list had grown even longer. I was especially late that night after chasing down an errant lamb who had wiggled his way through the back fence.

The house felt chilly as I pulled the glass knob on the kitchen door shut behind me. I always waited to turn on the furnace each year, perhaps trying to deny that winter was set to bluster its way in for half the year. Mr. Pickles, the giant orange tabby that had claimed the house as his, meowed at me from his perch on the upright piano before jumping down to crisscross between my legs.

The kitchen smelled of garlic and goodness as I grabbed a bowl from the cupboard and stirred the chicken soup in the slow cooker. If I hadn't had to do the extra chores, there might have been time to make some biscuits to go with it, but I was hungry and sitting down to eat was my single priority.

After ladling a generous portion of the soup into my bowl, I carried it over to the end table by the sofa and curled up under a fleece blanket. I picked up the bowl, dipped my spoon in and blew on the pieces of chicken, noodles, peas, carrots, and other vegetables, hoping to cool it down enough to avoid burning my tongue.

Just as the portion seemed safe enough to shovel into my mouth, Mr. Pickles launched himself from the floor toward my shoulder. He missed and hit my arm holding the bowl. He fell back to the couch, my hand lost contact with the bowl and the chicken soup landed in a splattered mess on the floor.

"Mr. Pickles." My voice sounded like an old school marm, even to my ears. "I thought we talked about not trying to jump so high anymore. You always miss, and we always end up with a mess."

Mr. Pickles twitched an ear before hopping up onto the back of the sofa and settling his girth into his best imitation of a bread loaf.

I cursed under my breath, grabbed some paper towels from the kitchen and went back to clean up the mess. I frowned as I leaned over the soupy puddle that formed around the upturned bowl.

Was that a mushroom?

It wasn't cut in a mushroom shape, but I couldn't think of anything else that I'd put into the soup it could be. The chicken I'd used was left over from a roasted chicken, and I'd shredded it all before putting it into the broth. None of the vegetables were white or cream colored.

I poked through the soup, finding more of the small mysterious pieces. There were even more of them in the slow cooker.

How had mushrooms made it into the soup? While I'm not opposed to mushrooms generally, they weren't something that were in the recipe handed down from my grandmother. I also hadn't bought any or been mushroom picking since the summer. Mr. Pickles lacked the opposable thumbs for knife use, even if he thought the soup warranted mushrooms.

The only explanation was that someone had come into my unlocked house and added them to the soup. I checked the dining room table and kitchen counter, but there wasn't a note from anyone who might have stopped by. Adding mushrooms to someone's soup seemed a little overly friendly, even in the best of times.

Nothing added up. Either I had somehow added mushrooms and didn't remember it or someone else had done it, and, if that were the case, it was just plain weird.

After cleaning up the living room floor, I bagged up a few of the mushrooms and put the slow cooker with the rest of the soup in the fridge.

After making sure to lock up, I climbed into my rusting Ford F-350 truck and backed out of the gravel driveway. On the way to pick up a fast-food sandwich in town, I dropped the bagged mushrooms off with a biologist friend.

***

The phone call the next morning wasn't reassuring. "Abigail, the mushroom pieces were definitely death caps. You didn't eat any of them, did you?" my friend at the U.C. Sierra Nevada biology department asked.

"No, no. They looked off in the soup."

"That's good, but, still, a close call. You didn't buy them any place in town, did you? If so, we need to alert people so that no one gets sick or dies from them."

"No, a friend dropped them off from some he'd collected," I lied. "He wasn't going to use any until later in the week. I'll make sure he knows right away and doesn't make the same mistake again."

We ended the call on wishes for each other's health, and I hit the end button with thoughts that my good health had almost been ended twice.

I could have explained away the first incident, but the second was harder. I could no longer deny that someone was attempting to facilitate my demise. I'd like to say that Charlie McGrath was the first person who came to my mind when considering potential assailants, but he wasn't. Nor was he even in the top ten. It wasn't until the process of elimination brought his name to the forefront and the realization that he had the means to have been behind both of my close calls. Why he had not followed through with either when it was clear they hadn't succeeded was perplexing but didn't necessarily preclude his guilt.

I had previously checked into records and gossiped around town enough to ascertain that Charlie's farm was doing as well as mine, but not so well that he'd want to push me out of the way to buy my farm. And, if I was not cutting into his profits, he'd be better off keeping me around than risking having someone else take over my farm who might disrupt both businesses. As we'd had no altercations or hard feelings lately, that left a personal reason for killing me unlikely.

For days, I wrestled with the questions and dilemmas. Should I confront Charlie? Call the police? Neither solution seemed wise. Charlie would just deny everything, while leaving him aware that I knew he was trying to kill me. Or maybe he was just trying to scare me. But why? No, the police weren't a good option for several reasons, including that I had no proof, the attempts could have been accidents, and when people start poking around, they tend to find things. Things that shouldn't be found. No, I was on my own. I'd have to learn why Charlie was trying to put me six feet under and then do something about it.

I went back through each incident, looking for something that might have precipitated it. I hadn't seen Charlie for months, except at a distance, and hadn't communicated with him either. We didn't run in the same circles and if there hadn't been a change to his circumstances, and town gossip suggested that there hadn't, there wasn't a reason to get rid of me for business reasons.

The only commonality seemed to be my presence in the back pasture, first while I was fencing it in and second when I went to locate the wandering lamb the day the soup had been poisoned. It wasn't a place I went to regularly as it was deep within my property, nestled up against the end of the cleared and cultivated land. I owned more acreage in the woods behind it, but the land there was wild, full of brambles, thorny vines, and trees.

A small pioneer cemetery was all that was left there. Beyond that, a steep ravine made the area potentially dangerous for any domesticated herd animal or Christmas tree shopper. I'd offered that part of the farm up to the nature gods and let it do its thing, without intervention from me.

Had Charlie set up an illegal pot farm back there, where I wouldn't notice it and it wouldn't be connected to him if someone stumbled across it? Was something else going on that I wasn't aware of?

I decided that further investigation was needed.

***

The final time Charlie McGrath tried to kill me, secrets came uncovered.

I waited until the darkness created by the new moon before turning my truck in the direction of the elderly couple, the Alberts, who lived on the other side of my farm. But, instead of visiting them, I took the old logging road that was just inside their property and pulled my truck to a stop behind a tangly mess of lilac bushes. The mass of branches, even bare, would disguise my truck if anyone decided to take a quick peek down the two-track of a road.

I picked up a small game trail and followed its winding path onto the back of my property. It didn't take me long to find what I was looking for, just not in the way I thought I'd find it.

Gingerly stepping toward the family-sized burying ground that clung to the steep hill, I hefted the shovel I carried a little higher. Mr. Albert had once told me that the cemetery was abandoned even before his parents had bought the property a century ago. Some days, I thought I should try to right the wrongs here, but the ghosts of the past were heavy, and I didn't like the idea of disrupting them any more than I had to. Some secrets should remain buried.

At first glance, nothing seemed out of place. Vines and brambles crowded the markers that still stood, and the tall grasses made it hard to see much beyond the wrought iron fence with finials at the top that surrounded the small plot of land. It didn't look like anything had changed since the last time I was here. I stepped gingerly through the gate, which protested loudly, hoping that it was cold enough that I didn't have to worry about stepping on a snake in the dark.

Two steps in, then three.

"You're an old ninny, Abigail," I said. "Nobody's been back here. Whatever Charlie is doing, if it's even Charlie, the dead are still resting." With a silent apology to the one I needed to disrupt, I set about to make sure she was still safe in her final resting place. As long as she was here, I had a hand full of aces, a secret that Charlie would continue to pay to keep quiet and a safeguard I could use to get him to stop trying to kill me.

Not long after I uncovered the first bones, I could hear the sheep gathering at the fence.

"Not now," I called to them. "I'll feed you later."

"Too bad there's not going to be a later, Abigail." Charlie's voice cut through the dark to my right. "I'm done paying, and if killing you is the only way to end your hold on me, then that's the way it has to be."

My eyebrows scrunched together as I slowly shook my head. "Charlie, I don't know what's gotten into you. You've been paying for my silence for what? Ten-fifteen years? Not once have I asked for more, and I've kept your secret all these years, just like I said I would. But, if you're not going to stick to your end of the bargain and keep trying to kill me, I'll be forced to go to the police to let them know that I found your missing wife's body buried out here on my property not long after you killed her all those years ago. They'll believe me when I say I just found her." I used the shovel to gesture to the hole I'd dug. The finger bones from his wife's left hand lay in the dirt; the rest of her still covered up.

"I'm done. I'm done paying you. I'm done worrying about if or when you're going to tell someone about what I did."

Had I goaded Charlie into trying to kill me? It hadn't been intentional, if I had. I enjoyed the monthly checks he dropped off like clockwork into the metal box outside my barn. Maybe the sheep and my being so close to the cemetery and his murdered wife's remains on a more regular basis this summer tipped the balance. Or maybe it would have happened anyway.

"Charlie, you don't want to kill me. People will ask questions and want answers, and those answers are bound to bring them straight to your wife, too. Two women from your life missing or dead? It won't matter that it's been years. They'll connect the dots, and you'll end up going down. We've got a good thing going. I haven't told anyone, and I won't, not as long as the payments keep coming."

For a moment, I thought I had him. His shoulders dropped just a fraction and his body started to turn back toward his house. I'd always thought he hadn't really meant to kill her back then, all those years ago. He wasn't normally violent or mean.

But something must have changed in him because he pulled a handgun out of his pocket and aimed it at me.

It was one of those moments where everything stands still. Charlie took a ragged breath, the gun in his hands shaking slightly as he clicked off the safety.

I swung the shovel, knocking the gun out of his hand, and then swung again to hit the side of his face. He fell to his knees, clutching the arm I'd hit to his chest. While he was down,

I felt through the grass and weeds until my fingers touched the cold metal of the gun. I raised the pistol, advanced on Charlie and leaned in close to make sure it would look like we'd struggled for the weapon. Then I pulled the trigger.

In the back of my mind, I wondered if I really needed to kill him. After all, none of his attempts on my life had been particularly successful. Maybe I could have given him a stern talking to and sent him back home. I didn't think he really wanted me dead, just not in a position to hold his secrets over him. But even bad aim sometimes hits, and I wasn't willing to spend my life looking over my shoulder, waiting for the next time he tried to kill me. I suppose I could have stopped making him pay instead, but a deal is a deal. Besides, even if he wasn't paying, I still knew his secret and that made me a threat to him.

When the cops showed up, they found the bones of Charlie's wife and, several feet away, Charlie's body. They never even bothered to question my story. To them, it was clear: I found the remains of Charlie's wife. He tried to kill me to shut me up. And I shot him during a struggle to save myself. A sordid mess of self-defense. There was probably enough truth in the story to make me sound convincing.

It was all a little unfortunate, and I'd miss Charlie's contributions to my quality of living, but some things can't be helped. I could always find another source of extra income.

Charlie McGrath would never get another chance to kill me because, unlike him, I made sure that the first time I tried to kill him, I did.

The 27 Club

Nan Mahon

Mick sat on the cement-covered grave and leaned back against the granite headstone. His fingers moved slowly across the frets of his Resonator guitar, but his eyes were looking up the cemetery's asphalt path at the woman walking toward him.

The ghost moon was a full white disk above and its glow caught her over-sized loop earrings as she walked. Her hair was long and blonde and her skirt swayed around her ankles, just above her sandals.

She grew nearer and her eyes met his in a moment of familiarity, but he did not know her.

"Hello," she said. "It's this side of midnight."

"Yes," he answered. "I guess it is."

"Not many come to visit at this time."

"You're here."

She moved closer, stepping off the asphalt, onto the grass. "I have people here. You don't."

Mick played a riff. "You know that how?"

She dropped slowly beside him, folding her legs under her. A July breeze lifted her hair and he stared at the low scoop of her blouse, where her breasts teased his mind. In the cleavage, a small piece of raw crystal hung from a thin silver chain around her neck.

"Play some blues," she said.

He smiled. "You know the blues?"

"That's why you're here, isn't it?" She brushed the strands of hair from her face, causing the multiple bracelets on her wrist to jingle and catch the flash of moonlight.

An ethereal quality about her caused him apprehension. "I know you from somewhere?"

"Just play something old. From the Delta."

Mick swept his dark brown hair from his forehead and combed it back with his fingers. Then he pulled a metal slide from his pocket and put it on his left ring finger. "What'd you want to hear? A standard twelve bar or the eight bar?"

She tilted her head to one side and smiled. "Play the eight bar, I like a quick turnaround."

He closed his eyes and started the chord progression, moving his fingers over the strings in that old, familiar way, so natural it was part of him. He sang in an imperfect voice with a hint of gravel and sorrow. The voice of the blues and the pain that gave birth to it.

He stopped and looked at her. Her skin was moist from the summer heat. It seemed soft and invited touching. Her eyes were so light they were almost translucent.

"What's your name?"

"Jasmine."

"You're beautiful."

She smiled, then pulled her legs up and wrapped her arms around her knees. "I know you come here every night after midnight."

He searched his mind to remember if he'd ever seen her before. "It's quiet here."

"That's not the reason you come."

Mick looked around at large crypts of the wealthy and flat headstones of the less affluent. Rose bushes were growing along the narrow road that traveled up low hills and parched leaves lay in the unkempt places. There were no new graves in this large burial place that held the remains of the historic men and women who built Sacramento so long ago. It was just off Broadway, where the traffic rushed by every day without a glance toward the tall iron fence, with gates that locked history inside.

"How'd you get in?" he asked.

"I told you I have friends here. How did you get in?"

"I can get past most any lock. My stepfather is a locksmith. He taught me the trade, said I would need a way to make a living if I was set on playing music. Good way to starve, he said."

She laughed a soft kind of laugh and leaned toward him so that her bare breasts fell against the low curve of her blouse. "Keep playing," she said.

He moved the slide across the strings and began an old Elmore James tune, "It Hurts Me Too."

After a moment she began to sing with him. Her voice was a light soprano, more beautiful than sad. He thought it sounded like a sweet breeze against the summer night. His guitar riffs seemed smoother as he backed her on the song.

"Sing with me," she said.

He joined his voice with hers and it seemed so right, the earthy gravel in his and the lightness of hers.

They ended the song and sat in silence. Mick didn't want to spoil the moment with talk. Jasmine moved closer and touched his hand where it lay on the guitar. Her eyes held his as she moved her fingers up his arm to his face. She leaned forward and met his lips. It felt like kissing cool satin.

Mick didn't move, didn't reach to hold her. He trembled and he wanted this thrill to last. But, something about her scared him. She seemed too perfect, too mysterious, too exciting.

"Hold me," she whispered.

"No. I can't." He couldn't explain his resistance, but he knew he shouldn't embrace her.

She laughed. "You're pretty special, Mick. No one ever says no to me."

It gave him chills. Who was she?

Jasmine broke the moment by jumping to her feet and kicking off her sandals. She put her arms above her head and twirled in the grass, dancing among the graves, her silver earrings and bracelets flashing in the moonlight. He watched as she moved around the headstones and began to play a fast blues tune. Their laughter and the music echoed in the silence of the cemetery.

When she finally came back to him and fell on her back on the grass, she said, "I know why you're here."

"Really?" He leaned on his guitar and looked over at her.

"Robert Johnson." She smiled and turned on her side to face him.

"How'd you know that?" he asked.

"I know. People told me."

"Yes, I come here because that's what Robert Johnson did."

"Ahhh, yes, Robert Johnson," she sighed.

"You know who he is?"

"Yes, I know him."

Mick thought she was mistaken about who he meant. "He was from Mississippi, down where the blues was born. They say he was always on the road and no one really knows where he is buried."

Jasmine smiled. "Some people do."

Mick was surprised that she knew about Robert Johnson. A musical legend to blues musicians, but most people didn't know his story.

"Robert loved three things in life," Jasmine said. "His music, women and whiskey. Got him killed at just twenty-seven."

"But, he was king of blues guitars while he lasted." Mick ran the flat of his hand over the guitar strings. "This is part of how he did it. He and his guitar teacher Ike Zimmerman would go to the graveyard in the middle of the night and practice so no one would complain."

"So, you come here at midnight hoping some of that greatness will come to you?"

"Something like that."

There was no lightness in her voice when she said, "How much do you value your soul?"

Mick felt a tinge of fear. "You talking about the myth that Robert sold his soul to the devil to become great?"

"Just a myth?" She gave him a sardonic smile. "A mediocre guitar player who disappeared one day and then came back as a great one. Do you find that strange?"

"He and Ike practiced every night in the cemetery."

"Yes, and he wrote a song about going to the crossroads."

"Jes' a song. Don't say nothing about trading his soul."

Jasmine swayed a little, as if she was hearing music even though the cemetery was silent. "Janis Joplin, Kurt Cobain, Jimi Hendrix, Amy Winehouse, Little Walter, Jim Morrison, Brian Jones and Robert are all members of the 27 Club. You ever wonder about that? The most talented all dead at 27."

Mick placed his guitar against a headstone. "It was drugs killed them all."

Jasmine twirled slowly to the music in her mind. "Hmm, yes. Drugs and alcohol. Fame is so short-lived."

"I don't know what you're tryin' to say." And yet, Mick knew exactly what she was telling him.

"Maybe Robert should tell you himself."

A black man stepped from behind a tall tomb and came toward them. His walk was measured, neither quick nor slow. He was tall and thin, wore an inexpensive, rumpled dark suit and his necktie hung loose against a soiled white shirt, stained fedora pulled down on his forehead.

Mick backed against the headstone as a current of fear and excitement almost paralyzed him. "Oh my God! Oh my God, Robert Johnson!"

Robert stopped a few feet from Mick and spoke in a Mississippi drawl. "You play the blues?"

"Yes sir," Mick said, even though he could see his idol was only a few years older than him.

"How old are you?" Robert asked as if he could read Mick's thoughts.

"Twenty-two."

They looked at each other for a long moment. Robert shook his head as if remembering another time. Maybe a time when he was that age, wanting to be the best.

"I don't have long," Robert said. "Let me hear what you got."

Mick's hands trembled as he reached for his guitar, placed the strap over his head and adjusted the instrument. He put the slide back on his finger, pulled a pick from its place between the frets, and looked into the deep brown eyes of a blues legend. Mick began to perform the only song that came into his mind, Robert Johnson's signature song.

Mick played the classic guitar blues introduction, a shuffle progression of the tried and true blues riffs. He sang in a clear voice with a touch of gravel and pain.

"Going down to the crossroads…everybody passed me by…"

It was a song of rejection, a plea for help. Mick poured his soul into the melody. He played his best riffs and the slide pushed them along.

"You can run, you can run…"
A man looking for someone to care.
"Tell my friend Willie Brown…"
Desperation.
"I believe I'm sinkin' down."

Jasmine stood, one finger to her cheek, a smile in her eyes, seemingly amused. Robert wore no expression as he listened to the song he wrote almost one hundred years ago.

Mick finished the song and waited, looking at Robert, almost praying for approval. He pulled the slide from his finger and shoved it into his jeans pocket.

Robert readjusted the hat on his head, tilting it a little. His expression didn't change, he didn't smile or frown. "You sing blues pretty good for a white boy," he said. "But, you got a ways to go on that guitar." Robert pointed his finger at the Resonator. "It's a fancy instrument, but it don't play itself."

Mick felt his dreams turn to dust. "I can take lessons, practice more like you did with Ike. I can get better, just like you did."

"Everybody got a bluesman they admire. Mine is Son House." Robert's eyes hardened as a cloud hid the moon. It seemed like a shadow came over him. "Most bluesmen can't read a note on a piece of paper. Cain't be taught what you got to learn. Greatness don't come from that guitar. It comes from your soul."

A man's laugh filled the air. A deep mocking kind of laugh without joy. The three of them looked toward the path and saw a man advancing on them. His suit was tailored silk and he strode with confidence. But his face was ugly and mean.

He stopped near them. "You want to be great, kid?"

Robert dropped his head and looked at the ground. Mick backed up against the headstone. But Jasmine turned to the man.

"What are you doing here, Satan?" Jasmine said.

"Easy pickings, girl," he answered. "Easy pickings."

"Leave him alone! You already have the greatest blues-man ever."

The man sneered. "Really?"

Mick looked over at Robert Johnson. Gone. It was as if he had faded into the night. At that moment, Mick realized who the other man was and it filled him with terror.

"You come here this side of midnight looking for something. Jest like Robert did at the crossroads. He found it. You can too."

"This one time, I am asking you to leave him alone," Jasmine said.

"Don't be stupid, bitch. Why would I leave him alone when he is so ready?"

Stunned into silence, Mick stood holding his guitar and listening as he realized they were talking about him. His mind was flooded with memories of Sunday school songs and Bible verses from his childhood. He remembered the pictures of Jesus blessing the children and others of Him knocking at the door of your heart. Jesus praying in the garden. The Last Supper. *Where is He now, while I'm facing the devil?*

"Whatta you think, kid. I can make you better than Robert Johnson ever was." The devil spoke directly to Mick, terrifying him.

"Here, try this." Satan tossed something to Mick and with simple reflex he caught it in midair. A slide made of gold and it gleamed in the pale light.

The sky had begun to fade to a light gray and shades of pink and gold touched the clouds. Birds fluttered from tree branches.

The slide felt warm in his hand and Mick slipped it on his left ring finger. He felt an energy surge from it. He adjusted his guitar and started to play. The slide seemed to move his finger so that he opened the song with a strong load-in, like a rushing freight train. Then he got control and slowed it down to a blues classic shuffle. He sang another Robert Johnson song.

"I got rambling on my mind...I got leaving on my mind..."

The slide moved on the frets crying out the song's pain.

"I hate to leave my baby...but she treats me so unkind..."

Lost in the moment of pure blues, Mick reveled in the ache in his voice and power in his fingers. The slide seemed to control his hand, creating difficult riffs he had never been able to accomplish before. Phrases and notes came like quicksilver to guitar frets. Mick realized he was just along for the ride.

Satan and Jasmine watched as he played. Satan smiled. Jasmine cried.

Mick went through the song a second time because the slide would not let him go. It glowed as it moved, as if it were on fire.

When he was able to finish the song at last, Mick pulled the gold tube from his finger and looked at it for a long time. Satan cocked his head and smiled.

Jasmine ran forward, grabbed Mick's hand and yanked the slide from his grasp. Pulling her arm back, she threw the piece of metal far across a row of graves, out of sight.

Satan laughed but anger touched his expression. "What do you think you're doing, girl? That won't change a thing."

"Don't listen to him, Mick," she said. "Go home and don't come here again."

Still euphoric from the music, Mick said, "Did you hear what I did?"

"You think *you* did that? You did nothing, kid," Satan said. "But, I can make it keep happening."

"But only for a while," Jasmine said. "In five years you will be twenty-seven. Do you want to be a member of The 27 Club?"

So *that's it*, Mick thought. *Will it be worth it to have five years of playing the greatest blues, instead of a lifetime of trying?*

"Come on, kid," the devil said. "Robert did."

"No, Mick," Jasmine pleaded. "Don't trade an eternity in Hell for five years of glory."

Mick looked into the distance where the slide had disappeared. The pink and gold streaks in the sky were growing, pushing out the dark. Birds began to call, and on the street, sounds of traffic became louder.

Instant fame or years of struggle? he wondered. His stepfather said music was a losing game. He could prove him wrong. Or would he, if he did nothing to earn it.

"It's almost sunrise, kid. Let's get this done," Satan said.

"No!" Jasmine pleaded. "Don't take a membership in The 27 Club."

Satan turned on her. "I told you to shut up!"

Mick placed the Resonator in its soft carrying case and slung it over his shoulder. "Robert Johnson said the blues got to come from deep in your soul. It's not the same if someone gives it to you." He stepped from the gravesite, onto the asphalt path and started toward the tall iron gate. "I don't believe I want a membership in The 27 Club," he said over his shoulder. "I'll pay my dues in the blues and take what comes."

He didn't look back, but he knew they were gone, vanished into the coming morning. No one would believe what just happened to him. No need to tell anyone.

Robert Johnson, he thought with awe. I looked into the face of Robert Johnson and saw sadness there. Maybe the legend of the crossroads is true.

Daylight was here now, lying across the freshly mowed grass. Things looked different to Mick as the sun made its way into the cemetery, all marble and cement, roses and asphalt.

He wondered if he had fallen asleep and just dreamed it all.

Mick cut across a narrow path that wound through the graves on the west side of the cemetery to the gate that opened onto Riverside Boulevard. Near the iron fence, the grass gave way to dirt, and something on the ground caught his attention. He stopped when the early sun rays hit the gold object so hard it seemed to burst into flame. Music, a one-four-five blues progression came from the fire.

He stepped closer. There on the loose gravel directly in front of him the golden slide shimmered in the sunlight.

Mick stared down at it.

The Secret of Thompson's Hill

Karen A. Phillips

Young reporter Gina Knox sat at her editor's desk, anxiously twisting the end of her ponytail.

Her work at the *Auburn Journal* had suffered since her mother succumbed to cancer just six months ago. She'd even missed a couple of deadlines. Her editor, Jim Larue, once told her he'd hired Gina because he saw potential in the young woman fresh out of college. He understood she was still grieving, but made it clear during a previous meeting, Gina needed to break out of her slump . . . or else.

While he talked, Gina's gaze traveled from the shine on Larue's bald head to the gleam of the dome atop the courthouse in Auburn, California. Early morning October sun cast a warm glow on the historic town founded during the Gold Rush. Gina wondered, as she often did, what the weather was like in New York City, where she planned to become a successful newswoman interviewing famous people, reporting breaking news. She recalled her mother's words, "Dream big, my little girl."

Larue cleared his throat. "Gina?"

"Yes, sir."

"I'm assigning you to cover the annual barbecue event tomorrow in Thompson's Hill."

Oh, no. He might as well send me to Siberia. "I thought we didn't cover small-town gigs. It's on the events calendar. Isn't that enough?"

Elbows on the desk, Larue leaned forward. In a serious tone he said, "I'm giving you one last chance to prove yourself, Gina." He held her gaze. "I'd like you to cover the event but also see what you can find out about some recent deaths. I've been getting phone calls from a woman who's convinced there's been, and I quote, 'foul play.' She won't leave her name. She called again when her brother mysteriously died. Said the police aren't interested. I've been in the business a long time and I have a hunch this isn't a joke. This could be your shot at a big scoop."

"I've never been to Thompson's Hill," Gina said.

He told her to allow sufficient time to get there as the road was treacherous and had taken many lives.

Gina marched through the warren of cubicles to the break room, chin up, ponytail swinging. *Act confident. You still have your job.* She had expected another Larue lecture, or to be fired, but instead, he'd dangled a strange and mysterious carrot.

She set her coffee in the microwave to reheat and looked up directions to Thompson's Hill on her cellphone. The smart plan would be to check out the area before the event. She decided to drive up there after she turned in her current article.

Dylan, the cute guy from the IT department, walked in and removed a sandwich from the fridge. "Happy Friday," he said. His T-shirt read KEEP CALM AND CYCLE ON.

"Ever been to Thompson's Hill?" Gina asked.

Dylan pushed long bangs out of his eyes. "Oh, wow. Yeah. Years ago on a bike ride. Gnarly road. Why?"

"My next mission. If I choose to accept it."

"A sense of humor is good in dire situations."

Gina sighed. "So, you heard my neck's on the chopping block."

Dylan focused on the sandwich he held, as if debating a response. "Gina, I've read your work and even I can see your heart's not in it." He looked up and met her eyes. "Not like it was."

Great, Larue and now Dylan. She didn't know whether to laugh or cry. "Life kinda sucks lately."

His face softened. "Hey, I'm sorry for your loss. Can't be easy."

Gina sniffed and managed a small smile. "Thanks. And thanks for reading my work. I appreciate it."

"Sure," he said. "One piece of advice? Thompson's Hill ain't for sissies."

"What do you mean?"

"It's the town motto. It's on everything: T-shirts, bumper stickers, coffee mugs. Stuff like that."

"Dorky."

"Yeah, but they're not joking. The place is creepy. Like being in a zombie movie. No one said hi. We went into the one and only store—that's where I saw all the T-shirts and stuff—got our snacks and vamoosed. Oh, and cell coverage is spotty at best." He pointed his sandwich at her. "Take pepper spray. Better yet, take some garlic and a wooden cross."

As he was leaving, he said over his shoulder, "And a gun with a silver bullet."

Back in her cubicle, Gina searched the archives for anything and everything regarding Thompson's Hill. Two hours later, she left work and made a quick stop at home to grab a protein bar and scribble a note for her dad. *On assignment. Might be late for dinner. Took Bella.*

Gina didn't have pepper spray, or a gun, but she did have a dog. Her yellow Labrador, Bella, jumped onto the passenger seat, panting with anticipation, her amber eyes searching Gina's face for a clue to their destination.

"You ready, girl?"

Bella barked in response.

They drove north up Interstate 80, native black oak and dogwood flamed in oranges, reds and yellows in the early afternoon sun.

Gina glanced over at Bella. "Want to hear what I learned about Thompson's Hill?"

The dog gave her a sidelong look.

"Thompson's Hill was founded in 1851 during the Gold Rush. At one point the town brought in $100,000 per week in gold. Can you believe that?"

Gina sped around a line of semis hogging the middle lane.

"In its heyday, the population was 10,000. Then the Gold Rush ended and several fires destroyed the town," she continued. "Now the population is only 200. They're so remote they're 'off the grid,' relying on solar power and generators."

At Colfax, elevation 2,425 feet, they exited the freeway. They took a bridge over the American River, water so clear you could see to the bottom. The road narrowed, winding uphill through dense brush and rock outcroppings. No guardrail protected them from plunging into the steep canyon below. Gina kept her eyes glued ahead, refusing to look down. *Why would anyone want to live this far out?*

When they finally reached Thompson's Hill, Gina gave a sigh of relief and relaxed her grip on the steering wheel. She drove slowly into town, passing ramshackle houses, lean-tos and sheds. Rusted vehicles sat abandoned in weed-choked yards. A man sitting on a porch stood up and unholstered his gun, watching her. On the other side of the street a curtain parted in an open window and someone aimed a rifle in her direction. *Dylan was right. This place is creepy.*

At the end of the main road, black wrought-iron fencing enclosed a large cemetery. Gina found cemeteries fascinating and made a mental note to check it out. Close by was a weathered wooden building with a sign that read GENERAL STORE AND APOTHECARY. According to Larue, her contact ran the store. Gina parked, then cracked a window for Bella. Cool, pine-scented air wafted in.

"Stay, Bella," Gina said as she unbuckled her seat belt and got out. She stood next to the car, taking in the surroundings. Thick forest encircled the town, blocking out the real world. Wind whispered through the trees. Sunlight filtered through the canopy, its fractured rays creating a magical quality.

The trip had only taken one hour, but she felt like she'd landed on another planet. The town was eerily quiet and Gina strained to hear any signs of life. As if on cue, a bird squawked somewhere in the branches and a squirrel scampered around the trunk of a tree. Bella whined to be let out.

Where is everyone?

She stepped onto the wooden porch that ran the length of the storefront. Two old rocking chairs sat empty, a small rickety table between them. An ashtray held a lone cigar butt. Gina went to the screen door, the boards creaking underfoot. Windows on either side of the door were covered with sale notices and flyers. A poster proclaimed: HILLBILLY BBQ! GET YER TICKETS NOW! The door squealed as she entered, then slammed shut behind her. *Bang!* Gina nearly came out of her shoes.

An old woman materialized, gripping a stout wooden cane.

The woman's hair resembled a large silver snake, coiled around her head and stuck in place by two red chopsticks— the only color in an otherwise somber outfit. A pair of reading glasses hung from her neck by a beaded string. Sunspots freckled her wrinkled face. Gray eyes peered upward from under penciled-in brows.

"Didn't mean to scare ya. Can I help with something?"

"Hi. I'm Gina Knox from the *Auburn Journal*. I'll be covering the event tomorrow. I thought I'd come up a day early and get a feel for the place." Gina offered her hand.

The old woman appraised Gina, then seized her hand in a firm grip. "Ester Thompson." She looked deep into Gina's eyes. "Lord, sweetie, I can feel yer pain."

Gina blinked.

"Was it yer mother?"

Gina nodded, too surprised to speak.

Ester finally let go of her hand. "Yer pulse is racing. I got somethin' that'll help." She went to the apothecary at the back of the store and searched the shelves. Bottles and jars held a rainbow of colors. Soaps, candles, and various tins which, according to the labels, contained salve, creams and lotions. A door with an EMPLOYEES ONLY sign stood partially open. Beyond was a dimly lit room. Beakers and Bunsen burners crowded a center table, the light from a high window reflected on glass and metal surfaces. Against the far wall was a wooden desk and a metal gun safe with a combination lock.

Ester handed Gina a small purple glass bottle labeled CALM. "Put one drop on the tongue. No more, seeing as yer driving."

"What is it?"

"Valerian root. An herbal tincture." When Gina hesitated she added, "It won't hurt ya."

Gina didn't want to offend the woman. Her mother had tried herbal treatments after refusing to continue chemo. *Why not?* Gina squeezed a drop onto her tongue and swallowed. The taste was earthy, woodsy.

"You run both the store and the apothecary?" She searched the walls for a license or certificate. "Are you a pharmacist?"

Ester's features darkened. "Don't need a fancy piece of paper," she scoffed. "I dabble in herbs, homeopathic solutions. It ain't rocket science."

"Fascinating," Gina said, trying to please. "I'd rather try a homeopathic remedy than some expensive drug."

"Most folks here would agree."

"But, don't they get pushback from their doctors?"

Ester gave her a patronizing smile. "These people can't afford health insurance. By the time they come to me it's too late. All I can do is manage their pain."

Heavy footsteps landed on the stoop. A large man wearing a red-checkered flannel shirt lumbered in and grabbed a six-pack of beer from the cooler.

"Afternoon, Garth," Ester said as she made her way to the register. "You gonna give me extra for yer tab? I can't keep the store open if no one pays on their credit, now can I?"

Garth scowled as he pulled cash from a wallet. "I'll want a receipt."

"Of course."

Ester went to the lab-cum-office and opened the safe. Gina spotted two rifles and a shelf with several binders inside. One spine read ESTATE PLANNING. Ester put the money into a bag, closed the safe door and spun the lock. She sat at the desk and made a note on a pad. She tore off a page, exited the room and shut the door.

Garth pocketed the paper and left.

Ester coughed. "Let's go sit so I can have a puff."

Outside she picked up the cigar butt and lit it.

Bella put her nose to the open window and sniffed.

Ester squinted. "That yer dog?"

"Her name's Bella. Okay if I let her out?"

"I reckon. Long as she don't wander. Folks round here don't take to strange dogs. They shoot first, ask questions later. Or not." She smiled, but there was no kindness in it.

As soon as Gina opened the door, Bella trotted over to Ester, who waved her away. Bella shook her head, then found a dry grassy patch to relieve herself. Gina removed a notebook from her purse and began interviewing Ester.

After the last question, Gina closed her notebook. The valerian root had taken effect. Gina felt so relaxed, she'd lost track of time.

Ester stubbed her second cigar out in the ashtray. Grasping her cane, she got out of the rocking chair and peered into the gloom. "Now where'd that dog get to? Damnation. I told ya not to let it run off."

Gina pulled a whistle from her pocket and blew. From around the corner of the building Bella appeared at a trot.

"Good girl. Now, sit." When Bella obeyed, Gina clipped a leash to her collar.

She looked for Ester, but the woman must have gone back inside the store. Gina put Bella back in the car and then decided to have a look at the cemetery.

The hinges of the wrought-iron gate cried out on opening, as if in pain. Gina made her way through a maze of graves. Using her phone, she took photos of the tombstones, many old and crumbling, the letters mostly illegible. There were several newer grave markers, the names and dates easy to read. *These people aren't even old,* she observed. One had died at age 52, and only three months earlier. Others were within the last five years. She took more photos.

A group of ornately carved monuments within a rock border caught her eye. Gina ran her fingers over the grooves in the largest stone, tracing the name, *Elijah Thompson.*

As if her touch awakened a demon, a gale force wind moaned through the cemetery scattering dry leaves, pine needles and twigs. Gina covered her face from the onslaught. Within seconds the wind abated, leaving Gina unsettled. She hurried from the cemetery.

Before leaving town, Gina returned to the store to buy a coffee mug for her dad.

Ester came to the cash register and frowned. "I thought ya left."

"I'm into old cemeteries. I saw a family buried there named Thompson. Are you related?"

Ester stood as tall as her aged body would let her. "Elijah was my great-great grandfather. Worked the mine till it killed him. The Thompsons made this town. And I won't let anyone forget it."

From Ester's frosty demeanor, Gina chose not to inquire about the number of recent deaths. She'd probably get more information doing her own research online.

That evening Gina sat across from her father at the dining table. Bella lay nearby, patiently waiting for crumbs. Gina told her dad about Thompson's Hill, but not the fact someone had pointed a gun at her or that Larue had given her a special assignment. The last thing she wanted was for her father to worry about her any more than he already did.

"Sounds like an interesting place," her father said. "I've heard of it, but never been."

"Believe me, it's hicker than hick. Hard to believe a big event is happening tomorrow." Gina set her fork down. "Dad, ever since Mom died I feel lost . . . at loose ends. Maybe if I'm where the excitement is, where important things are happening, I'll find myself again. I want to—"

"Move to New York and work at the *Times*," he finished for her. His brow furrowed with concern. "You will, honey. But first you have to prove yourself."

"I will. Then you'll be proud of me."

"I'm proud of you already." Sadness filled her father's eyes. "And so is your mother."

Gina wiped away a tear. Grief hung in the air, occupying space like an unwanted guest. She remembered the gift she'd bought in Thompson's Hill. "I have something for you." She ran to get the coffee mug, with Bella bounding after her.

Her father peered through black-framed eyeglasses and read the slogan THOMPSON'S HILL AIN'T FOR SISSIES. He chuckled at the cartoon of an old codger wearing a straw hat brandishing a shotgun. "If all the residents look like this old geezer, then I guess there's no chance you'll meet a nice young man in Thompson's Hill."

Gina smiled. "It's a good thing, because I don't need a distraction getting in the way of my dream." As soon as the words left her mouth, Dylan entered Gina's mind. She'd been thrilled to learn he'd actually read her work.

***

On Saturday, Gina returned to Thompson's Hill for the barbecue. She left Bella at home. She looked forward to interviewing the locals and tourists who came for the event. As for the cemetery, she'd researched the names and dates of the recently deceased on the internet, but all had died of natural causes. Yet, Gina sensed a story buried there. For the first time since her mother's death, she was excited.

Parking was more difficult than Gina expected, but she eventually found a space. She stood back and observed the festivities from afar. Booths offered food, drink, and homemade crafts. Several games entertained both children and adults. A three-piece band played bluegrass. Ester stood out with her silver dome of hair. She moved through the crowd like a minister after service, stopping briefly to exchange words, receive a hug, or clasp a hand.

Gina approached a booth where a thin man with a full moustache and beard sold chili.

"Care for some of the best chili on the Hill, miss?"

She paid for a small serving, introduced herself, then opened her notebook. "Can I ask you a few questions?"

They talked for several minutes about the barbecue, how many years the town had hosted it, and why he participated in it. Just when she was going to segue into asking about all the recent deaths, he started to get more customers. She thanked him for his time and tossed her empty container in the trash.

Gina then went to an old man sitting on a tree stump, his walker within easy reach. "Excuse me," she said.

He looked up with rheumy eyes and held a hand to one ear. "Eh? What's that you say?"

She spoke louder. "I'm Gina. From the *Journal*." A few people turned to stare.

The man indicated for her to sit on the unoccupied stump next to him.

She began her interview by asking how he felt about so many strangers visiting his small town. After a short time the old man's speech became slurred. Suddenly he convulsed and fell to the ground, twitching.

Gina jumped up. "Help! Someone!"

"Ester! Come quick!" A booming male voice called out.

The crowd parted to let Ester through.

"I'm here, Jeb. I'll help ya." She put a small bottle to his lips, holding the back of his head to help him swallow. She then waved at two men who helped Jeb to his feet.

"I'm so glad you came when you did," Gina said.

Ester glared. "What were ya jabbering on about got him so riled up?"

"Nothing. Just a few questions for my article. Will he be okay?"

Ester ignored her and went to Jeb, who took hold of his walker and they shuffled off.

A woman with dyed copper-colored hair came to Gina. "It wasn't anything you did."

Gina smiled. "Thanks. Ester acted like I had something to do with it. What's wrong with him? Is he sick?"

"Yes, very. Ester is treating him. I'm surprised Jeb's hung on this long. It was nice to see him outside, enjoying himself."

"I just asked a few questions for my article."

"What newspaper are you from?" the woman asked.

"*Auburn Journal.*"

The woman's face lit up. "Oh, thank goodness you came. I was about to give up on you guys."

"So, you're the one who left anonymous messages for my boss."

The woman glanced around, making sure they were out of earshot. "Yes, that was me."

Gina opened her notebook. "Can I have your name?"

"Mary Cates. C-A-T-E-S."

Cates. That was the last name of one of the people Gina researched last night. He was only 52 when he died.

"I saw a tombstone with the same name as yours. Samuel Cates. Was he a relative?"

Mary nodded. "Yes! That's what I told your boss on the phone."

Gina stared. "After I interviewed Ester I walked through the cemetery and noticed a lot of deaths within the last five years. The people weren't that old. From my research, there isn't a lot out there as to details. Most died from natural causes, like heart failure. On the surface, there isn't reason for concern. But to me, it sure seems odd."

Mary closed her eyes for a moment, then opened them and said, "Sam's my brother. Ester was taking care of him. I know she killed him. I just can't prove it."

Mary believed Sam had symptoms of mercury poisoning. Mercury contamination was common around gold mines, but Mary said the town's well water had been tested and results showed acceptable levels of mercury. She theorized Ester was obtaining mercury from the old mine. Ester murdered Samuel, and most of the others who were buried in the cemetery over the past five years.

Gina considered the situation. Ester had been helpful to her the prior day, both with the article and the herbal tincture. But then she thought about how Ester tried to blame her after Jeb got sick and how rude she'd been to Garth at the shop. Ester seemed to have a dark side.

"Why would she kill all those people?" Gina asked.

"Greed, plain and simple," Mary said. "She says she's helping folks who can't pay for a doctor. That's how it starts. Then her 'patients' become dependent on her."

Mary explained how her brother had lost his job due to his illness and then she had to quit her job to take care of him. They couldn't always afford basic necessities so Ester gave them credit at the store. When Sam's pain became unmanageable they went to Ester for help, but they couldn't pay. She said they could work something out. Before he died, Samuel made Ester the beneficiary of his estate to pay off his debt to her.

"She took everything he had and it still wasn't enough."

Mary got another job and was paying Ester when she could.

"I'm convinced Sam's not her first victim."

She asked Gina to help her get evidence to prove Ester's guilt, and together they formed a plan.

***

On Sunday Gina and Bella went back to Thompson's Hill, arriving at dusk. They went inside the store and found Ester with an elderly man at the register.

Ester handed him a paper bag. "Remember to take it three times a day. I wrote instructions on the bottle."

The man tipped his hat. "I don't know what I'd do without you, Ester. You're a lifesaver." He skirted around Gina and Bella on his way out.

"Well, I see yer back," said Ester, obviously displeased. "And the dog."

"Her name's Bella," Gina said. "I wanted to get a few more details about the town for when I write my story tomorrow."

At that moment, Garth came in. "I'm here to make another payment."

Gina took Bella down one of the aisles and pretended to browse as Ester and Garth conversed. Ester went into the office while Garth waited at the register for a receipt.

Gina twisted her ponytail with anticipation as she prepared for what was to come. Bella gave a low-throated growl. Gina turned to see Ester standing behind her.

"You startled me," Gina said, hand on her chest. Bella growled again, but Gina checked her with a tug on the leash.

Ester glared at the dog, then cocked her head at Gina. "Need more valerian root?"

"Oh, no. I'm good. Thanks."

Bang! The screen door announced the arrival of Mary Cates. Mary stood at the register next to Garth.

As soon as Ester walked away, Gina snatched several bottles from the apothecary and stuffed them in her purse.

"I'm here to make a payment," said Mary.

"About time," Ester said. She first handed Garth his receipt, then took Mary's money and went back inside the office.

Gina gave Mary and Garth a thumbs-up, then watched as Ester opened the safe. Gina unleashed Bella and took a green tennis ball from her purse. She threw the ball toward the screen door. "Fetch, Bella." In her pursuit, the big dog knocked against Garth who fell into a display of coffee mugs. Simultaneously, Mary cried out, "Ester! Help!" Mary then sat on the floor and clutched her head, moaning as if hurt. Ester came running, leaving the safe open. Garth pushed Ester who landed on top of Mary. The chaos was more than Gina had even hoped for.

During the melee, Gina rushed to the safe and threw the estate binder onto the desk. She thumbed to the C tab and discovered Cates and the form where Ester had been named as Sam's beneficiary. She took photos with her phone. Absorbed in her task, she didn't register Mary yelling out a warning until she noticed Ester's shadow, cane raised high, on the wall.

Gina shoved the phone into her back pocket just before Ester's cane came crashing down on her arm. She screamed out in agony.

In a rage, Ester swung her cane, breaking beakers, sending foul smelling fumes into the air. Silver beads of mercury bounced across the floor.

Cradling her arm, Gina knocked past Ester and ran out the office door. She glanced behind her and saw Ester pull a rifle from the safe. Gina headed to the front door at a faster speed.

Near the register Mary struggled to stand. Garth was nowhere to be seen.

Mary saw Ester with the gun and yelled to Gina, "Go! She's got a gun. Hurry!"

Gina took hold of Bella's leash, just as Mary tripped Ester, buying her precious time.

Gina smashed open the screen door and jumped in the car. She backed up and hung a quick U-turn, tires spinning on gravel. The car lurched forward just as Ester emerged from the store running after them. Gina clutched Bella's dog collar and stomped on the gas.

Boom! The back window exploded. In the rearview mirror Gina saw Ester standing in the center of the road, aiming the shotgun. Her hair had come loose and the silver strands fanned out from her head like writhing snakes. Garth appeared, towering over Ester. Gina returned her focus to the road and swerved to avoid taking out a fence. A second shot tore off the driver's-side mirror just before Gina careened around a curve and onto the main road. Halfway down the hill the front right tire left the pavement and the car plunged into blackness.

The whoop-whoop sound of the Life Flight helicopter reached Gina's subconscious. She awoke when Bella licked her cheek.

"We had to take both of you," the paramedic said. "You had a death grip on her collar."

Then all was dark again.

When Gina regained consciousness, she found herself in a hospital bed. A man wearing black-framed glasses hovered over her. Recognition dawned. "Dad?"

Her father smiled. "You're going to be fine. Just a few broken bones." He kissed her bandaged forehead. "I don't know what I'd do if I lost you, too."

The room was filled with flowers. She stretched for the card stuck in the nearest bouquet and winced.

He handed her the card. "You sure ain't no sissie. Get well soon. Dylan." Gina smiled. "How's Bella?"

"She's doing great. She sends her love." Her dad grinned. "The vet said she didn't have a scratch on her."

A knock at the door got their attention. A policeman in uniform and another man in civilian clothes stood in the doorway. The civilian showed his badge. "I'm Detective Osborne and this is Officer Dodds. Okay if we ask a few questions?"

Gina grinned. "I love questions. That's what got me into this predicament."

The corners of Osborne's lips ticked up in amusement. "You are one lucky lady. And something of a local hero." He consulted a notebook. "We have Ester Thompson in custody. Garth Jackson said he wrestled a rifle from Ester and subdued her after she shot at you twice. And Mary Cates heard your car crash and dialed 911."

"If it wasn't for those two, I might've been another one of Ester's victims," Gina said, then asked for her phone and purse. "I have evidence to give you."

She showed the photos on her phone to the Detective and gave him the bottles from the apothecary.

***

In December, Detective Osborne surprised Gina when he showed up at the *Auburn Journal* to deliver the toxicology report in person. The analysis of the bottles found heavy mercury content and, combined with the photos Gina provided of the beneficiary forms, the evidence convinced a judge to have Samuel Cates's grave exhumed. As Mary had suspected, the autopsy revealed his death to be from mercury poisoning. Other recent Thompson's Hill deaths were also exhumed, leading to Ester's arrest for multiple counts of murder.

When the Detective stood to leave, Gina handed him her business card. "A good reporter maintains a positive relationship with law enforcement."

He gave her an engaging smile.

As she admired his retreating backside the very thought of moving to New York was the furthest thing from her mind.

Presenting our 916 Ink author
Hugo de Léon

This Capitol Crimes 2021 Anthology represents a taste of the amazing talents of our membership. An additional dimension of our mission is to create outreach opportunities for others to explore the craft of writing. We are especially pleased to present you here with this reading bonus, *Dreamscape* by Hugo de León.

Hugo was selected from the students of 916 Ink's summer mystery writing workshop for youth to write a story for this anthology. 916 Ink is Sacramento's arts-based creative writing nonprofit that provides workshops for Sacramento area youth, grades 3-12, in order to transform them into confident writers and published authors.

If Hugo's story is any indication of the talents of this next generation, the future of the genre is in good hands. To learn more and support their work, go to 916Ink.org.

Dreamscape

Hugo de León

She couldn't believe it. Sure, Miss Betty had been in her eighties but she had been healthy and well. She had grown to know Miss Betty when she grew up in the community of which the older woman was the matriarch. Juliette stood on the hill overlooking the cemetery, the cold wind blowing through her hair, the sky foggy and gray. Down below her a sea of black cloth gathered around the casket rippled. The only sound was the ocean crashing against the shore about a mile away.

The funeral home was a small estate that had been a family business for as long as anyone could remember. Tall cypress trees stood sentinel on the edges, the path to the main building lit by glowing lights, hazy from the fog. Juliette stayed on the edges of the funeral because she couldn't quite comprehend that Miss Betty was dead. In their small community Miss Betty was always on her porch overlooking the crashing waves, telling stories to little kids.

She spun stories from the air, telling of times long before even she was alive yet always talking as if she had been in every moment. Everyone gathered around, wanting to hear stories of faraway lands and mysterious creatures. No one knew if they were true or not but that didn't really matter.

Miss Betty could conjure worlds of words and that was a very rare skill.

Juliette walked slowly down the muddy hill, trampled grass beneath her feet. The minister, Allen Treden, was speaking but she was only half listening as she made her way toward the crowd. Miss Betty's daughter, Annalise, sat in the back, her shoulders hunched over, crying silently. Annalise had inherited her mother's long red hair and heart-shaped face, but whereas Miss Betty was always smiling there seemed to always be something tragic happening to Annalise.

Miss Betty's casket was so unlike what she would want. It was a dark, shiny, mahogany, at least seven feet tall and very intimidating. But the worst part was that it was an open casket. Juliette had always been unnerved by them and obviously nothing in this funeral had been done according to her wishes. As she walked up she considered just turning back and sitting in the back. But she walked up to the coffin anyway.

Inside, lying serenely as though she was asleep was Miss Betty. Her face was off. It had so much make-up on it that it looked like her face was melting. She was wearing her favorite crimson coat and black boots. Her neck was adorned with a gleaming gold chain necklace.

But the one thing that really unnerved Juliette was the mark below Miss Betty's neck. The hospital said she died of heart failure, but the mark looked a lot like a gunshot. But that could not be true. There was no reason to murder Miss Betty. She didn't have money or friends in high places. Maybe it was just a scar that she had never seen before. She went back to the seats before anyone could see the mystified expression plastered on her face.

Juliette listlessly sat through the rest of the service and walked along the two mile path to the cemetery. She watched as the coffin was closed and lowered into the grave. Walking under the grove of cypresses, Juliette thought about if, and why, Miss Betty had been murdered. She got into her old gray pickup truck and drove along the rocky road down to the bluffs. She got out of the truck and walked down the least steep slope toward the beach.

The tidepools had always been her favorite places, especially the crabs scurrying around and fish coming in with the tide. The water here was relatively calm, the waves crashing softly but you could see out to the stormier seas, ocean spray covering the bluffs, carving caves into their sides.

She mulled over the funeral and what she had seen on Miss Betty's body. The tide swept over her feet, barnacles beneath them. The sand was wet from the night before and sea foam bubbled on the ground. She walked on the shore far away from the clutch of the riptide.

Taking in deep breaths of the misty air she strode back up the steep hillside through towering sequoias, their needles blanketing the forest floor. It was nearing November but these trees would never be completely bare. She needed to get back to her home in Fort Bragg before dark, when it would be dangerous to navigate the poorly lit cliffside roads.

She climbed back into her truck and took off. The road to her house was curvy but only three miles as the crow flies. The sunset was glimmering on the ocean, like a sheet of stained glass. After around twenty minutes she turned into her driveway. Her house was a little blue bungalow with a large garden and a wood front porch. The original owners had owned several properties along the coast and had sold this one for a dirt cheap price because they didn't want to figure out the repairs.

She plopped into her reading chair and fell asleep. The next morning she made breakfast and set out to work. She was going to figure out what had happened to Miss Betty. She grabbed her wool coat and headed out the door. The walk to Miss Betty's house was short, thankfully, because it was quite brisk outside. The winding roads were narrow and steep. The community had one parking lot that was near her house and you could walk from there.

Miss Betty's house was up on the hill, clustered with a few others. Weeping willows loomed over the walk, dropping leaves like tears. Miss Betty's house was the furthest out on the bluff. Around here the doors were never locked. She opened the rusted handle and walked up the creaky stairs. The rooms were bare, the walls whitewashed. Some bookshelves and tables had scattered papers in and around them but since she didn't know what she was looking for it was no help.

Suddenly she remembered something. There was an old leather-bound journal that Miss Betty had always carried around. There might be something useful in it. She started in the bedroom with its old wooden beams and the windows always open to let in the sea air.

The bed creaked and when she lifted up the mattress a cockroach scurried out. Nothing was around the bed. The dressers and drawers were bare, save for the long draping strings of ghostlike cobwebs. She went out into the dusky hallways, the lights long out and snuffed. She quickly got through the bathroom, guest bed, and kitchen. Next she went into the study. Miss Betty rarely let children into her private little library, for fear they'd ruin her collection of rare books.

It still smelled like cedar and a warm fireplace, even though there hadn't been a fire for days. Bookshelves lined the walls, towering over the ebony desk like great, shadowed trees. The walls were painted a deep red, the paint peeling away, showing signs of the ocean air that tore away at so many of the buildings around here. Cluttered piles of papers drifted across the desk.

One thing caught her eye though. Buried underneath old gift certificates and late tax fees was an old leather- bound journal with a gold encrusted symbol on its front. She dug excitedly through the junk to get to the book. It was about six inches long and stained a light olive green.

The title said *Ruina Mare*, Ruin at Sea, with a large embossed golden illustration of a ship being tossed around by brutal waves. Miss Betty never liked the water and didn't go near it. The sea near Fort Bragg never seemed swimmable. Sure, some divers went down in the bay but that had never seemed like a good idea.

The journal might just have been the only one left in a gift shop or museum. But Miss Betty always seemed to do everything with purpose. The first page stated in a font so curved and twisted she could barely read it.

Always remember, never forget, ghosts of the past will haunt the Dreamscape. The name of its sister will open the lock.

What was the Dreamscape? Who was its sister? What lock? And most importantly did this have anything to do with Miss Betty's murder? So many questions swirled through her head. Her head hurt intensely, so she went to sit down on the comfy leather chair. And as she looked around the room aimlessly something she saw made her practically jump out of her seat. A lock box.

Small and slightly rusted silver it was nestled between dictionaries and encyclopedias on a high shelf. She bolted to it, her feet kicking up flurries of papers. There was a stool in the corner, helpful because Juliette was quite short. She grabbed the stool and stood on it, her shoulders just at the height of the lock box.

It read simply, *My code is the sister of Dreamscape*. Well that was one mystery solved at least. This was the lock, now what was the key. She decided to start where she always started. In the library.

The Fort Bragg public library was a small brick building, the doors open and swinging in the wind. She dashed inside, into the warm, welcoming feeling of being surrounded by books. She walked up to the librarians desk.

Rosalie Diaz was the librarian on duty. She was nice and cheery but a bit of a gossip. Today she was wearing a crimson dress with lace sleeves.

"Hi Rosalie, how are you doing?" she said.

"Good, good, you? I heard about Miss Betty. So horrible."

"I'm fine."

"What are you here for?"

"Do you know anything about the Dreamscape?"

"I'm guessing you're not talking about psychology. I'm not sure of anything beyond some old rumors, but Pam might know more."

She waltzed back and when she returned it was with an older lady with frizzled white hair wearing an olive turtleneck.

"Hey Juliette, I'm Pam Fields, the senior librarian here."

"Hi, thanks for this. Do you know anything about the Dreamscape?"

Pam flinched when she heard it, almost imperceptibly.

"Where did you hear about that old thing?"

"Oh, just something Miss Betty told me about."

"Ah, well in that case I think there's a few books back in the history of Northern California section. I trust you know where that is?"

"For sure. Thanks for the help."

"Anytime"

And with that Pam left as soon as she had come.

She waved goodbye to Rosalie, then headed off toward the Northern California section. With huge stuffed bears and a painting of towering redwood forests on the walls it looked like a visitor center of a forgotten state park. The bookshelves towered over and around her. She looked for the word dream. A Pioneer's Dream, The Land of New Dreams, Dreamcatchers: A History, The Elena, The *Dreamscape*, and Other Shipwrecks off the Northern Coast. That was the one.

She flipped open the book and turned to the page about the Dreamscape.

...travelers with it to California. The last time the crew was seen alive was off the coast of Eureka. While approaching Fort Bragg the seas were calm and the ship seemed like it would make it safely to port. It is suspected a sniper or submarine blew out the hull. No one is believed to have survived in the freezing waters. In 1949 its sister ship the Olympia Rose sank in a storm off Gualala. We have a written account by the survivors of this wreck available at theolympianrose.com.

She slammed the book back on the shelf and raced back through the library and to Miss Betty's house. Then she stopped dead in her tracks. In the bedroom the light was on, illuminating the top floor. And she could hear someone moving things around in the cluttered rooms. She looked down at the small journal stuffed in her pocket, suddenly grateful she hadn't left it inside to be discovered by whoever was tearing apart Miss Betty's room. She ducked behind a hedge just in time as someone stormed out, crumpled papers thrown in their wake. All she could distinguish was a long black coat and dark boots.

When she was sure she was out of sight of whomever had been inside, she peered in the window to make sure there wasn't anyone there. She quietly slipped into the study. She entered the words Olympia Rose and held her breath, waiting anxiously. It opened slowly revealing a little slip of paper.

To Whomever May Find This,

I have kept this secret for over 60 years. No one has suspected that there were any survivors of the Dreamscape. On that very dark day I remember that I was standing on the main deck watching the sleek seals underwater. In Alaska it was harder to go out to sea. My village only had simple fishing boats with room only for the fisherman. I looked up to see that on a boat but 1/4 of a mile away there was a group of black-cloaked people standing on the deck. Each carried a large musket and as soon as I saw this I shouted out a warning. But from the boat their shouts overpowered mine.

"We are the order of the Midnight Sun and you will surrender the treasure your boat holds or we shall sink it."

No one on board knew what on earth they were talking about. I guess they didn't wait for an answer before they fired. The ship sank fast and the lifeboats were inaccessible by the time anyone thought to look for them. A strong current took hold of me and separated me from everyone else. A long piece of driftwood swept toward me and I held on to it until I washed ashore on the rocky beach. My family had come here before the Dreamscape and I made my way to their house. They welcomed me in and, horrified, I explained what had happened. They told me to keep it secret and to say that I had come on a different ship. And so I lived my life with this story, and only I know that the treasure, whatever it might be, is probably still at the bottom of the ocean in the captain's private quarters.

Sincerely,
Betty Sutherland

Juliette was stunned. Miss Betty had never even told her she was from Alaska much less on the shipwreck. It was astonishing how many secrets she had had. Well, at least now she knew where to look in the shipwreck.

She had no clue where she could get scuba gear or a wetsuit though, things that would definitely be essential. At least she could start by calling her mom. Juliette's mom, Ms. Romanov, was the manager of an outdoor supplies store in Portland. She couldn't drive up there but her mom might know where to get the things she needed.

"Hello, Mom, it's Juliette"

"Oh hey Juliette, I'm just closing up here, what do you need?" She could imagine her mother gruffly speaking into the phone while cleaning down the counters, disinfectant and camo coats galore.

"I was just wondering if you knew anyone around here who sells scuba gear and wetsuits?"

"Hmm...After Martin closed down the next best option would have to be Elliot's, just north of you, you know the one?"

"Thanks a lot. Love you."

"Bye!"

She drove to Elliot's and got the supplies. They were a little pricey but it was worth it. Then she looked at the map and saw where the *Dreamscape* had crashed. It wasn't far at all and a diving trip was going near there in an hour or two. Luckily her mother had made her do deep sea diving lessons a while ago, so she knew how to do it. She signed up for it and soon she was speeding over the grey water. When they got close to the *Dreamscape* she jumped in.

The water couldn't get through her wetsuit so she was insulated from the cold. Diving deeper down it grew darker and darker until the only light she could see came from her headlamp. Then she saw it. About fifty yards ahead was the hull inscribed with the words: THE USS *DREAMSCAPE*. It was intimidating and terrifying, so large it could have had a movie set in it. She went in through the main deck. Everything was eerily quiet in the water. But then inside she saw something.

Below there was a light in the passageway. Another headlamp. Someone else was on the ship. Quickly, she dove in the crack of the hull and tried to find where the captain's quarters might be. Schools of fish flitted through the halls where decades ago humans would have walked. The light was coming from the dining room. A figure in a wetsuit with the words Donovan & Co. on the front was gliding through the room. She tried to avoid getting her light near him but he saw her.

And then he chased after her. Underwater her movements were limited and her pursuer clearly had better equipment. She dove randomly through the hallways, trying to lose her pursuer until she saw a rotting door flung open with the vague words "Captain's Quarters." She swam in and dove under the bed. The man chasing her was just far enough behind that he didn't see her. He sped past continuing down the hall.

Once she was sure he was gone she started to look through the rooms. The main one was the bedroom. All the furniture was disintegrating and there was a lot of broken wood to look through and scour for the box. Then her leg hit something beneath the rotting sofa. It was hard and when she went to look at it, it was a metal box labeled: PRECIOUS CARGO.

Juliette could barely contain her glee. She sped up through the ship and it was only when she was near the surface that she looked back and her heart sank. The man pursuing her was but a few yards behind her and gaining ground. She decided she would rather fight him from above than below so she stopped and suddenly, catching him by surprise, hit him with the metal box. It must have hurt because she could feel the wave vibrations in the water. She got on the boat and back to shore. She couldn't wait to open the box.

On the beach she could see someone waiting for her. And then she saw it was a man in a Donovan & Co. suit. He was built like a wrestler, stocky with enormous muscles. He motioned for her to talk.

"Hey, I'll give you $500 for it. For my employer."

Warily, she declined. He tried to snatch it out of her hands but she avoided his grabs.

She ran up the street and dove over the corner. She was certain she was being chased but now that was actually an advantage. The man behind her took out a knife and started bolting at top speed. He stopped dead in his tracks after he realized he had followed her into the Fort Bragg police station.

A couple of officers were milling around. They all looked up when she ran into the room, pursued by the man with a knife. Before the man could run back out the door the officers surrounded him. One cop slapped a pair of handcuffs on his wrists and put him in a waiting cell. Then another cop took her into the back room to question her.

She told the cop everything that had happened. Strangely, he believed her.

A few hours later the cop came back and said "I have found a few of the answers you might want or need. What are your questions?"

"First, what was that treasure?"

"Ah, well it turns out that it isn't exactly a treasure in a conventional sense. It happens to be the only written histories of meetings between Native American chiefs and Russian explorers. These are going to be donated to the Museum of Native American Heritage."

"Who shot Miss Betty?"

"That would be the henchmen of Earl Donovan who is currently in police custody. They are also working with the modern day iteration of the Midnight Sun who didn't want that document to get to shore because it would endanger their order's standings with several powerful officials in San Francisco."

"Have you located the leader of the Midnight Sun?"

"No, but we have enough evidence to jail Donovan and his henchmen."

"Thank you."

"No, thank you for bringing this evidence to light. Everyone is very grateful for this."

And with that he left the room. She followed him out soon afterwards, the sky growing dark and storm clouds approaching. At last she had the answers for her questions. That night she went to sleep in her large comfy chair.

About the Contributors

Kathleen L. Asay is a mystery writer and editor and a long-time member of Capitol Crimes and Sisters in Crime. She has had stories in Capitol Crimes' three previous anthologies. Her first novel, *Flint House*, is set in Sacramento. A sequel is planned for release soon. www.kathleenlasay.com.

Donna Benedict has been a reporter, a radio announcer, a communications analyst, an English, journalism and creative writing teacher for 28 years—and now a short story author and novelist. Benedict's first full-length Romantic Suspense novel, *Queen of Charades* was published August, 2021. The mother of six is currently working on her second novel. She resides in Northern California.

Melissa H. Blaine has spent countless hours exploring and photographing cemeteries across the globe and even wrote her master's thesis in sociology on the topic of gravestones. She lives in Michigan where she's a certified leadership/career coach and nonfiction ghostwriter. Several of her short mystery stories have been published in anthologies.

Sarah Bresniker is a mystery writer and former librarian who lives in Northern California. She loves classic mysteries and exploring the natural beauty and fascinating history of the Monterey Peninsula. Her first short story was published in the 2021 Sisters in Crime Guppy Anthology and she is working on her first novel.

Jenny Carless began her writing career in environmental nonfiction and moved into corporate communications before tackling fiction. She loves wildlife, photography and travel—particularly in the African bush, which is the inspiration for most of her fiction. Here, she decided to explore the wilds of the Central Valley.

Hugo de León is 14 years old and entering eighth grade at Alice Birney. He enjoys rock climbing and playing with his dog. He has been writing short stories for as long as he can remember.

Chris Dreith's first published short story, "Old Soles," appeared in the Anthony Award Finalist 2020 Bouchercon Anthology, *California Schemin'*. "Unknown Male and Parts of Two Others" was inspired by an actual headstone in the Woodland California Cemetery. The nameless residents of this grave have been waiting a long time for their (fictional) story to be written.

Eve Elliot is a romance novelist and voice actress. Her first foray into crime fiction was the audio drama whodunnit *The Death of Dr. Davidson*, which she produced and directed with a full cast. *The One* is her first short story in the crime genre. She lives in Dublin, Ireland.

Elaine Faber is a member of Sisters in Crime, Cat Writers Association, and Northern California Publishers and Authors. She volunteers at the American Cancer Society Discovery Shop. She has published eight cozy mysteries and an anthology. Elaine's stories have won multiple awards, and are included in more than 20 anthologies and national magazines.

Stacie Giles turned to mystery fiction after retiring as a CIA analyst and adjunct university instructor in intelligence and comparative politics. Primarily a nonfiction writer with one published mystery short story, she enjoyed using her experience to help prepare this very creative volume.

Kenneth Gwin is a visual artist living in San Francisco. He is a fan of both mysteries and thrillers, with a special interest in espionage, conspiracies, and disinformation. He thinks everything you really want to know is behind that curtain. What's there, you ask? That's the mystery.

Kim Keeline freelances helping authors with marketing, web design, and more. Her first short story, "The Crossing," was published in the San Diego SinC anthology *Crossing Borders* and was a 2021 Derringer finalst for Best Short Story. Her second, "California Fold'em," was in the 2020 Bouchercon anthology *California Schemin'*. www.kimkeeline.com

Virginia V. Kidd has stories in *Capitol Crimes Anthology 2013* and *2017*. She is completing a humorous middle-grade book. She co-authored *Cop Talk: Communication Skills for Community Policing* and helped create *Memories of McClatchy Library*. In 2003 she was named Outstanding Teacher in Arts and Letters at CSU Sacramento.

Nan Mahon's stories appear in several Capitol Crimes and other anthologies. As a writer, band agent and stage producer, she learned a sense of the artist's struggle and tells those stories. Often gritty, her work gives voice to the disenfranchised and people living on the fringe of society.

Catriona McPherson, national-bestselling and multi-award-winning author, was born in Scotland but immigrated to the US in 2010. She writes a historical series set in the old country, a contemporary series set in the new country, and standalone psychological thrillers. Catriona is a former national president of Sisters in Crime. Vist her website at www.catrionamcpherson.com

Jennifer K. Morita spent the first six months of the pandemic baking bread and rolling sushi before finally writing the mystery she'd been plotting for years. A former journalist, she lives in Sacramento juggling freelance jobs with being a mom, revising her manuscript and pushing Girl Scout Cookies.

Karen A. Phillips enjoys writing mysteries, MG/YA fantasy, and poetry. She has several short stories published in various anthologies and is working on a full-length novel. She resides in Granite Bay, California, and serves on the Board of the Capitol Crimes chapter of Sisters In Crime.

Rick Schneider lives with his wife in Fort Myers, Florida where he writes full time when not hunting for the perfect sea-shell on the shores of Sanibel Island. He has published three mystery and suspense novels, including *Runners, Hidden in the Wind,* and *Succession.*

Terry Shepherd writes thrillers for grown-ups, detective stories for kids and collabs with his wife, Colleen, to teach youngsters how to protect themselves from pandemics and other mystery bugs. He lives and writes in Jacksonville, Florida.

Joseph S. Walker teaches college literature and has published more than fifty short stories. He has been nominated for the Edgar Award and the Derringer Award, and won the Bill Crider Prize for Short Fiction and the Al Blanchard Award. Follow him on Twitter @JSWalkerAuthor and visit him at www.jsw47408.wixsite.com/website.

Acknowledgments

This is the fourth anthology from the Capitol Crimes chapter of Sisters in Crime, and each one has involved a small village. There are so many people to thank for everything that went into this one, please forgive us if we leave anyone out.

First, we thank Sonja Hazzard-Webster for her determination to keep our anthology tradition going. Capitol Crimes Board President Penny Manson, along with Board Members Sarah Bresniker, Mary Griffith, Rae James, Karen Phillips, Frank Rankin, Rita Rippetoe, Marie Sutro, and Dänna Wilberg stayed committed to keeping up the momentum, as hard as it was without Sonja cheering us on.

Volunteering to read and critique 29 stories is a commitment, and we are so grateful to our judges, Janet Dawson, Sunny Frazier, Kaye George, David Hagerty, and Terry Shames, for being so giving of their time and expertise.

As a chapter, we wanted our anthology authors and readers to have a professional experience, and we were thrilled with Deborah J. Ledford's work as our copyeditor, bringing out the best in each of our selected stories.

Our fearless team of editors came together with the exact mix of talents we needed. Terry Shepherd knows how to get people excited about writing and reading using every medium imaginable, from video to voice work, to plain old words on the page. Kathleen L. Asay's keen eye for detail made everyone's writing stronger. We relied on Stacie Giles's wisdom and willingness to do the research when we needed to make hard decisions. Karen Phillips wore so many hats, all with grace and kindness, that she needs a new closet. Sarah Bresniker plotted out the deadlines and kept everyone on track. Each one of these amazing humans showed up, worked hard and found ways to have fun on Zoom!

Besides serving as a board member and an editor, Karen Phillips created a cover for us that is a work of art and also formatted the book for print and ebook versions. We would be lost without her!

Of course, none of this would be possible without our fantastic Capitol Crimes members. We are constantly in awe of the amazing talents, as well as the sense of community, to be found in this band of writers and readers. We hope that you enjoy the stories presented here and are inspired to be a part of the next Capitol Crimes anthology.

If you enjoyed the stories in this anthology, please leave an honest review. Reviews sell more books and the revenue helps our mission to educate and support those who enjoy reading and writing crime fiction.
—*Capitol Crimes*

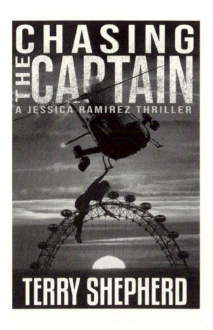
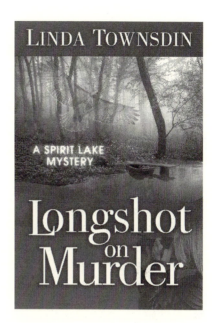

244

Ramirez & Clark
PUBLISHERS
CONGRATULATES
THE CAPITOL CRIMES
2021 ANTHOLOGY
AUTHORS

PROUD OF OUR BROTHERS AND SISTERS IN CRIME

RamirezAndClark.com

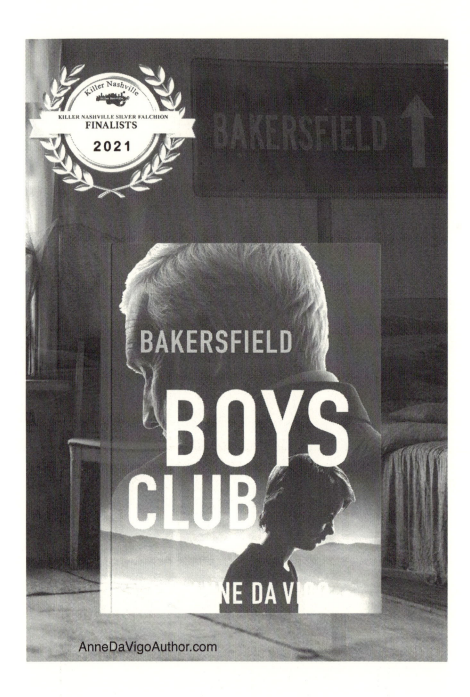

Bringing Words to Life

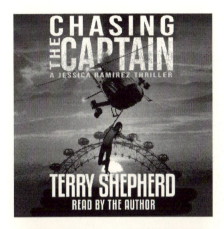
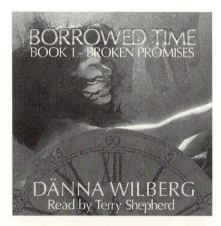
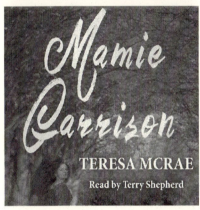
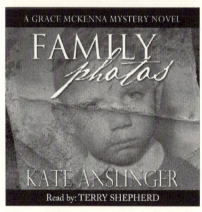

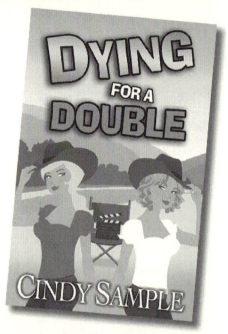

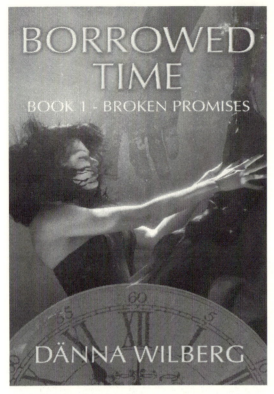

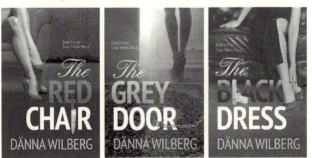

The Grace Simms Trilogy: *What do we really know about a person?*

Nancy Drew meets DEXTER

June Gillam

House of Cuts

A Hillary Broome Novel

JuneGillam.com